TRANSLATING KERALA

TRANSLATING KERALA

The Cultural Turn in Translation Studies

Meena T. Pillai

Orient BlackSwan

The publication of this book was funded by Centre for Cultural Studies, University of Kerala.

TRANSLATING KERALA:
THE CULTURAL TURN IN TRANSLATION STUDIES

ORIENT BLACKSWAN PRIVATE LIMITED

Registered Office
3-6-752 Himayatnagar, Hyderabad 500 029, Telangana, India
Email: centraloffice@orientblackswan.com

Other Offices
Bengaluru, Chennai, Guwahati, Hyderabad, Kolkata,
Mumbai, New Delhi, Noida, Patna

© Orient Blackswan Private Limited 2024
First published by Orient Blackswan Private Limited 2024

ISBN 978 93 5442 716 9

039193

Typeset in Minion Pro 11/13 *by*
Shine Graphics, Delhi 110 094

Printed at
Thomson Press, New Delhi 110 020

Published by
Orient Blackswan Private Limited
3-6-752, Himayatnagar, Hyderabad 500 029, Telangana, India
Email: info@orientblackswan.com

The publisher has endeavoured to ensure that the URLs for external websites referred to in this book are correct and active at the time of going to press. However, the publisher has no responsibility for the websites and can make no guarantee that a site will remain live or that the content is or will remain appropriate.

To Papa, whose life was spent as a translated being in a land far away from Kerala, and whose yearning for his home defined my own love for Kerala. Also, for teaching me to have the courage to stand up for my conscience and be the woman I am today.

Contents

Acknowledgements

This book comprises some of my early thoughts and work on translation, spanning nearly two decades. The current framework offers a shift in focus by putting those scattered pieces into a perspective that seeks to forge links between translation studies and cultural studies. Once again, I owe a debt of gratitude to the most professional of editors I have worked with, Sreenath Sreedharan, Managing Editor, Orient Blackswan, who literally shaped the book and put it into its current format. I thank Mahalakshmi Jayaram for the meticulous proofs. I am deeply indebted to the Vice Chancellor and Syndicate of the University of Kerala for their generous grant to the Centre for Cultural Studies that helped me contribute another book to the field of Kerala Studies. My thanks to my brilliant scholars at the Centre for Cultural Studies, University of Kerala, Sucheta Sankar, Meera C., Maalavika Ajayakumar, Jobson Joshwa, Sidharth M. Joy, Arya K., Arya A., Benita Acca Benjamin, Maria Viju and Abhirami S. R., for helping me with the proofs, and continuing to question my premises at every turn, making me turn a critical eye on my own work. This book comes at a rather trying juncture in my life, when I was beset with multiple personal crises. I thank all my friends and colleagues, Vishnu, Appu, Lakshmi Priya, Lakshmi Sukumar, Kalyani, Babitha and Gigy, who stood staunchly by my side in support. My love to Tara, Amrit and Ajish, for helping me dare to dream amidst adversities.

Publisher's Acknowledgements

'Is Gabriel García Márquez a Malayali?', *Translation Today,* vol. 5, nos. 1 & 2, 2008, first published under the aegis of *Translation Today.* Used with permission of the National Translation Mission.

'Gender and Translation', originally published as 'Gendering Translation, Translating Gender: A Case Study of Kerala' in *Translating Women: Indian Interventions,* edited by N. Kamala, published by Zubaan, 2010. Used with permission of the publishers.

'Translating the Subaltern', parts of this essay appeared in 'Translating the Nation, Translating the Subaltern', *Translation Today,* vol. 1, no. 2, 2004, first published under the aegis of *Translation Today.* Used with permission of the National Translation Mission. Parts of the essay were also based on an article that first appeared as 'On Marketing the Subaltern: Sales Tags for Postcolonial Margins', *Phoenix: Sri Lanka Journal of English in the Commonwealth,* vols. 10 & 11, 2013–2014. Used with permission of the *Sri Lanka Journal of English in the Commonwealth.*

'Autobiography as Translation', originally published as 'Translating Her Story: A Woman in Quest of a Language', *Translation Today,* vol. 2, no. 2, 2005. Used with permission of the National Translation Mission, Central Institute of Indian Languages.

'English and Postcolonial Translations', first published as 'The English Speaking Gendered Subaltern: Sales Tags for Postcolonial', *Journal of the School of Language,* Issue 15, Spring, 2011. Used with permission of *JSL.*

'Translating the Popular', previously published as 'On Adapting *Chemmeen*: Myth as Melodrama' in *Chemmeen,* translated by Anita Nair, New Delhi: Harper Collins, 2011.

'Translation as Adaptation', parts were first published as 'Taming the Fire: On Adapting Agnisakshi' in *Agnisakshi: Fire, My Witness* by Lalithambika Antharjanam, translated by Vasanthi Sankaranarayanan.

Oxford University Press, 2015. Parts were also previously published '*Pallivallum Kalchilambum* to *Nirmalyam*: Resurrecting the Word and the World', *Malayalam Literary Survey*, vol. 22, no. 1, January–March 2000. Used with permission of Oxford University Press and the *Malayalam Literary Survey*.

Cover Images

Back cover: Work by Waldo Saavedra. 2020 Regina Bernal Cataño. Courtesy of Creative Commons.

Front cover: Theyyam of Kerala. 2020 Shagil Kannur. Courtesy of Creative Commons.

Kodungallur Bharani Komaram. 2008 Challiyan. Courtesy of Creative Commons.

Thunchath Ezhuthachan. 2019 Rjwarrier. Courtesy of Creative Commons.

P. K. Rosy, the first actress in Malayalam cinema. 1901 unknown author. Courtesy of Creative Commons.

Kamala Das. 2010 Sreedharantp. Courtesy of Creative Commons.

Preface

Translating Kerala: The Cultural Turn in Translation Studies attempts to look at translation as a social and cultural act that transcribes, articulates, interprets and makes visible received structures of power as well as essentialised meanings inscribed within the ideational patterns and material realities of the everyday. This book, located at the interdisciplinary spaces of Kerala's cultural histories and the praxis of translation, is an academic endeavour that problematises/pushes the boundaries of the text and its contexts while also identifying the politico-economic structures that spill out into the silences and utterances of the text. The chapters in this book delve into seminal issues, ranging from the politics that constitutes various linguistic variables to the interpretative paradigms that render legible the experiences of the gendered and subaltern subject in Kerala, inaugurating new sites of critical dialogues between historical and cultural attitudes that traverse spatio-temporal differences. Hence, this project aims to unveil the polyphonic possibilities of the texts, destabilising the hierarchies between texts and their 'afterlives', texts and their contexts, texts and their actors/subjects.

The book attempts to puncture uncritical literary and popular discourses of development and progress attributed to Kerala by accentuating the politics that mediate articulations around 'translatedness' in numerous kinds of literary discourses that make and unmake the region. By positioning the text as a protean entity that always already leaps outside its material contours, the book looks at translation as an act of 'rewriting' (Lefevere and Bassnett 1990, 10), whereby the binding cultural tenets and ideological premises that constitute the translated (con)texts are unwound, reconfigured and exposed to scrutiny. To this end, the book looks at works of translation as a palimpsest that archives the region's evolving cultural tendencies, epistemic systems, transcultural engagements and linguistic mediations. Nevertheless, the book also acknowledges that the fraught encounters that translation makes possible in Kerala are too vast in scope and implication to be written down within the theoretical and methodological constraints of a single book.

The book begins with an introduction which discusses the critical lacunae that it seeks to address and the cultural exchanges that translation entails. Here, translation is viewed as a transdisciplinary and transgeneric process that engages with canonical and non-canonical texts in spelling out the contact zones that it inaugurates, revealing the socially inscribed filters of power that sift experiences and identities.

The second chapter titled 'Translation of *Les Misérables* and the Making of the Modern Malayali' attempts a critique of Nalappat Narayana Menon's translation of Victor Hugo's *Les Misérables* in three large volumes, published between 1925–28 with its phenomenally perceptive dedication where the translator says that *Paavangal* is dedicated to the miserables of Kerala. The chapter puts forth the argument that the translation strategies of Nalappat, including paratextual elements, usher novel forms of interpellation of the emerging middle-class Malayali readers, using *Les Misérables* without domesticating it, as a context for widening the horizon of readerly expectations. The translation thus became seminal in creating new critiques of diverse emerging social praxes that 'dehumanise' the human subject. In the process it inspired new idioms of prose, and new sets of novelistic forms and devices that would help 'write' universal forms of violence, suppression, indignity, and injustice into indigenous registers hitherto relatively isolated from critical reappraisals of more cosmopolitan forms of humanism.

The third chapter titled 'Translating Culture: Is Gabriel García Márquez a Malayali?' deals with the politics of translation by critically looking at the ways in which a text is strategically domesticated, acclimatised and assimilated into new cultures and vernacular registers. This chapter puts into frame translation as a process of intercultural communication whereby the shifting cultural priorities and ideological parameters that influence the process of translation in Kerala are explored by looking at texts as diverse as Premchand's *Godan*, Gabriel García Márquez's *One Hundred Years of Solitude* and John Bunyan's *The Pilgrim's Progress*. It argues that translation has been an important facet of Bhasha literatures' attempts to crystallise and strengthen themselves, by incorporating the experiments, strengths and resources of other literatures, and therefore, most of such translations have been largely 'acceptability oriented', adhering to target culture norms and often investing the foreign language text with domestic significance. The process of domestication of the translated text in most regional languages in India thus would begin with the very choice of texts to be translated to the act of translation *per se*, to continue in the process of reading and culminating in the review or the absence of it. Most translators, readers and reviewers of translations belonging to a minority linguistic community often find it convenient to deflect from the foreignness of the 'Translated Text' and focus instead on the degree of its conformity or opposition to dominant domestic ideologies and interests inscribed in it. Such agendas, strategies and interests are often determined by the function that is attributed to translation in that particular culture.

The fourth chapter titled 'Gender and Translation' looks at the linguistic incompetencies of Malayalam and cultural apprehensions in Kerala to critically dwell on the 'function' of translation as a radical political activity embedded within multiple structures of power. By examining the cultural distrust of translated feminist texts in Kerala, the chapter chooses 'absence' of texts itself as a point of departure to question the androcentric epistemological structures that fail to translate critiques of patriarchies and theories of feminism into the vernacular idioms of Kerala. It is an attempt to bring gender politics into translation theory and praxis in India. The chapter examines why in many parts of India, including the so-called highly literate state like Kerala, translating feminist texts have been considered scandalous. There is a covert fear of decentering of canons in the target language and culture, a paranoia towards bringing in an ethics of difference that is evinced in the resistance to translating feminist texts in India as illustrated in the case of Malayalam. Most often, as illustrated, what gets translated and how it is received in the target culture depends on how far the source text supports the ideologies and agendas of the target culture and whether translation strategies can be devised to tame the subversive elements in the text.

The fifth chapter titled 'Translating the Subaltern' attempts to study translation via the disjuncture between the writing subject and the enunciating subject, thereby suggesting that the marginalised subject is a 'being in translation'. Through the conflicting meanings, intentions and dialogues that the three versions of Nalini Jameela's autobiography make possible, the chapter attempts to problematise the locus of the agential voice by proposing that the 'speaking' subaltern subject is the result of a textual and mediated process of self-fashioning. It argues that the translating of marginalised selves is often a process involving plural subjectivities where authorship is only contingent—a wrestling over power between the enunciating subject and the writing subject with gradual intimidation of the former by the latter, since the former's knowledge of the conventions of literary genres is often seen to be regulated and 'subsidised' by the latter. It illustrates how such translations both facilitate and stall the subaltern's attempt to be a 'subject of history', to un-subaltern herself.

The sixth chapter titled 'Autobiography as Translation' refers to translation not only as a conscious act of linguistic negotiation but also as an embodied act of narrativising felt emotions. By looking at Kamala Das' *My Story* and *Ente Kadha*, two versions of her life story written by the writer herself in English and Malayalam respectively, this chapter looks at translation as a process of transcreation whereby the narrative subject has to engage with multiple linguistic, social, and moral registers, which are often at odds with each other, especially the language of thought, language of cultural reference, language of writing, and the language of moral majorities. Locating self translation of autobiographies as an act of writing the self from the source language of English to the target language of Malayalam, it analyses the various processes of reclaiming and recentering of identities in a new linguistic and cultural territory, and the politics of such recentering.

The seventh chapter titled 'English and Postcolonial Translations' attempts to look at postcolonial translation as a transplanting of sorts, where language serves not only as a medium of experience but also as the constitutive essence of the experienced reality. This chapter studies C. K. Janu's biography to understand how English, as a language of power and legitimacy, seeks to reproduce hegemonic structures of geopolitical power and stage cultural otherness for global consumption, explicating how translations often become an act of social validation, intricately connected to issues of differential linguistic currency, power and authority. This authority is further endorsed by the forces of institutionalised academics and a global publishing industry which offer the text of the subaltern certain currency. Thus, the power vested on the translator as an institutionalised power needs to be critiqued from various angles. One needs to look at the representation of the subaltern not as a simple act of representation but as a translation act contaminated by differential language power and mediated and constructed by institutional power. Using the ethnographic text *Mother Forest: The Unfinished Story of C. K. Janu*, it illustrates how the testimonio of an adivasi woman, who mobilised her people and led them to a historic protest against the government, agitating for land for the landless tribal people, can be co-opted by global marketing forces and hegemonic intellectuals who claim epistemological authority over textualised subaltern experiences. The chapter is also an attempt at critiquing postcolonial theory and translational practices which are becoming increasingly global in scope and ambition, and seek to privilege 'difference' as an eminently saleable commodity.

The eighth chapter, titled 'Translating the Popular' critically examines translation as a transgeneric act whereby the gendered subject of representation is configured in distinct ways, acknowledging the fact that different genres anticipate different modes of reception. To this end, the chapter views the radical dissimilarities in the portrayal of the character Karuthamma in Thakazhi Shivashankara Pillai's *Chemmeen* and Ramu Kariat's cinematic adaptation of the same to understand how the 'translated' female body becomes the signifier of culturally-coded feminine ideals. Using adaptation theory, it looks at the fissures and gaps that take place during the process of translating gender from fiction to film, and the issues at stake when the sign 'woman' is translated from the semiotic system of literature to that of narrative cinema. Analysing *Chemmeen*, which has been translated into most of the regional languages in India and a number of foreign languages and adapted into a highly successful movie, it critiques the gendered commodified systems of exchange that canonical literature and popular cinema often become, using translation as a tool for this analysis. This argument is carried over into the last chapter also.

'Translation as Adaptation: From Fiction to Film' looks at the literature/film interface in India and grapples with the issue of representational politics and the politics of representation in fiction and film, attempting to view translation as a transgeneric act. It delves into M. T. Vasudevan Nair's short story *Pallivaallum Kalchilambum* and its cinematic adaptation *Nirmalyam*, which celebrated its fiftieth year of production in 2023, to study how the film responds to the need of an era, a social, cultural and historical necessity that makes an adaptation possible.

In a state like Kerala, translation serves as a metaphor for identities in process, where the self is often a shifting paradigm of the constantly translated other. A land where during the pre-modern times a number of foreign cultures found a congenial soil, a people for whom travel and migration have become crucial markers of their modernity, Kerala and Keralites have come to be defined by numerous acts of translation that have shaped their social, cultural and political realities. Most of the essays in this volume—while covering the crucial issues in the general sphere of English translations in India—have out of necessity focused more specifically on the translations from Malayalam into English or vice versa because of the fact that these are the two languages that I am proficient in and competent enough to analyse in detail. However, they serve to highlight the numerous problems that all regional languages and literatures in India confront today *vis-à-vis* the broader contemporary notions of translation.

The topics, ranging from translating marginality to gender and representational politics, will, it is hoped, contribute to the field of translation critique by foregrounding the political dimensions of translational exercises. Though they address a range of approaches to the questions of what constitutes the politics of translation in India, the cartography mapped out remains incomplete in that there are yet other positions, debates and voices that need to be brought into the gamut of translational critique which have contributed to the creation of shared spaces in the new socio-cultural maps drawn out by forces of globalisation and liberalisation.

This book, in attempting to bring in gender and sexuality studies, theories of representation, popular culture, postcolonial theory, subaltern studies and minority literatures into the gamut of translation, hopes to contribute in charting a paradigm shift in the scope and focus of translation studies as a discipline in India. Thus, it seeks to dismantle translation studies as a discipline from the comparative literature and language framework, taking it closer to the cultural studies mode.

REFERENCES

Lefevere, Andre, and Susan Bassnett. 1990. "Proust's Grandmother and the Thousand and One Nights: The 'Cultural Turn' in Translation Studies." In *Translation, History and Culture*, edited by Andre Lefevere and Susan Bassnett, 1–13. London: Pinter Publishers.

ONE

Introduction

The Cultural Turn in Translation

In a land like India, where, according to the 2011 Census, there are a total of 121 languages, 270 identifiable mother tongues, 22 scheduled languages and 99 non-scheduled languages, any act of communication is bound to be political. The situation gets more complicated when viewed in the context of the fact that in most parts of India today, a child has to learn, in addition to the vernacular, two other languages, Hindi and English. Though Hindi is the official language of the Union and the respective regional language of each state its official language, English continues to be the single language with the most currency and power, the lingua franca that cuts across cultural, geographical and political borders. The satellite television boom and new digital media and technology have further encouraged Indians to appreciate the instrumental, regulative, interpersonal and imaginative purposes the English language can serve, as pointed out by Kachru (1983).

The complex and shifting matrices of such multifarious linguistic and social realities, while making translation an essential part of life in India, nevertheless imbue it with complex ideological, political and socio-cultural implications. This would require broadening the sphere of translation to include social, cultural and political crossovers and contexts in addition to transactions in language. In this broader sense, the term translation is often a contact zone that produces new transcultural texts, going beyond both the source and the target languages and cultures to create third spaces of enunciation and representation. To view translations fundamentally as a cultural exchange would also mean deconstructing the political concerns and agendas that are implicit in them. Translation, which occupied a liminal space in language departments, has traced a long trajectory of disciplinary growth to its current centrality in cultural and critical theorisation. This necessitates the need to supplant the linguistic slant in translation studies with a cultural turn that emphasises the fact that translation in India today is more about power, institutional, economic and ideological concerns and consumption patterns than about language per se or the poetics of translation. Often more than the translator's ideology, it is the complex network of market-driven economies, the agendas of publishing houses, the regulative and canonising roles of national academies, educational institutions and reigning political affiliations and patronages that govern both the choice of texts for translation and the translation process and presentation.

Translating Power, Language, and the Everyday

Stuart Hall's 'Cultural Studies: Two Paradigms' offered, on the one hand, the 'culturalist' paradigm, positing human experience as central to the cultural turn, drawing from the writing of Richard Hoggart, Raymond Williams and Edward Thompson. Hall's 'structuralist' paradigm pitched itself on a theory of ideology that was fundamental to the structural turn. However, both culturalist and structuralist paradigms are inextricably bound by issues of language. It has been pointed out that the structuralist turn itself had two turns, the linguistic and the ideological, the former through the rediscovery of the writings of Ferdinand de Saussure, and as applied first by Claude Lévi-Strauss (1968) to the structural analysis of myth, and the latter with Althusser using it to create a framework for his theories of ideology, and Stuart Hall and others applying this method to the study of contemporary myths in European societies and cultures (Scannell 2015, 645). For Althusser, 'the category of experience was the very home and heartland of ideology, for it was in and through "lived experience" that the "ideological effect" worked to produce individuals living their lives in an imaginary relationship to the real conditions that shaped and structured their existence' (645).

Michel de Certeau, in *Practice of Everyday Life* (1984), contends the emergence of a 'scriptural economy' that is born out of the intense dynamics between language and hegemony, whereby it is the 'mastery of language' that 'guarantees and isolates a new power, a bourgeois power, that of making history and of 'fabricating languages' (139). This would be an interesting premise to examine how some translations and certain cultural texts seem to accrue more authority than others. Certeau's critique of representations, positing it as the space of an absence, is an argument in sync with theorists of language like Derrida, where it is precisely in the absent 'other' that each representation finds its moral ground and legitimacy, an idea that gains traction in both cultural studies and translation.

Another essay by Hall, 'Encoding, Decoding', offers a theoretical framework to study how media messages are produced, distributed and consumed, particularly with regard to television. It would be interesting to use Hall's central premise to argue that the seemingly autonomous fields in the act of translation could possibly be underscored by 'complex structures of dominance' because writing and translating, as applied fields of communication, carry the imprint of cultural power relations. Thus, power relations at the point of 'production' of a text will roughly coincide with the power relations levitating around the points of its translation.

Cultural Studies and/as Translation

The very idea of 'translation' as an operational tangent of culture, and vice versa, is a crucial determiner in attempting to formulate a new axis to re-think cultural studies alongside its deep-rooted suspicion of disciplinarity that crystallises in and through numerous vectors of counter-disciplinary praxis. For an 'anti-discipline' that 'has never claimed scientific objectivity and rarely assumes that it possesses analytic methods that hold good across different cultures' (During 2005, 5), the institutionary exigencies that circumscribe the 'interdisciplinary eventfulness' (Herbrechter 2002, 2) of its political projectile have proved to be a complex impediment. This calls for a translative praxis—a locutionary archiving of culture in all its 'mobility', rendering cultural studies as a 'lingua franca for the global cultural studies community' (During 2005, 8). It entails a radical rewiring of cultural studies as a 'critical intellectual work' with 'no absolute beginnings and few unbroken continuities' (Hall 1980, 57)—a project of cultural criss-crossing that conversely affixes the idea that cultural studies is 'both the subject and the object of translation today (that is as a translator of ideas and as an academic discipline or a methodology translated into various national institutional contexts)' (Herbrechter 2002, 12).

What exactly are the stakes involved in construing the almost antinomian paradigms of 'translation' and 'culture' as forming an amphibian praxis? For one, it begets an implication that cultural studies has been 'hijacking' or usurping the domain of culture by means of overly theoretical and speculative or 'journalistic methods' (Katon 2018, 31). Furthermore, it entails a reanimation of the economies of exchange that cultural studies and translation share, having 'traditionally trodden separate paths, though both have been fundamentally concerned with the processes of communication and meaning' (Katon 2002, 177). Stefan Herbrechter thus makes an important point regarding cultural studies and translation where he says that

> the history of cultural studies—as a movement, an institution, a discourse, etc.—cannot be thought without considering the transfer of ideas, i.e. without a set of concepts starting with 'trans-': transnationalism, transdisciplinarity, translation. One reason why cultural studies suffers from, but also continues to indulge in, the sometimes obsessive problematisation of identity, orthodoxy, and canonicity is that its origins lie in translation, or in the 'inbetween'. (2002, 9)

Thus, both cultural studies and translation carry and are, in turn, defined by the ontological and epistemological tensions around 'in-betweenness'. This ontological and epistemological hybridity that goes against disciplinary logic also involves protracted battles to lay bare the struggles over processes of meaning-making that further require higher degrees of methodological reflection.

Herbrechter has pointed out that the phrase 'the translation of cultural studies' implies both subjective and objective aspects, whereby it means cultural studies translates and is also being translated, carrying the normative-political, ethical and historical-geographical dimensions (2002, 8). He argues that some urgent questions arise out of this problematic: what should cultural studies translate? Is there, apart from a politics of translation (i.e., translation as strategic appropriation), an ethics of translation (something that demands translation)? What has cultural studies been translating (which involves a critique of cultural studies' translation choices and practices; a historical and geographical analysis of cultural studies as both the product and the producer of translations)? Which processes of translation are responsible for cultural studies (for its history, its evolution and institutionalisation and, maybe, today, for its dissemination)? (8).

Whether it be the translation of cultural studies, translation in cultural studies, or translation as cultural studies, what it offers is the scope for a critique of the asymmetrical fields of cultural politics in which all translations occur, rendering meaning, representation and referentiality tenuous, contingent and fragmentary. Invoking the inconclusive, repetitive, and fragmentary nature of translation that both Walter Benjamin and Borges emphasised and supplementing it with Foucault's genealogical analyses, José María Rodríguez Garcia (2004) points out that 'the goal of the translator, who has now become a cultural mediator occupying a concrete subject-position, is to enable the visibility of the contradictions within and between texts rather than naturalize the perceived similarities' (5).

The disciplinary traversings between and within translation and cultural studies paradigms have not always been commensurable. This fraught nature of exchanges and translations is dovetailed by a condition of ex-centricity that ought to inform the idea of interdisciplinarity. It is crucial to consider this in terms of what Mieke Bal (2002) terms as the 'travelling concepts'. The conceptual 'intersubjectivity' (22) required to surpass the dogmatism of discipline and methodology has been a recurrent feature of translation and culture studies, having witnessed several aptitudinal 'turns' and 'shifts' historically. The emphasis on 'culture' as a referent and a translative praxis has opened up proximal faultlines between both disciplines. However, as Zwischenberger (2019) points out, the deepening narratives around 'cultural translation' have harboured certain tendencies to look past the discipline of translation studies, sidelining it once and for all. The reifying of culture as a mere technique has made for an uneasy dualism of translation as an 'elementary culture technique in cultural translation in contrast to the linguistically fixated translation concept' (263). Though there has been a certain overdetermination in this regard, the criticism against translation studies is not entirely misplaced. Zwischenberger notes that translation studies, as a discipline, despite the numerous 'inward turns', lacks a full awareness of its potential and of the need for such an outward turn (265). The projectile around the 'transculturality of translation' (266) is yet to be fully spelt out.

Affect and Translation

In the age of ChatGPT and other Artificial Intelligence and Machine Learning capabilities, the scrutiny of cultures and translations gets mired in the digital, where the affective could be foregrounded as a definitively human condition, at least until affective computing emerges in the future. Kaisa Koskinen, in *Translation and Affect: Essays on Sticky Affects and Translational Affective Labour* (2020), substantiates how translation is a mode of affective labour, one that is 'based on emotional and visceral responses to an equal degree as on cognitive reasoning' (55), arguing that 'engaging with affect is therefore of extreme value in understanding translating and interpreting as complex, interpersonal, situated and embodied forms of human communication' (29).

Moreover, the cultural turn in translation underscores an affective economy that creates a generative drifting of affective forces between works and mediums (Hodgkins 2013, 2). In seeking to look at the production, circulation and consumption of cultural texts within the networks of the market, social desire and institutional hegemonies, the cultural turn in translation studies would need to necessarily engage with the affective forces that are crucial to creating a use and exchange value for the product of translation as a concrete materialisation of labour that operates within institutional monopolies, such as publishing or copyright. Within the field of cultural studies and cultural materialism, one significant early attempt to locate affect and structures of sentiments in the necessary sociality which gives shape to them was taken up by Raymond Williams (1977) through his notion of the 'structures of feeling'—those modes of feeling which emerge at a specific moment in history but are not yet articulated as thought. The elements of sociality and potentiality implied here are emphasised by contemporary scholars of affect, such as Zizi Papacharissi (2015), who, in reference to Williams' coinage, highlights 'the potential that lies in that which is emergent and the power or agency that may derive from the volatility of social experiences in the making' (115).

'Lost in translation' is a phrase with deep affective resonances that universally acknowledges the inability of the translated text to completely articulate the lived experiences of the source text without substantial 'losses'. This is similar to Williams' conception regarding structures of feeling, a kind of practical consciousness around lived experiences, which are non-semantic and cannot be articulated with the forms of language available to those experiencing them. Williams points out that there is indeed 'frequent tension between the received interpretation and practical experience', and this tension, emblematic of a semantic inconsistency, is the symptom of a structure of feeling which cannot be articulated in itself (Williams 1977, 130). He locates structures of feeling in 'the endless comparison that must occur in the process of consciousness between the articulated and the lived' (Williams 2015, 168). It can be argued that this semantic tension is carried into the act of translation, too, often as 'an unease, stress, a displacement, a latency: the moment of conscious comparison not yet come, often not even coming' (Williams 1977, 130). Thus, the originary impulse of a translation, it could be argued, resides in such structures of feeling, 'which is indeed social and material, but each in an embryonic phase before it can become fully articulate and defined exchange' (131).

In many ways, this ties up with Walter Benjamin's thesis on history, where he says that 'to articulate the past historically does not mean to recognize it "the way it was"'. It means to seize hold of a memory as it flashes up 'at a moment of danger', which offers 'a striking if fleeting image of lived experience which may be vastly different from our mediated perceptions of what we think lived experience to be' (1969, 255). The cultural turn in translation, it could be safely surmised, is an attempt to re-vision the seizing up of this memory of the images of lived experiences as it flashes by.

Benjamin speaks of translation in terms of a fluidity that mirrors the organicity that one could trace in the 'relationship between life and purposefulness' (72). The 'purposiveness' of this endeavour, however, cannot be sought in the finality of its life; it becomes apparent only in the 'expression of its nature, in the representation of its significance' (72). This can be read in conjunction with Williams' conception of the affective structures and substrates, the patterns of feeling that need redeeming to deal with the disjunctive schemas that demand the 'immediate and regular conversion of experience into finished products' (Williams 1977, 129). It is crucial to locate translational activity as affectivity not defined in terms of a 'habitual past sense' but as a 'formative process' distinctively captured within a 'specific present' (129). The rendering of translation as an 'anticipative, intimating-realization' (129) is crucial to understanding the structured economies of affect that the translation industry engenders. This also entails a radical shift from the 'bipolar focus on either the author and the translator, or the source text and the translation' (Koskinen 2020, 39). As Koskinen observes,

> The contemporary, networked translation industry provides constellations of mutual dependence where translators, project

managers, revisers, terminologists and IT people and other parties are in constant, albeit often virtual and indirect, contact. The communicative situations entail multiprofessional expertise, and translators and interpreters need to bring their professional mediational competences to the common table and secure a firm footing among other experts. These networks of relations provide a second layer of affective labour, tangential but not directly derived from the contents of the translatorial task at hand. (39)

It is in this complex web of power dynamics that the historical materialist approach, as espoused by Benjamin (1969), gains special valence in acts of translation. It helps view all 'cultural treasures' with 'cautious detachment', marking a paradigm shift to the cultural turn in translation, whereby it becomes necessary to estimate such texts as owing 'their existence not only to the efforts of the great minds and talents who have created them but also to the anonymous toil of their contemporaries' (256). Thus, Benjamin sees the affective labour, both individual and social, in acts of textual production, whether it be acts of writing or translating. His words embed an ironic prophetic warning to all cultural critics, writers and translators when he says,

> There is no document of civilization which is not at the same time a document of barbarism. And just as such a document is not free of barbarism, barbarism taints also the manner in which it was transmitted from one owner to another. A historical materialist, therefore, dissociates himself from it as far as possible. He regards it as his task to brush history against the grain. (256)

Benjamin's theses on history thereby offer valuable lessons to the translatorial method, not to see the text as 'an eternal image of the past' (262), but to use it against the grain in order to blast open the 'continuum of history' (261).

The conceptual and empirical methods and acts of translation, as they emerge and proliferate in different ages, are valuable resources to study the crystallisation of cultures, as also the formations, practices and institutions through which they invoke affect in order to either stabilise hegemony or create a counter-cultural move against dominant ethos and aspirations.

Translation and Kerala/Translating Kerala

Translations could be an important node for studying ideations around nation, region, place or space, looking at how they map canonical texts, elite and popular cultures, gender and sexuality, caste, race, language and ideology. Peter Jackson, in his seminal book *Maps of Meaning*, proposes the idea of geographical 'cultural materialism'. His proposition draws sustenance from Raymond Williams and his theory of culture as materially produced within specific historical and spatial contexts. Space and place are crucial to the concept of culture, and translation as a field of cultural politics needs to be re-visioned in the context of 'territorial structures'. One could use translation as a tool for re-animating thoughts on cultural geography, drawing on the theoretical legacies of cultural studies in order to remap the contours of geographical and cultural sensibilities. Kerala, as a small yet distinctively complex terrain with polyphonic possibilities around composite engagements between translation, cultural and social geography, and cultural theory, offers great scope for analysing how people make sense of this small strip of land by looking at the symbolic landscape of its translations. The 'morphology' of Kerala (borrowing the idea from Carl Saueur) goes beyond its landscape of a long coastline and languid backwaters of tourism narratives, or the fragile Western Ghats of ecological discourses, or its developmental paradoxes, in order to think of it in a morphological sense, one that 'mediates between objective space and subjective place' and which 'may help to overcome both objectivism and subjectivism in sciences, by showing how both subjects and objects mutually imply each other in a process of reciprocal formation, constitution, and conditioning' (Furia 2022). Translation, I argue, would be a vital cog in such analyses, which, through multiple acts of mediation between languages, representations, lived experiences, and rituals and practices, would emplace material and symbolic forms of culture in their emergent, dominant or residual forms within objective space and subjective place.

The history of the Malayalam language reveals the multifarious strength and richness that acts of translation brought into it, giving great momentum to the use of the language itself, its script, narrative and stylistic forms, and semantic engagements. Reading tastes and the conventions of writing in Malayalam have been immensely shaped by the aesthetic intentions, linguistic deployment and political directives of translational efforts.

Between the twelfth and nineteenth centuries, Malayalam saw the emergence of new plots, narrative forms/genres and efforts in multiple kinds of translation and adaptation. An overarching dominant mark of this period is an attempt to summarise or elaborate Sanskrit *itihasas* and *puranas*, an act once considered sacrilegious. A mediaeval cultural logic is seen to be operative here, which sought to address the nascent desires of emerging cultural ecosystems and their ideological requirements. This cultural logic cannot be demarcated as an offshoot of a new culturescape. It was a latently available residue, one that is 'active in the cultural process, not only and often not at all as an element of the past, but as an effective element of the present' (Williams 1977, 122). However, within this residual cultural framework, fidelity to the source text was not much of a concern. The notion of originality was not yet central to the determination of literariness. Literature had not yet taken a concrete shape as a discourse in the rather fluid pre-modern oral-aural-scriptural terrain with no binding boundaries. Translation as an autotelic play for evolving, storing and circulating knowledge was never static and, in a sense, internalised a dialogic dynamicity that did not function on the writer/translator binary. The lisible economy configured by the autotelism of the 'translated' text enabled a juxtapositive polyphony, dismantling the structurality of the text even as it counterposed the rigidity of what Certeau called a 'scriptural economy' (1984, 137).

Malayalam received the genres of *sandesakavya, maha kavya,* and *champu* from Sanskrit during this pre-modern period, adapting their forms. Generally, this period can be termed as one of 'tradaptation', a median that forms between translation and adaptation, locating itself at a 'particular conjuncture of memory and intentionality with respect to the language(s) of the past and of the future' (Knutson 2012, 114). This pre-modern fluid and generative methodology, one that refused the customised translation methods to follow in later periods of time, evolved transcreative practices from within the source text, in and through the dialogues with the cultures of its adaptation. Such translations are thus acts of cultural performativity, claiming untrammelled freedom in experimenting with form, language, genre and style. Ezhuthachan's *Adhyathmaramayanam* took unrestrained liberties with Valmiki's *Ramayana*, writing it into the orality of everyday cultures, even while paradoxically standardising its script. In contrast, his 'tradaptation' of the *Mahabharata* epic as *Mahabharatham kilippattu* takes a 'sacrilegious freedom' bordering on what could have been deemed 'profane' then (and thereby rendered impossible today) by minimising and summarising the *Bhagavad Gita* in just two lines.

Translation in the context of British imperialism sought to place the language question openly within the matrix of hegemony, seeking to instil a cultural authority that would aid and abet the colonial logic of the binary between the enlightened colonial 'self' and the 'native other' in need of civilisation. Interestingly, several social, educational, religious and economic transformations elevated the position of prose in Malayalam-speaking society. As can be inferred from the central tenets of the infamous Minute on Indian Education by Macaulay, a new prose style became prominent—one that was Malayalam/Malayali in terms of the language but English in taste and approach. Of particular interest are the Bible translations that unfolded in the context of proselytisation efforts, which can also be placed at the root of a significant rupture in the history of translation cultures in Kerala. First of all, the idea of fidelity towards the source text became important. The notion of fidelity is a colonising logic that interpellates a subject through multiple structures of subjugation. The almost institutionalised veneration of notions around what constitutes 'chaste' faithfulness to the revered 'original' seemed to draw inspiration from an evangelical code of ethics. Thus, the definitive virtue of fidelity became important, both to the body of translation and the body politic. It sought to tame and limit the subject by prohibiting any act of transgression, where individual freedom is to be interred for the well-being of the Commonwealth. Interestingly, coinciding with the move to fidelity came the propensity towards linguistic usages outside a Hindu vocabulary, impelled by a missionary zeal for translation. The publication of Bible translations into Malayalam, a process which began in the early nineteenth century, used vernacular frames of the language to construct new iterations around quotidian experiences, thus laying bare the issue of language as a site of political struggle over meaning-making (see George 1972; Thomas 1989). Saurabh Dube (2016) finds two overlapping processes, one of the fabrications of colonial cultures of rule and the second one of the fashioning of a vernacular Christianity that lay at the heart of evangelical entanglements in India, which unfolded 'complex making and unmaking of historical forms, social identities, ritual practices, and mythic meanings—enacted over time' (162). In attempting to trace the manner whereby the catechists simultaneously thought through colonial categories and vernacular idioms, Dube argues that they deployed literal readings of the Scriptures, producing 'a surplus of faith in the Word', while conceptually translating the terms of evangelical Christianity and Western civilisation, whereby their 'writings register the everyday life of colonial power and evangelical authority—processes where subaltern subjects worked upon crucial distinctions of empire and evangelism, saturated with dominance, to instate such representations, while making them bear unsanctioned and recalcitrant meanings' (163). He calls this 'a struggle for construing meanings of the past and the present through dominant categories and apprehensions of the Bible, through vernacular frames and their distinct uses, ever bound to the one and the other', and sums up that before 'scholarly niceties of "agency" and "resistance", it is these terms of struggle and such making of meanings that are terribly important' (163).

The history of imperial dominion is itself a history of translation, implicated in issues of language, culture and identity. Thus, the catechist logic that translations of the word of God could not be transcreative in that it presupposes an immanent and transcendent 'uncorrupted original', cemented and strengthened notions around fidelity during this period, even as they sired novel moulds of prescriptive, archetypal literariness that determined the form and function of vernacular translations. These discursive figurations imagined by and through print modernity ratified new pedagogical milieus, situating the vernacular languages at their vantage points. This begot new aptitudinal registers that eventually coalesced to form new disciplines of inquiry that were thoroughly institutionalised, 'Malayalam Studies' being one of them.

'Malayalam Studies' as a disciplinary inquiry, conceptualised in the grid of colonial modernity, laid the ground for new prosaic ideations, which were not necessarily literary. This supplemented the lacunae around genre in the vernacular registers and even provided the originary impulses for literary prose in Malayalam. The early prosaic writings in Malayalam religiously followed the prose prototypes available in English, with no notable exception, even as journalistic writings followed suit. The newspapers and periodicals like *Rajyasamacharam* (1847), *Paschimodayam* (1847) and *Vidyasamgraham* (1864) relied upon English dailies for news content and directly translated news items and articles. It should be noted that at this stage, Malayalam prose found a footing of its own through resistance and conformity with the stylistic translations from English. The Malayalam language itself is Janus-faced at this point, looking outwards to the possible translation ethos of English, even while turning inwards, and forming alliances with other Indian languages to forge a nationalist idiom. Interesting cases in point are John Bunyan's allegory *The Pilgrim's Progess* as *Paradesee Mokshayathra* (1849) and the translation of the Bengali novel *Phulmoni aur Korunar Biboran* as *Phumoni Ennum Koruna Ennum Peraya Randu Sthreekalude Katha* (1858). Malayalam does not entirely break away from forging new translational inquiries around the question of genre in the following decades, as illustrated by the attempt to translate the genre of the novel through a work such as *Indulekha*.

In the Preface to *Indulekha*, Chanthu Menon establishes that it is not only science books that deserve to be translated and read but also novels. In the eighteenth chapter of the novel, the characters discuss the ideas introduced by science books. The unique nature of literariness put forth by this chapter later became integral to the novelistic culture in Kerala (see M. V. Narayanan's *Pathinettaam Adhyayathinte Bakkipathrangal*).

It is evident that the attitude towards prose translations into Malayalam changes considerably with the translation of *Les Misérables* by Nalappattu Narayana Menon as *Paavangal* (1925). This translation ushered in a paradigm shift in Malayalam, creating an affective-cultural turn in its translation ecosystem. It allied with new social, cultural and affective imaginaries forged under the aegis of nationalist struggles, agrarian uprisings, socialist upheavals and progressive literary movements. Its folkish evocativeness contributed to its mass appeal, thus metamorphosing into the lore of the land itself. It thus embodied the cultural affect of a period, a metaphor for its zeitgeist (Rajasekharan 2022).

Kerala was reconstituted in a post-Independence India in the wake of nationalist modernity and the linguistic reconfiguration of states. Even during the time of the erstwhile principalities of Travancore, Cochin and Malabar, a cultural imaginary of Kerala can be deciphered, where the region was simultaneously constituted out of the micro-nationalist narratives that circulated within the discursive spaces of literature, translations, cultural beliefs, institutions and practices. At this point, translations from Russian, French, Bengali and Marathi languages debuted in Malayalam, outside the power configurations of English and Sanskrit, which had been the languages of ideological hegemony and control. In translation, this moment of transformation creates a new cultural ethos, which is also the embodiment of a new social desire in India—the possession of a new nationalist spirit. At this historical moment, Soviet literature made powerful inroads into Kerala, which was also coeval with Jawaharlal Nehru's efforts to bring about a socialist leaning within the Indian National Congress. Soviet literature also helped in laying a foundation of ideas and tastes that helped the Communist movement, which became a strong political current in Kerala in the decades that followed. The landscape of alienation, loss and fragmentation that characterised the cultural terrain of post-independence Kerala found its political and aesthetic tenor in transcreations and translations such as that of T. S. Eliot's 'The Waste Land' in the decades of the 1960s and 70s. Boris Pasternak's *Doctor Zhivago*, published in 1957, was translated into Malayalam within three years in 1960 by a popular writer like Muttath Varkey. This was a period subsequent to the election of the first Communist government in Kerala, of fomenting resentment against Communist administrative policies and anti-Communist sentiments, finding in the translation of *Doctor Zhivago* an apt vessel for mobilising countercultural imperatives, where the Malayalam translation provided an ideological buttress for the anti-Communist sloganeering of the Liberation Struggle in Kerala.

The rise of Dalit, Subaltern and Women's Studies in academia, alongside the proliferation of poststructuralist theory with its peculiar problematic of the impossibility of representation and the enigmatic knots it creates for translation, all complicated the translational landscape of Kerala. The cultural turn at this juncture was characterised by escalated scrutiny and polemics around the asymmetrical fields of power that underscored any translational practice. The many movements built around identity politics were increasingly fuelled by politically active constituents. The waning of the aura built around the binaries of source and target, original and translated, left the field of translation open to the takeover and replacement of what Walter Benjamin calls 'cult value' by 'exhibition value', pushing it into the value system of the commodity. This need not be entirely negative in that new networks of circulation and review, enhanced by new medialities like the turn to the digital, increased both the visibility and consumption of translations, creating a sensitivity towards both the need for 'understanding the structures of translation (fields, production networks, institutional hierarchies, etc.)' and the 'need to "live with" translation, attuned to its "concrete and living" nature, and the often obscure "hopes, habits, instincts, needs, presentiments" of the people involved' (Koskinen 2020, x).

With globalisation and the liberalisation of markets post-1990s, novel translations became a staple for the culture industry in Kerala. Alongside British, American and Latin American texts, translations of West Asian, African and Islamic literatures became a booming market. On the flip side, translations from Malayalam began charting a reverse journey, finding a niche readership in English while also becoming viable economic models built around translation awards, the publishing industry, and the aspirations of booming diasporic populations, putting the spotlight on the pecuniary possibilities of the affective labour built around the various processes, practices and products of translation. The many travels of the Malayali diaspora across the globe also created more affective fields of consumption around intercultural fields such as translation.

REFERENCES

Bal, Mieke. 2002. *Travelling Concepts in the Humanities: A Rough Guide.* Toronto: U of Toronto P.

Benjamin, Walter. 1969. *Illuminations.* Translated by Harry Zohn. New York: Schocken Books.

Certeau, Michel de. 1984. *The Practice of Everyday Life.* Berkeley: U of California P.

Dube, Saurabh. 2016. "Colonial Registers of a Vernacular Christianity: Conversion to Translation." *Economic and Political Weekly* 39 (2): 161–71.

During, Simon. 2005. *Cultural Studies: A Critical Introduction.* London: Routledge.

Furia, Paolo. 2022. "Space and Place. A Morphological Perspective." *Axiomathes* 32: 539–56.

Garcia, José María Rodríguez. 2004. "Literary into Cultural Translation." *Diacritics* 34 (3/4): 2–30.

George, K. M. 1972. *Western Influence on Malayalam Language and Literature.* New Delhi: Sahitya Akademi.

Hall, Stuart. 1980. "Cultural Studies: Two Paradigms." *Media, Culture and Society* 2: 57–72.

Herbrechter, Stefan, ed. 2002. *Cultural Studies: Interdisciplinarity and Translation.* Amsterdam: Rodopi.

Hodgkins, John. 2013. *The Drift: Affect, Adaptation, and New Perspectives on Fidelity.* London: Bloomsbury Academic.

Jackson, Peter. 1989. *Maps of Meaning: An Introduction to Cultural Geography.* New York: Routledge.

Kachru, Braj K. 1983. *The Indianization of English: The English Language in India.* Oxford: Oxford UP.

Katan, David. 2002. "Mediating the Point of Refraction and Playing with the Perlocutionary Effect: a Translator's Choice?" In *Cultural Studies: Interdisciplinarity and Translation,* edited by Stefan Herbrechter, 161–77. Amsterdam: Rodopi.

———. 2018. "Defining culture, defining translation." In *The Routledge Handbook of Translation and Culture,* edited by Sue-Ann Harding and Ovidi Carbonell Cortés, 17–48. London: Routledge.

Knutson, Susan. 2012. "'Tradaptation' Dans le Sens Québécois: A Word for the Future." In *Translation, Adaptation and Transformation,* edited by Laurence Raw. London: Continuum.

Koskinen, Kaisa. 2020. *Translation and Affect: Essays on Sticky Affects and Translational Affective Labour.* Amsterdam: John Benjamins.

Narayanan, M. V. 2011. "*18-aam Adhyayathinte Bakkipathrangal* (Afterlives of the Eighteenth Chapter)." *Bhaashaposhini* 35(4): 37–44.

Rajasekharan, P. K. 2022. "*Malayaliyee Jeevithathilekk Valicheringa Oru Vivarthanathinte Katha* (The story of a translation which threw the Malayali into the realities of life)." *Prasaadhakan Magazine* 9 (109): 29–34.

Papacharissi, Zizi. 2015. *Affective Publics: Sentiment, Technology, and Politics.* Oxford: Oxford UP.

Scannell, Paddy. 2015. "Cultural studies: Which paradigm?" *Media, Culture & Society* 37 (4): 645–54.

Thomas, P. J. 1989. *Malayala Sahityavum Christianikalum* (Malayalam Literature and Christians). Kottayam: DC Books.

Williams, Raymond. 1977. *Marxism and Literature.* Oxford: Oxford UP.

———. 2015. *Politics and Letters: Interviews with New Left Review.* London: Verso Books.

Zwischenberger, Cornelia. 2019. "From Inward to Outward: The Need for Translation Studies to Become Outward-going." *The Translator* 25 (3): 256–68.

TWO

Translation of *Les Misérables* and the Making of the Modern Malayali

In 1925 a novel appeared in the literary firmament of Kerala, radically transforming its literary and moral landscape. This was Nalappat Narayana Menon's *Paavangal*, a translation of Victor Hugo's *Les Misérables*, a French historical novel published in 1862. Hugo in the Preface to the novel had said,

> So long as there shall exist, by reason of law and custom, a social condemnation, which, in the face of civilization, artificially creates hells on earth, and complicates a destiny that is divine with human fatality; so long as the three problems of the age—the degradation of man by poverty, the ruin of women by starvation, and the dwarfing of childhood by physical and spiritual night—are not solved; so long as, in certain regions, social asphyxia shall be possible; in other words, and from a yet more extended point of view, so long as ignorance and misery remain on earth, books like this cannot be useless. (1887, xv)

These words were prophetic in that this classic from nineteenth-century France became one of the most influential novels in shaping the political and moral contours of a modern Malayali reader. It creatively contributed to the nascent sub-national aspirations of a region by firming up the vectors of its aspirations around a universal humanism, offering the cosmopolitan registers for a radical critique of oppression and dehumanisation within the class dynamics of its coalescing social fabric taking shape under its emergent and multiple modernities. The protagonist Jean Valjean's conviction to life imprisonment and nineteen years of hard labour for the crime of stealing a loaf of bread for his starving family would strike a chord in a society which was still reeling under the impacts of natural calamities like the devastating floods of 1924. The Spanish Flu of 1918 caused the death of nearly twenty million people in colonial India. The brunt of these early twentieth-century calamities was borne by the poor from the lowest sections of society. In the 1920s, alongside pandemic-induced uncertainties, the failure of the southwest monsoons resulted in famine-like situations in many parts of the region. Provinces under British India including the Central Provinces, or what is today Maharashtra, Chhattisgarh and Madhya Pradesh, and the United Province or modern Uttar Pradesh, actually declared a famine, while the Bombay Presidency was also seriously affected (Viswanathan 2020). Madras Presidency registered a mortality rate of 15.8 per thousand. An article on the severity of the Spanish Flu reads thus:

> The economic strain due to war-time inflation and commodity shortages further exacerbated these difficulties by making essential commodities such as food and kerosene dearer, and thus beyond the reach of the vast majority of the population. Although not directly related to the disease, parts of Madras Presidency witnessed food riots in September 1918, indicating the extent of economic deprivation that was rife among the Indian population of that period. (Viswanathan 2020, n.p.)

Nalappat's *Paavangal* was translated into a soil tilled by the angst of such socio-economic upheavals and a resultant social scape ridden with anxieties around penury and deprivation, one that was also percolated by discourses brought in from the rest of India, by the tools of modernity such as the railways and the rise of print journalism. As observed elsewhere, the novel in Malayalam is as much a genre of modernity, as a critique of it, whereby as a discourse of regional modernity it may be considered:

> a mode of literary production whereby the dominant elite under colonial rule could construct its anxieties and aspirations as those of a nation or region. As a result, some of the impelling motives of attempting the novelistic form of writing arise precisely from the discursive terrain of its origins under western colonialism and imperialism, which necessitates the need to reimagine and reshape gendered subjectivities and native economies of desire as well as to

write them into more modern paradigms of significations. (Pillai 2012, 53)

After the early reform projects around caste in the first two decades of twentieth-century Kerala, the thirties witnessed multiple coalitions around class. For example, Meera Velayudhan speaks about coir workers in Aleppey, eighty per cent of whom were estimated to be Ezhavas, being influenced by the egalitarian and rationalist ideas of K. Aiyappan and E. Madhavan, where 'the workers under the leadership of the TLA (Travancore Labour Association) began to perceive their common interests as workers as evident from the resolution passed at the annual conference of the TLA in 1937' (1991, 66). She has argued that the economic interests of all labour organisations comprising of people from different communities and religions appeared to have been similar, there seemed to have been no relevance for religious or communal interests (66). However, it needs to be pointed out that during this time the Congress Socialist Party was gaining influence among the coir workers and there was an 'attempt to win over the workers to its political platform which sought to link the anti-savarna struggles with the anti-imperialist movement, through the development of the independent class organisations of workers and peasants. The general strike of workers in Alleppey in 1938 was decisive in facilitating this shift' (66).

Hugo's *Les Misérables* is as much about the formations and fomentations around class as it is a political education of the bourgeoisie that would address them to renounce their tacit collusion with the hegemonic practices of the emperor. A staunch critic of the Second Empire of Napoleon III, Hugo found freedom in exile. Hugo's exile, which would eventually become a voluntary act and which he embraced unto the triumph of liberty after the collapse of the French empire in 1870, was in a sense an act of satyagraha, as was his protagonist Jean Valjean's long march to the freedom of the soul, relentlessly fighting the soullessness of the state that Gandhi would go on to repudiate so vehemently. It is indeed interesting to note that a year after his magnum opus revolving around the act of stealing a loaf of bread found a voice in Malayalam, the salt satyagraha would be launched by Gandhi in 1930, when the poorest of Indians would be forbidden from producing salt, and instead forced into paying heavy taxes for putting salt into their daily bread. That Gandhi possessed a well-thumbed copy of *Les Misérables* is proof enough that the historical realism of the novel, set amidst the political turbulences of a nascent French nation had many echoes in the troubled ideations around a political India and its beleaguered regions in the early decades of the twentieth century.

Ironically enough, Hugo, who knew no English and had remarked that 'when England wants to chat with me, let her learn my language' (Mah), was able to find a strong foothold in Kerala and imperial India through the English translation of his work, which Nalappat would later translate into Malayalam. Earlier too, translations had left indelible marks on the evolution of Malayalam literature. Early translated works in Malayalam such as Archdeacon Koshi's *Paradesi Mokshayatra* (1847) and Basel Mission's *Sanchariyude Prayanam* (1847)—both translations of John Bunyan's *Pilgrim's Progress*—and Ayilyam Thirunal Ramavarma's translation of Kalidasa's *Shakunthalam* as *Bhashashakuntalam,* can be considered as proto-forms of the Malayalam novel. These translated works are emblematic of the fact that prose works were gaining salience among readers, and writers were growing fond of the prose form. The development of a modern prose style in Malayalam is inextricably linked to the growth of the Malayalam novel, where the earlier lengthy sentences in archaic prose style, deeply influenced by Sanskrit literature, were significantly altered by the realistic prose style close to the spoken form of the language, propounded by translations attempted by many missionary enterprises (Irumbayam 2012, 48–50).

The birth of the novel in Kerala coincided with multiple attempts to re-imagine the region in novel ways—discursively, symbolically and rhetorically re-configuring its spatial terrain through new imaginaries around the self, other and region that helped human subjects reckon with a new sense of individuation and community consciousness. 'The beginning of the novel in Malayalam as elsewhere in the world also coincides with the experience of "privacy" and the coming into existence of the notion of private space' (Pillai 2012, 54). Appu Nedungadi's *Kundalatha*, published in 1887, is regarded by many as the first novel in Malayalam. However, it has been argued that Chandu Menon's *Indulekha*, published in 1889, is 'the first well-shaped Malayalam novel' (Rajan 2000, 117). *Indulekha* was itself the product of a failed attempt at translating Benjamin Disraeli's *Henrietta Temple* into Malayalam. *Indulekha*'s Preface records Chandu Menon's confession that his original attempt was to imitate the genre of the English novel, in short, write 'a novel book' in Malayalam somewhat resembling the 'English novel book' (1965, 2). C. V. Raman Pillai's trilogy *Marthanda Varma* (1891) was published two years after *Indulekha*, and together with the sequels *Dharmaraja* (1913) and *Rama Raja Bahadur*, published in two volumes in 1918–19, 'the trilogy is considered the first and the best of historical romances in Malayalam' (Pillai 2012, 54). Noted critic Gupthan Nair called Raman Pillai 'the lone star in the firmament of Malayalam literature' who produced the three all-time great historical romances in Malayalam fiction (1992, 6). It has been argued that at a crucial moment in Kerala's history, *Indulekha* and *Marthanda Varma* 'kindled an interest in history in the reading public', where *Indulekha*'s focus was on contemporary history, 'critically evaluating moribund tradition and the changing fortunes of the Nair house-hold and the role of women in society and a home under the impact of the West' (Paniker 1998, 21). However, *Marthanda Varma* was located in a far more distant past that invoked heroic traditions. In strikingly diverse ways, these two masterpieces appealed to the readers of the times as 'the local manifestations of a spirit of Pan-Indian Renaissance', thus becoming 'landmarks in the cultural history of Kerala' (Paniker 1998, 21).

However, many of the novels like *Meenakshi* which followed in the literary footsteps of *Indulekha,* seeking to address the emerging middle-class aspirations, did not live up to *Indulekha*'s popular aesthetic appeal, and though the historical romances of Raman Pillai received much legitimacy and currency among the reading public, they remained largely highbrow. Thus, that for more than three decades after *Indulekha* and *Marthanda Varma* Malayalam prose remained curiously immune to any rich and startling influences, until the appearance of Nalappat's translation of *Les Misérables*, speaks volumes about how the simplicity and translucence of his prose had captured the Malayali reading public's imagination, and the sway it would hold in firming the terrain of Malayalam prose. Interestingly enough, *Indulekha* and *Marthanda Varma* sought to reform the subjects of both nascent modernities and earlier feudal systems respectively, while in contrast *Paavangal* sought to address the human subjects erased/banished by both modernity and feudalism, inscribing them squarely into the depth and breadth of a more 'humanist' novel form without compromising on the moral questions this humanist vision engendered. Thus, the resultant experiments with the form of the novel and its stylistic devices feed on and are strengthened by the growing affective economies around universal human emancipation. The formlessness, rather the fluidity of form, of the novel thus outruns the epic genre in Malayalam in charting a new cartographic excess for human subjects, inscribing new worldviews that underscored an anthropocentric immediacy, and having for their cornerstone the autonomy and dignity of the individual self. Thus, at a crucial juncture in the history of the region, *Paavangal*, by writing the specificities and universality of oppression and injustice, invokes an 'idea' of the human as both embodied and aspirational, stringing 'being' and 'becoming' on the dynamic and kinetic form of the novel, helping lay bare the dehumanising and alienating effects of capital, and systems of labour and production.

In 1921, Kesari Balakrishna Pillai had translated Balzac's *Eugenie Grandet,* under the title *Shandilya*, crafting a new language of critique in Malayalam prose for addressing what he perceived as the debased materiality of a rising bourgeois that was gradually overpowering the values of an earlier age of moral consciousness and ascetic strength. Though Kesari's translation is considered 'domesticated', there is an 'ethics of difference' that functions to form 'a resistance against ethnocentrism and racism, cultural narcissism and imperialism, in the interests of democratic geopolitical relations' (Venuti 1995, 20). The translations of this period can be seen as attempts at shrugging away the ideological baggage of British colonial domination, carefully hand-picking writers like Victor Hugo, Guy de Maupassant, Honore de Balzac, Stendhal, Anton Chekhov, Anatole France, Henrik Ibsen, August Strindberg, Luigi Pirandello, Marcel Proust and Franz Kafka, among a host of other non-English authors. This anti-British slant of translational ideology, however unconsciously impelled, was most evident in Kesari Balakrishna Pillai and Nalappat Narayana Menon. Raveendran has argued that the translations by Kesari, Nalappat and Changampuzha represent 'a sort of turning point for the history of literary translation in Malayalam', pointing out that though 'their broad literary humanism and their unconscious subscription to the principles of hermetic aesthetic would have made it impossible for them to take an overtly anti-colonial stand', nevertheless, there is the possibility of 'a tinge of nascent Euro-centrism in their obsessive interest in European writing' (2009, 220). He further elaborates that 'it is possible to look upon their systematic espousal of an international sensibility and their choice of non-British literature to elaborate this sensibility as having prepared the ground for the subsequent development of Malayalam literature in general and of translation in particular' (220). Raveendran comments on Malayalam translators' fascination for African, Caribbean and Latin American literatures during the post-Independence era, as well as 'for the "socialist" models of writing in European literature', pointing out that the process of cultural decolonisation that seems to have 'gained momentum in recent writing in Malayalam associated with new dalit and feminist initiatives can be said to owe a great deal to the developments outlined' (220).

Though much of this is indeed true, the claims around their hermetic aesthetic remain contentious due to the fact that behind the curtains in the Kerala of that period intense social reform projects were happening. Moreover, the appearance of several journals in Malayalam, the rise of print journalism, reading rooms and libraries, all attest to the emergence of new kinds of reading subjects. Ramakrishnan has argued that many of these journals contributed significantly towards 'the deepening self-awareness of the literate middle class which came to be increasingly mobilised both politically and socially' (1999, 37). Creative interpretations such as translations, and the very choice of what to translate can be seen as political acts, helping the language engage in a Bakhtinian dialogism that would mount trenchant critiques around pre-existing epistemological, literary and aesthetic values and traditions.

Paavangal, in three large volumes, published during 1925–28, was translated from English and not French, and the performance arc in the target language remained very different from the original source language of French. Published by Mathrubhumi from Kozhikode (Calicut), the first edition of the first volume came out in 1925, and its second edition in 1957, a few months after Kerala was formed as a state by the State Reorganisation Act, and the year in which the newly born state went into the first legislative assembly election to elect its first democratic government, which by popular mandate turned out to be a Communist-led one. However, the translator had passed away in 1954, before he could see his work go into the second edition. The Preface to the translation begins with an apology for what the translator considers his extreme presumptuousness in thinking that he could at all translate this sublime work of literature with his meagre linguistic repertoire. He goes on to elaborate that there were more than six or seven English translations, of which he chose the one that was most elaborate, and almost completely in sync with the original source as per experts in French. This translation by Isabel F. Hapgood, published in 1887, is famous for its numerous illustrations, and more than seventy explanatory footnotes. Nalappat particularly refers to the fact that he chose an 'unabridged' version, which explicates his determination to do justice to the original. The evident awe with which he approaches Hugo's masterpiece, his sanctification of the source text, almost consecrating it as a 'secularised scripture' (Narayanamenon 1957, 235), and the constant anxiety to preserve the classic as a classic, all point towards a normal refusal on the part of the translator to go beyond the concept of fidelity to the original. However, Nalappat's translation process in practice refuses to follow the often overlapping translational forms that such reverence takes, as listed by Venturi, 'ethical simplification—which is carried out in obeisance to the sanctioned values of the target society' and 'linguistic simplification—which erases, elevates and homogenises the different linguistic varieties of the source' (1995, 236). In his averred intentions to use the French pronunciations of names, he points out that since both French and English are foreign languages for Malayalis, it would only be befitting that one uses the French original. Pointing out the manner in which the original is bonded with French and European histories, he admits that those who had till then indulged in reading practices that did not exert pressures on the heart and the intellect would find his translation taxing. For such 'fainthearted readers' Nalappat attaches the translation of a letter written by Victor Hugo to his Italian translator M. Daelli, and points out that the walls so proudly built by the narrow-minded have no value for the Master who crafted this universe, and that no matter what be the histories of nations, the histories of the humankind remain essentially the same. Hugo's letter to Daelli, written on 18 October 1862, is literally translated by Nalappat and included after the Preface. It dedicates *Les Misérables* to all republics

> ... which have slaves as well as to Empires which have serfs. Social problems overstep frontiers. The sores of the human race, those great sores which cover the globe, do not halt at the red or blue lines traced upon the map. In every place where man is ignorant and despairing, in every place where woman is sold for bread, wherever the child suffers for lack of the book which should instruct him and of the hearth which should warm him, the book of Les Misérables knocks at the door and says: 'Open to me, I come for you'. (Hugo 'Letter', web n.p.)

Nalappat was obviously captivated by Hugo's logic that 'At the hour of civilization through which we are now passing, and which is still so somber, the miserable's name is Man; he is agonising in all climes, and he is groaning in all languages', since this very same passionate brief about universal humanism animates his Preface too.

Nalappat in his Preface even appeals to the curiosity and large-heartedness of his readers to put the footnotes to good use (differentiating his own from that of Hugo's with asterisks). One can see that the translator is not just translating, but revealing the function he attributes to his translation, moulding literary tastes and crafting a new 'Malayali reader', armed with what Hugo calls 'a new logic of art, and of certain requirements of composition which modify everything, even the conditions, formerly narrow, of taste and language, which must grow broader like all the rest' (Hugo 'Letter'). He reiterates with his source text and author that, whether French or Malayali, misery concerns us all. The function of his translation is to remind his Malayali reading public that 'ever since history has been written, ever since philosophy has meditated, misery has been the garment of the human race; the moment has at length arrived for tearing off that rag, and for replacing, upon the naked limbs of the Man-People, the sinister fragment of the past with the grand purple robe of the dawn' (Hugo 'Letter'). For the burgeoning middle-class readers of the period, Nalappat reveals how translation can become a tool to enter global discourses.

Thus, it is that nationalists, socialists, anti-caste revolutionaries, and all other kinds of readers find an affective footing in *Paavangal*, with a burgeoning love for simplicity of language and life, and a 'Hugoesque' patriotism, not for the emerging nation, but for humanity at large.

One of the most remarkable paratextual aspects of *Paavangal* is its dedication. The work of translation is dedicated to 'the miserables of Kerala' (1957, n.p.), a bold act of interpellation which in one broad sweep implicates the readers of the translation into a deeply humanist vision. Kerala, at that time, was witnessing the rise of a community of newly literate middle class. Their sensibilities were shaped by new forms and genres such as the newspaper, textbooks, periodicals and literary criticism. Many of them also came to constitute the intellectual core of the nationalist movement in Kerala. This bourgeoise middle class played a crucial role in constituting literature as a discourse as well as wielding it in creating new ideations around the structure of relations within the institution of family. This emergent social collective, forging complex, contingent and relatively different attitudes, and shifts in perceptions, lifestyles and dispositions, imagined themselves as different in their orientations with the value systems, ways of life, or sensibilities, of those engaged in physical labour, mainly agricultural labourers and a manual workforce. The translation of *Les Misérables* unveiled a novel experiential terrain within a newly unfurled cosmopolitan literary map that made possible new dialogic engagements between the *universal* and the *indigenous* around issues of hunger, poverty, morals and social position in a fast-changing world. The poverty of a thief's family, the universal war between good and evil, the priest who recognises the thief's hunger despite being located in a position of power, and the status of a saviour accorded to him, were elements that found an echo in the new middle class.

Hugo's humanism also echoed Marx's idea that 'we must make the actual oppression even more oppressive by making [the people] conscious of it, and the insult even more insulting by publicising it' in order that people be taught the courage to be shocked by themselves (Marx 2000, 74). *Les Misérables* is, at its very core, the rendering visible of dehumanising and oppressive structures and practices in social life in order that people are shocked by recognising themselves in the other. The Marxian premise that what appeared to be singular or isolated forms of suffering and injustice had to be made visible in order to reveal the universal nature of human suffering and injustice is exemplified by Hugo through the plight of Jean Valjean who epitomises the essential human condition of oppression and suffering, so much a part of the very quality of being human. Bipin Chandra has argued that when it came to peasant mobilisations during the phase of India's nationalist movements, even the political left failed to mobilise the anti-feudal and economic consciousness of the peasants towards anti-imperialist goals (1979, 355–56). Interestingly enough, Nalappat's translation seems to address, in however tangential a manner, the dehumanising conditions which both feudal and imperial forces had colluded to nurture in India, attempting to induce a self-reflexive social critique of the concept of the human in both socialist and nationalist discourses and mobilisations. Nalappat, through delineating Hugo's approach to humanism, dwelling at length on its operative paradigms, both within the translation as also its paratextual elements, creates a framework for a deeper empathy for all kinds of struggles against dehumanisation, agrarian revolts, peasant mobilisations, nationalist movements and socialist uprisings. In fact, V. T. Bhattathiripad has written about his deep indebtedness to this man and said that it was Nalappat who taught him the greatness of humanism, leading him out of the dark corridors of Brahmanism where he was stumbling in blindness. If in front of all the fire and brimstone of the radical revolutionary reform movements that was ushered into the Namboothiri community, including the boycotting of the veil, mixed feasting for all castes and widow remarriage, we find the formidable presence of Bhattathiripad, behind him stood the indomitable humanist, Nalappat Narayana Menon (Vasudevan 2022).

It was a translation that created a new linguistic, social and literary imaginary. Significantly, the absence of caste as an irritant in a new secular and political imaginary might have contributed to making the translation itself more appealing. The novel's close scrutiny of class posited humanism as a creed. Kalpetta Balakrishnan (2005) has pointed out that Keralites understood the oceanic expanse of the novel form from Nalappat's translation, wherein he closely adhered to the cultural specificities and sentimentalities of the source text, undertaking a literal translation of several usages such as 'born with a silver spoon', presenting with utmost bravery alien phrases and unknown ideas to Malayali readers. In this sense he can be called a curator of the early-nineteenth-century French culture, people and ideals, proffering new cultural sensibilities without losing their substance in all their totality (184–90). In the process, Balakrishnan claims that Nalappat in attempting to present a critically enlightened way to look at society, its structures and the repercussions they engendered in the experiential lives of people, influenced and engendered the progressive, humanist and social reformist ideals which became the cornerstone of the 'Jeeval Sahithya Prasthanam' and later 'Purogamana Sahithya Prasthanam', the progressive writers' movement of the 1930s—influencing the likes of Kesari, Thakazhi, Kesavadev, Bhasheer, Pottekatt and Uroob. Though nationalistic underpinnings are salient in the early works of Pottekatt and Uroob, they also attest to the tenderness and allure of the novel form that was a hallmark of Nalappat's translation. K. M. Tharakan also cites *Paavangal* as an influential text that, by focusing on the miseries of the hardworking, oppressed people and the inherent goodness of humanity, ignited the creative imagination of the writers belonging to the progressive writers' movement in the 1930s (2005, 74). In 2012, as celebrations reverberated across Europe marking the 150th anniversary of Victor Hugo's magnum opus, sesquicentennial celebrations were organised in Kerala too. A newspaper reports that 'Hugo's novel had a pivotal role in moulding the socio-political sensibilities of erstwhile literary luminaries in Malayalam, including Basheer, Thakazhi and Kesavadev. Poet Vallathol's remark that *Paavangal* should be read in front of the *nilavilakku* (ritual lamp) as if devouring a sacred text is a befitting testimony to the novel's influence in the society then' ('Re-reading' 2012). Many translations/adaptations of *Les Misérables* have appeared in Malayalam including a movie *Neethipeedam* in 1977. However, Nalappat's translation has acquired a canonical status, becoming part of school and college curriculum. The brilliance of the translation is that without any act of domesticating the original, it created an affective sphere that wrote Malayali readers into new communicative and experiential terrains. This is probably the reason why writers like

N. S. Madhavan have called it the first modern Malayalam novel (2006, 71). As long as the Malayali harkens, borrowing Hugo's words, to the cries of the miserable groaning in many languages, caught in prejudices, superstitions, tyrannies, fanaticisms and blind laws lending assistance to ignorant customs, *Paavangal* lives on, not as a translation, but as a living landscape populated by the distinctive characters and experiences of the people of Kerala, where Jean Valjean becomes a prototypical Malayali, on the run across multifarious spaces, diasporic at home, exile elsewhere, emerging out of the sewers of civilisational waste and urban uncanny, as the triumphant spirit of the modern that overpowers the darkness of dehumanised social and religious practices and cesspools of oppressive habits and customs.

<h2 style="text-align:center">REFERENCES</h2>

Balakrishnan, Kalpetta. 2005. *Malayala Sahitya Charithram*. Thiruvananthapuram: The State Institute of Languages.

Chandra, Bipin. 1979. *Nationalism and Colonialism in Modern India*. Hyderabad: Orient Longman.

Hugo, Victor. 1887. Preface. *Les Misérables*, xv. New York: Thomas Y. Crowell & Sons.

———. 'Letter to M. Daelli.' *Sparknotes*, https://www.sparknotes.com/lit/lesmis/full-text/letter-to-m-daelli.

Irumbayam, George. 2012. *Malayala Novel Pathompatham Noottandil* (Malayalam novel in the nineteenth century). Thrissur: Kerala Sahitya Akademi.

Madhavan, N. S. 2006. "*Priyapetta Vijayanu*" (To Dear Vijayan). In *O. V. Vijayan: Ormapusthakam* (O. V. Vijayan: A Memory Book), edited by P. K. Rajashekharan. Kottayam: DC Books.

Mah, Ann. "Where Victor Hugo Found Freedom." *ChinaDaily*, https://www.chinadaily.com.cn/travel/2012-08/13/content_15671774.htm.

Marar, Kuttikrishna. 1979. *Sahithyavidya* (Literary Education). Kozhikode: Mararsahithyaprakasham.

Marx, Karl. 2000. *Karl Marx: Selected Writings*, edited by David McLellan. Oxford: Oxford UP.

Menon, Nalappat Narayana, trans. 1957. *Paavangal*, by Victor Hugo. Kozhikode: Mathrubhumi.

Menon, O. Chandu. 1965. *Indulekha: A Novel from Malabar*, translated by W. Dumergue. Kozhikode: Mathrubhumi.

Nair, S. Gupthan. 1992. *C. V. Raman Pillai*. Thrissur: Sahitya Akademi.

Paniker, Ayyappa. 1998. Introduction. *Marthanda Varma*, by C. V. Raman Pillai, 11–23. Thrissur: Sahitya Akademi.

Paul, M. P. 1958. *Gadyagathi*. Kottayam: SPSS.

———. 1991. *Novelsahithyam*. Kozhikode: Poorna.

Pillai, C. V. Raman. 1998. *Marthanda Varma* (1891), translated by B. K. Menon. Thrissur: Sahitya Akademi.

———. 2003. *Rama Raja Bahadur* (1918–1919), translated by Prema Jayakumar. Thrissur: Sahitya Akademi.

———. 2009. *Dharmaraja* (1913), translated by G. S. Iyer. Chennai: Tranquebar.

Pillai, Meena T. 2012. "Modernity and the Fetishizing of Female Chastity: C. V. Raman Pillai and the Anxieties of the Early Malayalam Novel." *South Asian Review* 33(1): 53–75.

Pillai, N. Krishna. 2016. *Kairaliyude Katha* (Kairali's Story). Kottayam: DC Books.

Rajan, P. K. 2000. "Three Heroines: Indulekha, Sita and Gauri—A Study in Feminine Consciousness." In *Comparative Literature: Essays in Honour of Professor B. Q. Khan*, edited by Bijay Kumar Das, 117–25. Chennai: Atlantic.

Ramakrishnan, E. V. 1999. "From Region to Nation and Beyond; Allegories of Power in Malayalam Fiction." In *Rethinking Development: Kerala's Development Experience, Volume I*, edited by M. A. Oommen, 36–44. New Delhi: Institute of Social Science and Concept Publishing Company.

Raveendran, P. P. 2009. "Decolonization and the Dynamics of Translation: An Essay in Historical Poetics." *Indian Literature*, 53 (4): 214–25.

Sucheth, P. R. 2012. "Re-reading of *Paavangal* can awaken a new political conscience." *The New Indian Express*, https://www.newindianexpress.com/states/kerala/2012/oct/08/re-reading-of-paavangal-can-awaken-a-new-political-conscience-413414.html.

Tharakan, K. M. 2005. *Malayala Novel Sahithya Charithram*. Thrissur: Kerala Sahitya Akademi.

Vasudevan, V. T. 2022. "*Namboodiri Samudhayathil Nadanna Viplavathkamaaya Ellaa Sambhavangaludeyum Munpil Njaanayirunnu Enkil Pinnil Naalapaattundaayirunnu*" (If I stood at the forefront of all revolutionary events within the Namboodiri community then Naalapaattu led from the other end). *Samakaalika Malayalam*, https://m.samakalikamalayalam.com/malayalam-vaarika/essays/2022/

may/19/about-the-personal-relationship-between-vt-bhattathiripad-and-nalappattu-narayana-menon-149514.amp#amp_tf=From%20%2 51%24s&aoh=17009824592830&referrer=https%3A%2F%2Fwww. google.com.

Velayudhan, Meera. 1991. "Caste, Class and Political Organisation of Women in Travancore." *Social Scientist* 19 (5/6): 61–79.

Venturi, Paola. 2009. "'David Copperfield' Conscripted: Italian Translations of the Novel." *Dickens Quarterly* 26 (4): 234–47.

Venuti, Lawrence. 1995. *The Translator's Invisibility: A History of Translation.* London: Routledge.

Viswanathan, V. 2020. "The 1918 'Spanish' Flu Pandemic in India and Eerie Similarities to COVID-19 in 2020." *Newsclick*, https://www.newsclick. in/Spanish-Flu-Lessoons-for-India-in-COVID.

THREE

Translating Culture

Is Gabriel García Márquez a Malayali?

In 'The Task of the Translator', Walter Benjamin (2007) raises a very pertinent question—'is a translation meant for readers who do not understand the original?' (59). This would perhaps reflect the lacuna of proposing translation as a site for mere transmission, disregarding its cultural and political iterations. Translation in itself is an activity dependent on its relationship with a cultural system as the act of translation is foundationally as cultural as it is linguistic. It does not take place in a vacuum, and it is the target culture's needs and objectives that largely govern any translational activity, whereby it becomes a semiotic process, involving much more than the transfer of 'meaning' contained in one set of language signs into another set. In 'Fearful Asymmetries: A Manifesto of Cultural Translation', Tomislav Z. Longinovic (2002) poses some interesting questions about how 'hybrid forms of cultural interaction "translate" and domesticate particular political practices?' (5) through a process involving a whole set of extra-linguistic criteria.

Translated literature has maintained a key position in the literary polysystem in most Bhasha literatures in India. For example, for the relatively small and less dominant linguistic group of Malayalis, on the tip of the Indian subcontinent, translation has often been an activity of inclusion and assimilation as well as resistance and subversion. Almost all the early translations in our regional literatures strove to promote native registers, dialects, discourses and styles, in the process uniformly struggling to erase the foreignness of the source text. Translation has thus been part of Bhasha literatures' attempts to crystallise and strengthen themselves, by incorporating the experiments, strengths and resources of other literatures, and therefore, have been largely oriented towards acceptability, adhering to target culture norms and often investing the foreign language text with domestic significance. This 'ethnocentric reduction' (Venuti 2008, 15) or domestication of the source text to the target text often adopts a 'transparent, fluent style' (Yang 2010, 77) to minimise the strangeness of the source text. However, the process of cultural appropriation, many a time, leads to the erasure of differences of culture, as the priority is on the target text rather than the source. This process of domestication begins with the very choice of texts to be translated to the act of translation *per se*, continues in the process of reading, and culminates in the review or the absence of it. The translation is thus never 'impartial' but is shaped by the power dynamics at play, and the 'scandals of translation are cultural, economic and political' (Venuti 1998, 1). Translational acts are political in that even as they open windows 'on another world' and, 'often not without a certain reluctance', they bring foreign influences to penetrate 'native culture', resulting in ensuing challenges and subversions (Lefevere qtd. in Ruano 2018, 258). Manoeuvering the transactional flows of ideas, affect and cultural artefacts between the local, regional and the global, translation is as much about identities and national formations as it is about the cultural imaginaries around spatial deployments and investments in historical moments. The idea of a region like Kerala is the result of multiple translational/transcreative imaginations that use symbolic structures to code political possibilities and exclusionary implications, simultaneously creating and interpellating 'Malayali' subjects in the process. However, a critical regionalism would help one infer that a Malayali is born not just out of a linguistic configuration but also from the regionally inflected manifestations of the 'other'. Each act of translation, in that sense, is an act of reconciliation between the local and the universal, performing the inherent paradox of a dialectical tension between them.

Malayalam, which belongs to the Dravidian family of languages, is the mother tongue of over thirty million people, most of whom live in Kerala but many who are also dispersed across the globe. It has been pointed out that like Malayalis, Malayalam has also been open to foreign influences, in turn nurturing a literature that 'reflects this spirit of accommodation', over centuries building a tradition, 'which even while rooted in the locality, is truly universal in taste' and 'remarkably free from provincialisms and parochial prejudices that have bedevilled the literature of certain other areas' (Paniker 1998, 9). Malayalam's basic Dravidian stock has been embellished by 'elements borrowed or adopted from non-Dravidian literatures such as Sanskrit, Arabic, French, Portuguese and English', with the earliest of such associations being from Tamil, though Sanskrit 'accounts for the largest of the "foreign influences" followed closely in recent times by English', creating a 'broad based cosmopolitanism' which is 'a distinctive feature of Malayalam literature' (9).

Malayalam literature has been greatly influenced and transformed by translations, and innumerable authors and great books have all found a space for themselves in Malayalam through translation. The first conscious literary endeavour in Malayalam and probably its first epic poem, *Ramacharitam*, believed to have been penned in the twelfth century CE, can be called a translation and is a retelling of the *Yudha Kanda* of *Valmiki Ramayana*. Probably the first translation of the *Bhagavad Gita* into a modern Indian language was into Malayalam by Madhava Panikkar, one of the Niranam poets in the fifteenth century. In the same century, Niranathu Rama Panikkar translated the *Ramayana* and the *Mahabharata*, which became renowned as *Kannassa Ramayanam* and *Kannassa Bharatam*. During this time, Sankara Panikkar made a remarkable condensation of the *Mahabharatam* and called it *Bharatamala*.

In the sixteenth century, Thunchathu Ezhuthachan, considered the father of Malayalam poetry, translated the *Ramayanam* and the *Mahabharatam*. His *Adhyatma Ramayanam* and *Srimahabharatam* used the *killippattu* form, where he devised a new narrative technique of using a bird or 'kili' as narrator of the poems. Ezhuthachan's bird can thus be treated as a metaphor for the process of translation itself. However, scholars like Ayyappa

Paniker (1998) have pointed out that Ezhuthachan was not a mere translator but that '... in fact he follows the earlier Kerala writers in freely elaborating or condensing the original as he thinks proper. The celebration of this freedom gained in poetic creation is what enlivens and ennobles the hymns interspersed in his works' (30). Thus, translation is always 'doubly contextualized' (Lefevere and Bassnett 1990, 11) and is one of the many 'rewritings' ensuring the 'survival of a work of literature', whereby the original text cannot be considered as a 'monolithic' statement by the author, but a 'polyphonic' (Tabakowska qtd. in Lefevere and Bassnett 1990, 10) entity in itself.

It would be worthwhile to examine what was the function attributed to translation in that age by these ancient scholars. Cheeraman, the translator of *Ramayana* in the twelfth century, expounds his aim in writing *Ramacharitam*. He says, '*Uzhiyil cheriyavarkariyumarura cheyvan*', meaning to enlighten the common folk of this world. The Niranam poets also had the specific purpose of Dravidianization of Aryan mythology and philosophy, and together 'they constitute the strong bulwark of the Bhakti movement, which enabled the Malayalis to withstand and resist the onslaught of foreign cultures' (Paniker 1998, 23). As Devy (1993) points out, these 'translations were made without any inhibition, and they rarely maintained a word-for-word, line-for-line discipline'. The categories useful for the study of these translations are not 'the T L and the S L' or 'the mother tongue and the other tongue' (149). The writers attempting such 'vernacular rendering of Sanskrit texts treated both the languages as their "own"', and even while evincing 'a sense of possession in respect of the Sanskrit heritage', used translation as a tool to 'liberate the scriptures from the monopoly of a restricted class of people', thus making them 'a means of re-organising the entire societies' (149).

One cannot but agree with Devy here and assert that no theory with an exclusively linguistic orientation can be adequate to understand the magnitude of translation activity in Kerala at that time.

Many theorists of translation too have looked at the issue of domestication from different angles that trace distinct trajectories. Benjamin (2007) observes that translation ought to be on the outside of the 'language forest', and the 'echo' in its own language should be able to send the 'reverberation of the work in the alien one' (76). In that sense, the ST (source text) and the TT (target text) must remain as 'fragments' of a 'greater' (78) language as well as the culture that the former represents. Friedrich Schleiermacher in his lecture *On the Different Ways of Translation*, argues that translations into different languages should sound different because 'if all translations read and sound alike, the identity of the source text would be lost' (qtd. in Yang 2010, 78). Venuti proposed an 'ethnodeviant' way to 'restrain the ethnocentric violence of translation' (qtd. in Yang 2010, 78), foregrounding the identity of the ST. Rudolf Pannwitz notes that often the error of the translator is that 'he preserves the state in which his own language happens to be instead of allowing his language to be powerfully affected by the foreign tongue. Particularly when translating from a language very remote from his own he must go back to the primal elements of language itself and penetrate to the point where work, image, and tone converge' (qtd. in Benjamin 2007, 81). While attempting to expand and deepen one's language by means of the foreign language, translators oftentimes do not realise 'to what extent this is possible, to what extent any language can be transformed, how language differs from language almost the way dialect differs from dialect; however, this last is true only if one takes language seriously enough, not if one takes it lightly' (qtd. in Benjamin 2007, 81).

Benjamin's concerns with seriousness around notions of language crystallise in the modern era in Kerala, where the first play in Malayalam was a translation of Kalidasa's *Abhijnana Sakuntalam* by Kerala Varma Valiya Koyitampuran in 1882. The first attempt at writing a novel was again a translation titled *Ghataka vadham* (*The Slayer's Slain*). O. Chandu Menon's *Indulekha* (1889) believed to be the first perfect novel in Malayalam was also the result of an attempt to translate the English novel genre into Malayalam. Even the first book printed in Kerala in 1821 was a translation titled *Cheru Paithangalude Upakarartham Englishil Ninnum Paribhasha Peduthiya Kathakal* (Stories Translated from English for the Benefit of Little Children). The Bible translations under the leadership of Herman Gundert and Benjamin Bailey also played a great role in shaping Malayalam prose.

It is also significant to note that very early in the history of Malayalam there started a plethora of translations from other Indian languages into Malayalam. The first translation of a Tamil text was into Malayalam in 1595—the prose translation of the *Thirukural* by Aikaramatho Panikkar. There were numerous translations of the *Gitanjali* into Malayalam. Most of the great poets and writers of Malayalam were also able translators. Kumaranasan's translation of *Ramayana* for children, Changampuzha's and G. Sankara Kurup's translations of Omar Khayyam's *Rubaiyyat*, Sankara Kurup's translation of *Gitanjali* in addition to the pioneering works already mentioned merit special attention.

To say that translated literature has always maintained a key position in the literary polysystem in Malayalam would thus not be an exaggeration. For the relatively small and less dominant linguistic group of Malayalis, translation is as much an activity of inclusion and assimilation as resistance and subversion. One can thus safely surmise that in the context of Kerala, translation can be 'readily seen as investing the foreign language text with domestic significance ... because the translator negotiates the linguistic and cultural differences of the foreign text by reducing them and supplying another set of differences, basically domestic, drawn from the receiving language and culture to enable the foreign to be received there' ("Translation, Community, Utopia", 468).

It can be argued that the process of inscribing domestic, linguistic and cultural values to a foreign text steers the production, circulation and reception of the translated text, and culminates in the review or the absence of it. Thus, the review too in such a context is often seen to be inscribed with domestic intelligibilities and ideologies. This could be one of the reasons why translation reviewing has never been given much importance in Malayalam.

A reviewer of any translation should first seek to answer why a particular work was chosen for translation at a particular point of time. This attempt to correlate the principles of selection to the literary systems of the source and target culture would provide valuable insights into the position and role of the translated work within a given culture and language. Instead, most reviews in Malayalam treat these works not as translations but as works 'natural' to Malayalam, thus negating their foreignness and making them prey to too easy an appropriation into the oeuvre of Malayalam literature. Such reviews and readings in turn promote annexationist translations and sanctify imitations, adaptations, and paraphrasing, often without acknowledging the original. Reviews are often seen to treat the translated work as a domestic inscription rather than one that bears the function of intercultural communication.

Here I would like to cite the example of the renowned critic Kuttikrishna Marar's review of the Malayalam translation of Premchand's *Godan* by Divakaran Potti (1957, 92–97). The review is a vitriolic attack on Premchand, whose ideologies and aesthetic ideals were antithetical to Marar's. It is a battle between Premchand, the social reformist writer, and Marar, an unstinting champion of the values of classical criticism. The review is nowhere a review of the translation of *Godan* but a battle of two clashing ideologies taking place in Kerala society of the fifties. Marar's review makes possible only a domesticated understanding of Premchand, and his rating of Premchand is inversely proportional to the degree of subversiveness that Premchand induces in the domestic. Marar remains immune to the question of whether the translated *Godanam* communicates the basic elements of the narrative form of the original or to the analysing of shifts in translation or to the level of transmission of the invariants or even to the argument of whether invariance is at all possible in a translation from Hindi to Malayalam.

It is easy for the translator, reader and reviewer of a minority linguistic community to deflect from the foreignness of the "Translated Text" and focus instead on the degree of its conformity or opposition to dominant domestic ideologies and interests inscribed in it. Such agendas, strategies and interests are often determined by the function that is attributed to translation in a particular culture. In the case of a reformist work like *Godan* that had received a wide readership all over India, the translation could become the site for reviewers like Marar to challenge or contest the upcoming trends of an era of change. Thus, Marar uses *Godanam* as a context to foster a community of readers who would oppose the progressive socialist and reformist trends in literature in Kerala. For this, he adopts a universalist stance, rejecting the specificity of the translated work and focusing instead on its broad and general aspects. What Marar in fact attempts to do is to position *Godan* in the novel tradition of Malayalam and attack Premchand for not conforming to the norms and conventions of this tradition. Thus, what Marar finds in the translational discourse of *Godanam* is a subversion of his own critical conventions that he seems to mistake Premchand for one of his Malayali adversaries of the Progressive Writers' Forum.

Such a lack of perception on the part of reviewers stems, I feel, not from the lack of knowledge of the nature and scope of translation or its norms, but rather from a willing suspension of such norms in the larger interest of a socio-cultural function attributed to translation by a cultural community. Translation does not take place in a vacuum, and it is the target culture's needs and objectives that largely govern the translational activity taking place in that culture. Thus, when the translational behaviour and responses taking place within a culture start manifesting certain regularities, one can safely surmise that the norms that particular culture attributes to translation have manoeuvred different shifts of validity and reached a fairly stable axis of normativity. Translations in Malayalam are largely 'acceptability-oriented' and adhere to target culture norms. For example, the large amount of Russian and Marxist literature which found its way into Malayalam is beyond doubt due to the popularity of leftist ideology in the state. Thus, the translation policy regarding the 'choice' of what to translate seems to predominate other translation norms like operational norms and textual-linguistic norms that govern the relationship between the ST and TT and the selection of linguistic material to formulate the TT, respectively.

Any translation, which, according to Berman (2000), ought to be 'a trial of the foreign' (284), often becomes its negation, acclimation and naturalisation. Often the most individual essence of the ST is radically repressed, and this is where one feels the need for proper reviewing and reflection on the ethical aim of the translating act of receiving the foreign as foreign. A review that does not respect the linguistic and cultural differences of the ST in fact, promotes bad translation ethics and helps in creating a tribe of ethnocentric translators. The absence of proper reviewing and studies of translation could also lead to the neglect of translation norms, which further pave the way for weak, entropic, lack-lustre translations.

Kerala, as a land which from ancient times has witnessed extensive foreign influence and interactions with Chinese and Arab travellers to the Portuguese, Dutch, French and English colonial interventions, has remained remarkably open to the complex heterogeneity of the historical and cultural discourses thus generated. In the twentieth century, one can see two things which probably brought in a definite agenda to translation activity in Kerala and connected the pre-modern with the modern. The first is, of course, a compulsive need to be part of a pan-Indian consciousness in the backdrop of the Independence struggle and the awakening of a spirit of nationalism. The second is the anxiety of a small socio-linguistic group to negotiate the boundaries between the local and the international during its engagement with the language of modernity. These contradictory impulses signal the rise of translation from other Indian languages like Bengali and Hindi on one side and from foreign languages on the other. Nevertheless, this rise in translation did not create a corresponding theoretical discussion of translation studies or create the need for a realistic historiography of translation criticism. Kerala and its people, having been exposed to multiple languages and cultures, have a 'translating consciousness' as Devy (1992) would call it. But this consciousness has been made so familiar and humdrum that it has not been thought worthwhile to invest any effort in discussing the aesthetics of translation or its theorisation. Thus, translation, which should have brought in a new strength to Malayalam literature, falls short of this function by remaining constricted by an overpowering native culture and unhoned by sharp critical tools. Therefore, the failure to capture the vital and transitory energy of a cross-cultural enterprise in any systematic framework also leads to the lack of evolving an appropriate methodology for studying translation. This leaves the average reader seriously crippled by neither knowing what to expect of a translation nor having any critical tools to judge it. Though any critical analysis of Malayalam literature cannot overrule the great role of translation in shaping its literary tradition, it is indeed a shocking revelation that there have been no studies of the history of literary translation or its critical postulates, nor does it find any serious mention in any of the prominent texts on literary criticism in Malayalam. Thus, there is an imperative need for a reorganised historical perspective of literary criticism in Kerala with a more punctilious scrutiny of the process of assimilation of the 'foreign' and 'other Indian' traditions and texts into Malayalam.

Even as we acknowledge the fact that Kerala as a region experienced wave after wave of alien influx from time immemorial, one is reminded of Devy's statement that

> Colonial experience releases several conflicting tendencies in the colonised society. It simultaneously creates a revivalistic romanticism and a hardheaded political pragmatism. This simultaneous release of several conflicting tendencies results in a strange, superficial cultural dynamics. A colonised culture becomes violently progressive and militantly retrogressive, and in consequence, tends to remain static. In order to understand this cultural immobilisation an appropriate historiography is of prime importance. (1992, 4)

This violent progression and militant retrogression are evident in the profusion of translations in Malayalam as well as in the apathy to study them with critical rigour and review them, relentlessly probing motivations, methods and alignments. Translation is a voracious activity in Malayalam, but this untrammelled appetite, coupled with the lack of efficacy of the intellectual tools of Malayalam literary criticism to review or assess the process and act of translation, leads to a state of literary dyspepsia. Though it can be said that translation in Kerala has a history of nearly eight hundred years, the continuing practice has not given rise to any significant and original translation theory. Such theorisation would have helped bring in some critical rigour in the analyses of translation praxis. Dalton S. Collins (2008) points out that since the early 1970s, a cultural emphasis has initiated a rebellion against past and present colonialist and ethnocentric scholarship in translation. He writes that within this cultural turn, 'attention is paid to representations of the Other and to how these representations relate to our construction of the Self', where 'the Other is distinguished from the Self through difference, that is, through aspects with which we do not self-identify' (334). Collins further argues that 'the injection of "cultural studies" into translatology and work dealing with the connections between language and culture' adds a new cultural angle to the dimensions to the translator's 'always-present dialogic dilemma' (334).

It is against such a theoretical backdrop that I place translations of Gabriel García Márquez's work such as *Ekanthathayude Nooruarshangal* (*One Hundred Years of Solitude*), which, without acknowledging the original Spanish language or culture from which it was translated into English and not revealing whether it is a translation of the Spanish original or the English translation by Gregory Rabessa, in fact situate themselves in an ambivalent space between two languages and cultures. No review of the translation has raised the question of what the direct source text of the Malayalam translation is, whether it is the Spanish *Cien Anos de Soledad* by Márquez or the English *One Hundred Years of Solitude* translated by Gregory Rabessa.

If the Malayalam translator has used the English translation, is he equipped to translate the inscriptions of the original Spanish text or has he been forced to adopt the English version as 'the transparent vehicle of universal truth, thus encouraging a linguistic chauvinism, even a cultural nationalism?' (Venuti 1998, 92). Thus, what is called for urgently is proper reviewing of translated texts so that the issue of translation is not side stepped in the process of celebrating the taming of the foreign by over-valorising the native language and culture.

The translation (Velayudhan 1984) of *One Hundred Years of Solitude* carries two studies of the original which again fail to anchor the text in its historical and cultural context resulting in a translation which appears free-floating and unhinged from the specificities of history to occupy a universal realm that transcends linguistic and cultural differences. Thus, the fact remains that Márquez in Malayalam translation was one of the most favourite authors for Malayalis, who loved him as their own, the translations selling like hot cakes, so much so that by the time he received the nobel Prize in 1981 he had become a household name in Kerala. DC Books had published three of his most significant novels in Malayalam—*One Hundred Years of Solitude, Love in the Time of Cholera* and *Strange Pilgrims* among a host of other writings. *Ekanthathayude Nooruvarshangal* has an unbeatable record of having gone into 26 editions by 2021. Even small publishing houses like Shikha had done brisk business by publishing many of Márquez's stories in translation. When Márquez died in 2014, Facebook and Twitter (now X) were inundated with tributes to his memories from Kerala, with one such tweet encapsulating the emotional connect: 'Tributes to Gabo, the only Nobel Laureate in Malayalam literature! Bid Adieu to Kerala's own Márquez' (https://www.newindianexpress.com/cities/kochi/2014/apr/19/Marquez-Leaves-an-Indelible-Mark-on-Malayali-Hearts-601946.html).

However, the huge market, or rather a translation industry, feeding the popular appetite for Márquez, often resulted in crude, jaded and often slipshod translations. *Living to Tell the Tale* is translated as *Kadha Parayanoru Jeevitham*, which means 'a life to recount a tale', a translational mishap in the very title. In a similar vein *Strange Pilgrims* becomes *Aparichitha Theerdhadakar* or pilgrims who are strangers. The semantic shift from unusual, curious or odd to that of being unacquainted with someone betrays a lexical/cultural gap that is bridged by applying familiar tropes. One can see here an attempt to appropriate the ST, where the translation/translator fails to 'serve the purpose of expressing the central reciprocal relationship between languages' (Benjamin 2007, 72) and culture, resulting in the target culture remaining curiously unaffected by or immune to the source culture.

The growing market considerations have an enormous influence on translation practices. Many publishing houses have built a reputation on translating foreign titles leading to the 'phenomenon of *bestsellerisation*', and the censorship rights are no longer governed by the state, but by the market, which can result in a growing tendency to resort to 'conventional, sometimes even stereotypical, representations of foreign cultures' (Benmessaoud and Buzelin 2018, 160). These market-oriented translations are governed by short-term goals and the search for the sale of translation rights that starts well before the original is printed, is far from rare. Interestingly, these market strategies are not solely driven by the logic of economy, but the political and cultural dimensions of power relations remain crucial vectors. As Venuti (1998) notes, translation remains a form of writing 'depreciated by the academy, exploited by publishers and corporations' (1), and domesticated translations have virtually become the norm for corporate publishing houses.

The grave handicap of studies and reviews not recognising a text as translated leads to a seriously limited and provincial understanding of texts. Reviews of translations in Malayalam thus need a double focus and should aim to look at the foreign text and culture as well as the translating text and culture. Such reviews could then generate translation discourses and methodologies that would help view culture not as a monolithic concept but as a space where heterogeneous histories and languages commingle and also seek to look at the differential levels of power and privilege under which such activities take place. Such reviews could help reveal how 'different forms of reception construct the significance of the foreign text, and also which of these forms are dominant or marginalised in the domestic culture at any historical moment' (Venuti 1998, 94). Reviews, which can unravel the varying degrees of subordination, which most translations inflict on the source, would thus help reveal the hierarchy of domestic values that produce appropriative movements in the translation encounter and assess the cultural and political significance of such attempts at domestication. Thus, reviewing need not limit itself to linguistic and stylistic scrutiny, but delve into the ideological apparatus that governs the translation and further probe into the politics of translation, and how it assisted in the course of canon formation.

The influence of Chinese, Portuguese, Dutch and British cultures in Kerala and the immigration of Keralites in large numbers to all parts of the world in the twentieth century raises certain fundamental questions about identity. In the context of a booming Malayali diaspora which contributes to large flows of global capital and ideas in the State, the term Malayali has itself thus become the epitome of hybridity, of in-between-ness that postcolonial critics like Bhabha celebrate. Within the discourse of hybridity that so permeates the Malayali psyche, it is possible to argue that translation is also an act of subversion, which seeks to topple the originality of the original. Thus, translation could also be a devouring, a ritualistic eating to assimilate the vitality of the source text, in the process rejuvenating the target language and literature. Such 'vampire translations', which have thrived in Kerala, reject the concepts of 'imitation' and 'influence' and come to represent today a typically postcolonial attitude towards cultural dialogues with dominant ideologies and attitudes. Susan Bassnett (2002) comments, 'The images of translation as cannibalism, as vampirism, whereby the translator sucks out the blood of the source text to strengthen the target text, as transfusion of blood that endows the receiver with new life, can all be seen as radical metaphors that spring from post-modernist post-colonial translation theory' (155). But I would argue that such translations were in currency in Kerala even before the knowledge of post-colonial theory and are a powerful statement of instances of native resistances to colonial power hierarchy be it Sanskrit or English which privilege a particular text as 'original' and relegate the 'other' as translation.

It is Western literary and critical theories that have suffered most at the hands of such 'vampire translations'. Social, literary and philosophical theories ranging from structuralism, cultural materialism, feminism, post-structuralism and deconstruction and a host of other ideas formulated by eminent philosophers and critics from the West have found their way into Malayalam indiscriminately and over-zealously with no proper introduction or acknowledgement, through translations, adaptations and paraphrasing.

It is interesting to note in this context that the translation of John Bunyan's famous allegory *The Pilgrim's Progress* into Malayalam titled *Sanchariyude Prayanam* (1849) and later alternatively called *Paradesee Mokshayathra*, engendered many debates over the name of its translator, some attributing it to Hermann Gundert the illustrious German missionary, scholar, lexicographer, Indologist and translator, since the translation was found in the Tuebingen University Library amongst the printed and handwritten source materials from the collection of Hermann Gundert and his Basel Mission colleagues. Gundert also wrote one of the most significant Malayalam grammar books, *Malayalabhaasha Vyakaranam* (1859), as also a Malayalam-English dictionary (1872), alongside pioneering contributions in the field of Bible translations into Malayalam. The translation has, however, also been attributed to Rev. Joseph Peet, another missionary scholar in British India. In the Malayalam translation of the *Pilgrim's Progress*, the hero Christian, as he traverses through the valley of blood, bones, ashes and dead men, comes across 'Rakshasas' he had not met in the English version, called 'Vigrahasuras'. A little further on, Christian meets 'Mohammed Rakshasa', born more than a thousand two hundred years ago, and the arch-enemy of the 'Vigrahasuras'. Even as such translations might leave one appalled today, they speak volumes about the necessity of making translation visible as an intensely political activity, and in the absence of any concerted critique or efforts to study it, force a reassessment of the cultural and pedagogical practices that might rely solely on such translated texts. However, even as I argue that translation in Kerala is an intensely political activity, often without the Malayali being conscious of it being so, there is still the need to theorise its political and cultural implications and study the different methodologies that could effectively be used to make it truly interdisciplinary and intercultural. The scant attention that critics and reviewers have given to translation policies and strategies has given rise to many conceptual inadequacies in dealing with translations in one of the most translating/translated regions in India, as well as the ensuing lacunae around concrete methodologies to tap its subversive potential.

REFERENCES

Bassnett, Susan. 1993. *Comparative Literature: A Critical Introduction.* Oxford: Blackwell.

———. 2002. *Translation Studies.* London: Routledge.

Benjamin, Walter. 2007. "Task of the Translator." In *Illuminations,* translated by Harry Zohn, 69–82. New York: Schocken Books.

Benmessaoud, Sanaa, and Hélène Buzelin. 2018. "Publishing Houses and Translation Projects." In *The Routledge Handbook of Translation and Culture,* edited by Sue-Ann Harding and Ovidi Carbonell Cortés, 154–76. London: Routledge.

Berman, Antoine. 2000. "Translation and the Trials of the Foreign." In *The Translation Studies Reader,* edited by Lawrence Venuti, 284–97. London: Routledge.

Collins, Dalton S. 2008. "Linking Translation Theory and African History: Domestication and Foreignization in 'Corpus of Early Arabic Sources for West African History'." *Canadian Journal of African Studies/Revue Canadienne des Études Africaines* 42 (2/3): 331–46.

Devy, G. N. 1992. *After Amnesia: Tradition and Change in Indian Literary Criticism.* Hyderabad: Orient Longman.

———. 1993. *In Another Tongue: Essays on Indian Literature in English.* New Delhi: Macmillan.

Lefevere, Andre, and Susan Bassnett. 1990. "Proust's Grandmother and the Thousand and One Nights: The 'Cultural Turn' in Translation Studies." In *Translation, History and Culture*, edited by Andre Lefevere and Susan Bassnett, 1–13. London: Pinter Publishers.

Longinovic, Tomislav Z. 2002. "Fearful Asymmetries: A Manifesto of Cultural Translation." *The Journal of the Midwest Modern Language Association* 35 (2): 5–12.

Marar, Kuttikrishna. 1957. *Danthagopuram*. Kerala: Marar Sahithya Prakasam.

Paniker, K. Ayyappa. 1998. *A Short History of Malayalam Literature*. Trivandrum: Department of Public Relations.

Ruano, M. Rosario Martin. 2018. "Issues in Cultural Translation: Sensitivity, Politeness, Taboo, Censorship." In *The Routledge Handbook of Translation and Culture*, edited by Sue-Ann Harding and Ovidi Carbonell Cortés, 258–78. London: Routledge.

Venuti, Lawrence. 1998. *The Scandals of Translation: Towards an Ethics of Difference*. London: Routledge.

———. 2000. "Translation, Community, Utopia." In *The Translation Studies Reader*, 468–88. London: Routledge.

———. 2008. *The Translator's Invisibility: A History of Translation*. London: Routledge.

Yang, Wenfen. 2010. "Brief Study on Domestication and Foreignization in Translation." *Journal of Language Teaching and Research* 1 (1): 77–80.

FOUR

Gender and Translation

Gender and translation, as two key markers of postmodern conceptualisations of identities, are critically interlinked and contiguous in that subjects are in constant processes of being both 'gendered' and 'translated'. Acts of translation happening between two languages cannot but be gendered because languages themselves are gendered, ingrained with loaded belief systems, value judgements, ideological practices and historical antecedents that are etched with sub-cultural differences, privileging dominant loci of socio-cultural and sexual identities. A 'woman' thus constituted in this hegemonic imaginary is always already delimited in terms of subversive translational acts. Thus, a crucial question that informs literary and cultural acts of translation would be to look at how women's ambiguous relationships to language inform translational practices where there are qualitative and quantitative differences in the production and maintenance of gender hierarchies in the Source Language and the Target Language. While conceding that language is phallogocentric, as Irigaray (1985) would argue, and some more so than others, a feminist translational praxis would try to seek out the multiple political acts of mediation that naturalise gender oppression. This would mean that 'there would no longer be either a right side or a wrong side of discourse, or even of texts, but each passing from one to the other would make audible and comprehensible even what resists the recto-verso structure that shores up common sense' (80).

Malayalam, the official language of the state of Kerala, is a language whose idiomatic, symbolic and communal references seem abundantly inscribed with patriarchal logic, paving the way for numerous historical silences, omissions and elisions of the feminine. So, even translating words like 'sex' and 'gender' become exercises in procrustean linguistic torture by which feminists in the language are often made the target of ridicule. Like many other languages, Malayalam too is ill-equipped to express many words around emerging queer politics in the state, as also those around the intersectional space produced by race, class and the wide spectrum of gender. A South Indian Dravidian language deeply influenced by Sanskrit, Malayalam displays a considerable amount of gender prejudice, both sedimented over time as also contemporary and emerging. The conceptual systems of the language are informed by 'kyriarchal' categories of thought 'which grapple with multiple, intersecting and co-constitutive structures of power and oppression' (Osborne 2015, 137) that internalise and validate various structures of dominance, including gender, class, sexuality, race, nationality and religion in everyday lives.

For example, the theocratic wisdom as encoded in a popular sloka in Sanskrit attests to the ideal 'everyday' roles of women thus: '*Karyeshu Manthri, Karmeshu Dasi, Rupeshu Lakshmi, Kshamaya Dharithri, Sneheshu Matha, Sayaneshu Vesya, Shadkarma Nari Kuladharma Pathni*', meaning an ideal woman should be a minister in practical affairs, a slave in action, Goddess Lakshmi in beauty, Mother Earth in patience, and a sex worker in bed. Here, woman as an analytical and epistemic category can be seen to inhabit diverse, interlocking, and co-constitutive fomentations of power and subjugation that surround and work through the spectrum of subject positions available to her. This is inherited and arduously glorified in the Malayali's linguistic and cultural repertoire, such as in the popular film song '*Karyathil Manthriyum, Karmathil Daasiyum, Roopathil Lakshmiyum Bharya*' (*Raakuyilin Ragasadasil* 1986), numerous leitmotifs of which circulate and gain currency and sanctity in the social and cultural registers of Kerala. In this context, it is important to understand Kerala as a space where women still labour to perform their 'gender' through a constellation of socially sanctioned micropolitical activities that inscribe repetitive acting out of moral codes of conduct and sartorial prescriptions. The advent of Feminist Theory and Women's Studies into this fraught terrain engendered a 'popular' disapproval and disdain as writ large in the aesthetic, cultural and social fabric of the state, in spite of widespread acceptance within academia. This antipathy, though predictable within the scopes of hetero-patriarchal gender regimes, acquires a new valence when read against the state's long tryst with progressive social reform. Despite recording positive trends across many conventional indices of gender development, a phenomenon credited to the 'Navodhanam' or social renaissance of the late nineteenth and early twentieth century, close scrutiny of certain 'dimensions of well-being' highlights 're-formed' and emerging systems of gender inequities in the state (Kodoth and Eapen 2005, 3278).

Interestingly, even as Marxist and liberal humanist ideologies have long entered popular circulation, 'feminism' is earmarked for criticism as a 'foreign theory'. As Jasbir Jain (2011) points out, the reifying of feminism as a Western import, alongside the 'concept of the nation and the creative form of the novel', obliterates the relevance of feminism as a 'sociopolitical reality' (1). But then, a mere celebration of 'fragments' in terms of 'difference and plurality' is not where the stakes lie; it is about gauging and responding to the mediational interfaces through which 'entire packages of ideas and institutions such as nationalism or democracy, free market or socialism, Marxism or feminism' were received (Chaudhary 2011, xiv–xv). The various social, religious and agrarian reform movements which arrived in Kerala in the wake of modernity and the Kerala Renaissance created an atmosphere conducive to a larger democratic, secular, political culture, which, on the flip side, nevertheless continued to hide a patriarchy that staunchly resisted any attempts to shake its base. The 'radical reconfiguration of the socio-spatial dynamics following the Kerala renaissance in the nineteenth century has covertly solidified the upper-caste and familial moorings of ideal femininities' (Pillai 2022, 178). So, the moral/ethical structures and socio-cultural codes of Kerala society are marked by a deep sexual hypocrisy that is more covert and, hence, more difficult to dislodge than what is apparently overtly patriarchal elsewhere in the country.

It is ironic that the same society, which voted the political Left to power as its first elected government, continues to denigrate 'feminism' in all its popular discourses, oftentimes alleging that it is a 'foreign theory' which does not refer to or include the specificity of Malayali experience. This is particularly surprising, considering that 'modern notions of gender as they emerged in Kerala were neither exclusively global nor local' (Devika 2019, 80). As J. Devika notes, if

> the language of modern gender began to spread in the late 19th to early 20th-century Malayali society with claims of universal relevance, the language of feminism appeared within that society in the late 20th century. By the 1990s, feminism in Kerala was beginning to be irrevocably pluralised. By then, the global discourse of women's empowerment and gender mainstreaming was firmly entrenched in Kerala. (80)

And yet, the very 'progressive' politics and radical emancipatory movements that shaped the publics of the state did not sufficiently address questions regarding the emancipation of women. Gender becomes subsumed in issues pertaining to linguistic, religious and ethnic identity formation. Many feminists have looked at the gender paradoxes of Kerala's progressive politics (see Saradamoni 1994; Mathew 1995; Kodoth and Eapen 2005; Mukhopadhyay 2011; Devika 2014). For example, it has been argued that Kerala's 'relatively better position on women's property rights has obscured from view the progressive decline of the material basis of women's well-being', where its 'admittedly radical land reforms bypassed married women's independent rights and failed to consider especially vulnerable categories of women' (Kodoth and Eapen 2005, 3279). Thus, even those women who were part of radical emancipatory movements and agitations in Kerala have often complained that progressive politics need not sufficiently address the emancipation of women. As Rekha Raj (2013) notes in her analysis of the predicament of women Dalit activists, more often than not, 'these women are the "other"—leaving no options than to be depicted as violent, aggressive, extremist women or as the poor victims of state violence and upper caste exploitation', forced to make 'right claims and seeking recognition from the mainstream' (61). Like the woman question in the Indian national movement during the Independence struggle, in Kerala too, gender becomes subsumed in issues pertaining to linguistic, caste, religious and ethnic identity formations. Feminist politics here has oftentimes become entangled in the conventional structures of academic discourse, and though Kerala has witnessed a number of activist movements that inscribed feminist praxis and translational acts at the grassroots level, nevertheless it could only partly address the spiritual mystique created around the tyranny of the 'intimate' and the familial. Moreover, at an intersemiotic level, there is a significant absence of translation of feminist theory into both academic discourse and everyday praxis. Pointing out that no language is gender neutral, whereby the fundamental framework of literature remains patriarchal, Devika critiques the manner in which women's writing and the ways in which they puncture existing frameworks of patriarchal literary aesthetics remain 'undiscussed', instead placing the female authors on a pedestal and tagging them in a way favourable to the male dominated realm, which gets reflected during the selection of works for translations also. Translation is a purposeful act of creating an equivalent of a message in a semiotic and cultural code, which is different from the original, with the aim of producing an effect equivalent to the one produced by the original. So, it is not the semantic import of a text, its 'fidelity' or 'accuracy' that need to be stressed here but its 'function'. It is in studying the function of a translation that one realises how translations are resisted owing to their potentially subversive socio-cultural and political agendas. Malayalam has historically evinced considerable resistance to translating feminist texts and feminist theory into the language, as is evident from the scant translations in this area. As Lawrence Venuti says,

> Translation is scandalous because it can create different values and practices, whatever the domestic setting. This is not to say that translation can ever rid itself of its fundamental domestications, its basic task of rewriting the foreign text in domestic cultural terms. The

point is rather that a translator can choose to redirect the ethnocentric movement of translation so as to decenter the domestic terms that a translation project must inescapably utilize. This is an ethics of difference that can change the domestic culture. (1998, 82)

This fear of decentering of canons, a marked paranoia towards this ethics of difference can be read into the resistance to translating feminist texts into Malayalam. A translator who lives in the target culture and communicates in the target language is oftentimes not in a position to translate a text freely from a source language that has created a radical change in the source culture. Moreover, if the set of addressees that the translation hopes to address is constituted of a group whose power interests are subordinated by a more dominated group, the act of translation is again resisted. The small tribe of feminist translators who initiate an ethics of difference that deflects the mechanical reproduction of prevailing norms is countered by a notion of cultural loyalty. So, in the end, it is only by being marked as virtually disloyal to one's domestic cultural codes that the feminist translator is able to commence their translation project. As Lori Chamberlain points out,

> ... in some historical periods women were allowed to translate because it was defined as a secondary activity. Our task as scholars, then is to learn to listen to the 'silent' discourse—of women, as translators—in order to better articulate the relationship between what has been coded as 'authoritative' discourse and what is silenced in the fear of disruption or subversion. (2000, 82)

The significant absence of feminist translations in Malayalam where translations of Márquez and Neruda abound, where *Mein Kamph* and *Harry Potter* have been translated, where Marx and Engels are easily available, speaks volumes about how feminist writings have been co-opted or sidelined. When the canon and market decide what texts are to be translated, those that destabilise cultural and ideological norms and question dominant discourses and hegemonies often do not fit the bill. For example, Simone de Beauvoir's seminal work *The Second Sex* (1949) was translated into Malayalam only in 2017, nearly seven decades after its publication. It is interesting to speculate why Helene

Cixous's essay 'The Laugh of the Medusa' was never translated into Malayalam. Virginia Woolf's *A Room of One's Own* has been translated, as has *Mrs Dalloway,* though the latter was published only in 2023, nearly a century after its original publication. And yet, *Orlando* does not have a Malayalam translation till date, revealing a profound linguistic and cultural inability to touch the daring of Woolf's feminist historiographic excess or its gendered moral ambivalences.

By not translating feminist texts, the translators of Kerala are in fact capitulating to a male logic of non-translation as collaboration. Feminist translations would seek to puncture such collaborative silences by making available to a reading public texts that have raised problematic questions on sexualities, which have posed complex perspectives of gender and language, and given voice to the contradictions in existing male traditions in other cultures and languages. Thus, for example, though the number of women translating from Malayalam has risen in the last few decades, a conscious feminist translation praxis can be attributed to very few translators. Devika, for one, points out that her translations are 'attempts to bring out the female writings from the narrow interpretations of Malayalam literary criticism', which highlights a feminist project (https://englisharchives.mathrubhumi.com/specials/world-translation-day-2021/feminist-writersmalayalam-literatureinternational-translation-day-2021-1.6046016).

Lori Chamberlain speaks of the importance not only of translating but of writing about it, making the principles of practice part of the dialogue about revising translation. It is only when women translators begin to discuss their work—and when enough scholarship on previously silenced women translators has been done—that we will be able to delineate alternatives to the oedipal struggles for the rights of production (2021, 327).

The project of patriarchy in Kerala is strengthened by simultaneously not translating Helen Cixous or Adrienne Rich or Chandra Talpade Mohanty or Ruth Vanita or Tarabai Shinde or Ismat Chughtai, while translating the complete works of Amish Tripathi, which serves to give more currency to gender stereotypes that rationalise the historical logic of male domination. Post 1990s, one does find a significant increase in the number of women translating from Malayalam to English. Gita Krishanankutty's translation of M. T. Vasudevan Nair's *Kaalam*, as also the short stories and autobiographical essays by Lalithambika Antharjanam; Vasanthy Sankaranarayan's translations of Lalithambika Antharjanam's *Agnisakshi*; C. N. Sreekantan Nair's *Kanchana Sita*; Matampu Kunhukuttan's *Bhrushte* (Outcaste); Kovilan's *Thattakam*; P. Vatsala's *Agneyam*; Sara Joseph's *Oorukaval* (The Vigil); Prema Jayakumar's translations of Madampu Kunjukuttan's *Ashwathama*; M. Mukundan's *Daivathinte Vikrithikal* and Malayatoor's *Yakshi*; Catherine Thankamma's translation of Narayan's *Kocharethi* depicting the lives of Arayas, as also the first Dalit novel *Pulayathara* by Paul Chrakkode; J. Devika's translation of K. R. Meera's *Aarachaar*; Rajasree's *Kalyaniyennum Dakshayaniyennum Peraya Randu Sthreekalude Katha*; Ambikasuthan Mangad's *Enmakaje;* E. V. Fathima's translation of Subhash Chandran's *Manushyanu Oru Amukham*; Gracie's *Baby Doll* and co-translation of M. Mukundan's *Delhi: A Soliloquy*; Ministhy S.'s translation of V. J. James' *Nireeswaran*; K. R. Meera's *Unseeing Idol of Light* and *Poison of Love;* Jayasree Kalathil's translation of S. Hareesh's *Meesha*; Nisha Susan's translation of K. R. Meera's *Qabar*; Shahnaz Habib's translation of Benyamin's *Jasmine Days*; and Sangeetha Srinivasan's translation of Sarah Joseph's *Budhini* are just a few examples of the rising number of women translators and a selection of their translations from Malayalam to English.

That could be a number of reasons for the entry of more women translators, the primary one being the opening up of Indian markets as part of liberalisation, which marked the entry of new and international publishing houses.

> There are intense writings going on in Indian languages. In the absence of good translations, these remain unknown outside their language circles. Now the scenario is changing. Excellent English translations are coming up, and major publishers are willing to publish them. Translations free Indian language writers from their

isolation and anonymity and help them to be part of the Indian mainstream literature. (Fathima. https://www.aboutamazon.in/news/books-and-authors/translations-free-indian-language-writers-from-isolation-and-anonymity)

Alongside this could be the changing connotations of what is often called 'Indian English Literature'. This is partly due to a rising interest in regional literatures or bhasha literatures. P. P. Raveendran (2023) points out that 'Indian literature' has been conceptualised by literary scholars both 'as the artistic realization of an essential spirit of Indianness that binds all Indian bhashas together', and 'as a politically significant blanket concept that brings together discrete literary formations, each centred on a bhasha with its own canons and traditions'. He argues that though there are 'conceptual differences between the two formulations, both agree, in principle though not always in practice, on a relation of egalitarianism among the different languages with room for each bhasha to thrive independently of the others', since the Constitution of India guarantees equal state patronage for all Indian languages even though 'government policies and historical links between languages as well as the power relations that in practice exist between them have sometimes led to tensions between bhashas' (98).

Moreover, there has been a significant rise in the awards instituted for translation—the Crossword Award, DSC Prizes, JCB Awards, etc., which have afforded the activity a new visibility and legitimacy. Just to cite a few examples—Gita Krishnankutty received the Katha Award for Translation twice, in 1993 and 2000, and also the Crossword Award for Translation in 1999; Fathima E. V.'s translation of Subhash Chandran's *Preface to Man* (2016) won the V. Abdulla Translation Award in 2017 and the 2018 Crossword Book Award for Fiction in Translation; Shahnaz Habib's translation of Benyamin's *Jasmine Days* won the JCB Prize for Literature in 2018; Ministhy's translation of V. J. James's *Anti clock* was shortlisted for the JCB awards in 2021, while her translation of *Nireeswaran* won the Vayalar and Kerala Sahitya Akademi awards; Jayasree Kalathil's translation of Sheela Tomy's *Valli: A Novel* was shortlisted for the JCB Prize in 2022.

The crucial question that remains in this context is, what ought to be the ideal relationship between feminism and translation? Having more women translating does not necessarily entail that they are engaged with feminist translational praxes. A translation might yield feminist readings when the translator consciously seeks to critique dominant modes of gender representations by choosing what to translate and deciding how to translate it, or by refusing to reduce the text to the hegemonic intentions of its author, intervening through feminist discursive strategies to problematise its *a priori* meaning. The feminist translator thus could seek to demystify the grand notions of 'fidelity' in translation and pose the text as the site of a gendered struggle in language, for control over the process of signification. Such a translation might consciously focus on bringing a more 'woman-centric' slant to the language, choosing linguistic strategies which could prioritise the articulations of female experiences that stretch beyond the limits of patriarchal discourses, while using subversive textual methods like footnotes or forewords to critique cultural hierarchies exclusionary to women's concerns that are embedded in the original. It is not 'dynamic equivalence' that such translations would aspire to but a 'reader-focused shift of coherence', which is linked to 'a change in reader audiences through translation' (Blum-Kulka 2000, 304) and not to the process of translation *per se*.

Such a shift in focus would help the translator study deeply the difference in normative systems of the source language audience and the target language audience and help her overcome the potential strategies of resistance devised in the target language. It is only through using a reader-based shift of coherence that the subversive ideologies of gender studies and feminist theory can be made palatable to an audience whose horizon of expectations often fail to envisage such 'culturally alien' concepts.

Translating feminist theory is an interesting case in point. Critical theories from the West have occupied a central space in Malayalam literature without any of the seminal treatises ever getting translated other than a few exceptions. Feminist theory has often been paraphrased or adapted by mainstream writers and critics to introduce new concepts or new ways of reading. A good example is the introduction by noted literary critic K. Satchidanandan to Sarah Joseph's collection of feminist short stories *Papathara*. Paraphrased theoretical works are governed by a need to introduce new interpretative modes, and are grounded on more 'acceptability-oriented' translational practices than 'adequacy-oriented' ones. While Satchidanandan's brilliant translation carved a new landscape of feminist theoretical possibilities for Malayalam, one does not find many more of such radical translational efforts. Moreover, domesticated translations of feminist theorists often bring the author to the language of the reader while the reader never moves to the source language and its cultural frameworks that necessitated the critique in the first place. 'It is only when we force the reader from his linguistic habits and oblige him to move within those of the author that there is actually translation. Until now there has been almost nothing but pseudo translations' (Gasset 2000, 60).

Nabakov says that paraphrastic translations that 'conform to the notions and prejudices of a given public' (1941, 16) constitute the worst evil of translation. He goes on to say, 'The term "free translation" smacks of knavery and tyranny. It is when the translator sets out to render the "spirit"—not the textual sense—that he begins to traduce his authors. The clumsiest literal translation is a thousand times more useful than the prettiest paraphrase' (2000, 71). Such paraphrastic translations resist the source language and culture, and fail to make a holistic analysis of the structure of the source text, in the process deforming it. This is a kind of crude mastication in order to digest it into another system, domesticating an ideology by domesticating the text and the writer under the guise of transmissibility, which serves to systematically negate the possible subversive and critical landscapes of the source text. Such paraphrases and adaptations, I argue, seek to free the translator of any collaborative responsibility—moral or ethical—in the ideology brought forth into the target language and culture. Domesticated translations that render docile aggressive texts to a target audience, in effect cater to the needs and tastes of that audience and elide over the issues of how linguistic and cultural differences are negotiated in translation and how they can offer means to challenge cultural and institutional hegemonies. This necessitates putting translational acts into perspective, not as isolated or individual efforts, but as attempts that share a conceptual system and are connected through invisible strands of a cultural relationship. Itamar Even-Zohar's arguments that translated works correlate 'in the way their source texts are selected by the target literature' and also 'in the way they adopt specific norms, behaviour and policies' (2000, 193) used in the source literature, become valid in this context. Granted that translations play a great role in shaping the literary polysystem, what gets translated depends on the literary model prevalent at that time or the emerging trends that are shaped by the popular or the avant garde.

In this context, it would be interesting to examine how the writing of one of the pioneer thinkers of feminism, Simone de Beauvoir, has been translated into Malayalam. Significantly enough, it is not Beauvoir's *The Second Sex* but her lesser known *Memoirs of a Dutiful Daughter* that has been translated by Nitya Chaithanya Yathi into Malayalam as *Simone de Beauvoir: Avarude Kathaparayunnu* (Simone de Beauvoir Tells Her Story). Yathi calls it an 'abridged' translation and the shift in emphasis from 'Memoir' to 'Story' denotes a muting of authentication, a denial of the conferring of authority to the writer. The translation thus begins with a hijacking of voice, a wresting of agency from the woman author. Here one can decipher the politics of translation where the translator 'cannot engage with or cares insufficiently for the rhetoricity of the original' (Spivak 1993, 181). The translation falls flat because there is no attempt on the part of Yathi to recreate either the tone, or the spirit of the *Memoirs*. In the Malayalam translation, ironically, there are instances where the reader sees a 'Beauvoir' articulating male desire and speaking in the masculine voice.

The opening page of the book highlights five excerpts from the book. The first is a gross mistranslation that begins thus: 'I would stroke the plump breasts that women covered in Satin. But what attracted me more were men with mustaches. I knew by heart their tobacco smell. Their voices were deep. How strong were their arms...' (1988, 8), where the original is actually an early childhood recollection of Beauvoir that reads thus: 'My parents' friends encouraged my vanity. They politely flattered me and spoiled me. I would stroke the ladies' furs and their satin sheathed bosoms. I admired even more the gentlemen with their mustaches, their smell of tobacco, their deep voice, their strong arms that could lift me nearly up to the ceiling' (Beauvoir 1958).

All five excerpts are in a similar vein, focusing on what must have appealed to the translator as Beauvoir's 'untrammeled' 'feminist' desire, her libidinous attraction for both male and female bodies.

This valourisation of the signs of the masculine in translating an overtly feminist writer is a strategy calculated to ensure a reductive reading of the text, fitting it into the Malayali's stereotypes of the 'feminist'. One sees a too ready male desire to take a woman's text out of its framework and flaunt it as a prototype that one needs to be wary of importing from the West. Thus (man)ipulated, (man)handled, the text comes out mutilated. Such translations may generally be called bad translations but my argument is that there is a political need to understand the sexual politics involved in this act of 'appropriative penetration' and 'capture' of the woman's text, the deliberate attempt to diffuse its ideology and contravene its purposes. That the translator fails to understand the budding feminist sensibility in the text is perhaps pardonable. That there is no desire to valourise the writings of a woman like Beauvoir is also understandable. But then why translate? Why Beauvoir? That Beauvoir is a sign Yathi is ill equipped to read or decipher is illustrated by the translation itself, which does not evince any intention to bring to the target audience the vibrantly new ideas of a feminist memoir. If at all, he has used translation with a specific patriarchal cultural agenda—of painting the portrait of a 'feminist' and making her the object of his gaze. That, as a male translator of a woman writer, Yathi puts himself in a position of dominance can be safely surmised from the cover and blurb of the book where his photograph and name are given more prominence than Beauvoir's. The first page has a small photo of Beauvoir carrying her signature under which come the five excerpts, which spill over to the next page, flaunting what could be read as 'feminist' bodies and passions. The excerpts bring out a Beauvoir objectified and reduced to the images of a woman who is all tears, transgressive desire, and body. Yathi's photo, in contrast, has him posing majestically among books, thus seemingly conferring him with an intellectual value that is denied to Beauvoir. Moreover, the context of Beauvoir's writings is not introduced properly with just a line stating that she is the most eminent woman in the intellectual arena of our century. Deficient in providing the background of her ideas or writing, the translator has further taken random liberties, deleting sections and mistranslating at will. The ending is what comes out as the most problematic. Beauvoir in original ends her book thus: 'She has often appeared to me at night, her face all yellow under a pink sun-bonnet, and seeming to gaze reproachfully at me. We had fought together against the revolting fate that had lain ahead of us, and for a long time I believed that I had paid for my own freedom with her death' (1958, 360). Yathi translates this as: 'Afterwards too I saw her. In my dreams—not once but many times. Always she had a pale yellow face. There was a red handkerchief tied to her head. She would gaze at me. It seemed as though there was some vague reproach in those eyes. My Sassa' (1988, 214). Why these deliberate mistranslations of the tenor and content of the original? The willful attempt is to focus solely on the lesbian tone of the early memoirs of a feminist theorist and philosopher, who has attempted to record her emotional and intellectual birth pangs, as though lesbianism is the single marked trait of her character! It is ironic that such a text had to suffer distortions at the hands of a gender-biased translator whose translation strategy is overarchingly patriarchal. Thus, Yathi's attempt at linguistic castration of the seminal ideas of Beauvoir, his attempt to render her writing 'impotent' to an audience whose cultural orientation is only too willing to lap up the image of a feminist as 'provocative', 'promiscuous' and 'unnatural' is what this 'abusive' translation of the *Memoirs of a Dutiful Daughter* reveals. It is also interesting that a parallel publishing house like Mulberry Books, Calicut (Kozhikode), notwithstanding its ethical intent, becomes a co-conspirator in this attempt to translate a 'woman' back into the language of patriarchy. The skewed representation of Beauvoir's autobiography and the ideological slanting in portraying a 'free' woman, reveals a translation strategy that domesticates gender politics and caters to the mainstream Malayali readers' version of reality that is essentially male chauvinistic. Thus, Beauvoir had to be fitted into the stereotype of 'women who transgress'. The result is a translation laden with the normative values of the target language and culture, underscoring and legitimising its rigid patriarchal registers.

Even a preliminary examination of the translation scenario in Kerala shows us plainly that the most popular foreign translations are from Latin American literature, and within India from Bengal. These two have gained mass appeal within Kerala because they address the cultural, moral and political issues that concern the Malayali population in a way that is self-referential. As Venuti opines, such translations reinforce the values of that particular readership and 'reveal much more about the domestic culture for which it was produced than the foreign culture which it is taken to represent' (1998, 125). In this context the fact that Afro-American writings and African literatures have not gained the same currency is worth taking note of. The languorous pace of Latin American lives narrated in simple, transparent Malayalam creates an illusion of reality that finds an echo in every Malayali's mind—an echo that resonates with the Malayali's own cultural codes, stereotypes and values. Malayalam's translational landscape resonates with textual domestication practices where the translated text is inscribed with the 'cultural and political values that currently prevail in the domestic situation—including those values according to which the foreign culture is represented' (Venuti 1998, 126).

What gets translated and how it is received in the target culture depends on how far the source text supports the ideologies and agendas of the target culture, and whether translation strategies can be devised to tame the subversive elements in the source text. Leela Sarkar has translated Mahasweta Devi's *Aaranyer Adhikar* and *Hazar Chowrasir Ma* and numerous translations of Devi have found their way into prominent Malayalam literary journals and publication houses along with the large corpus of works from Bengal. And yet most of these translations of Devi's works have not gained her the critical acclaim as a feminist writer in Kerala that a translator like Spivak has acquired for herself in English. It is not what is translated, but how it is used to unsettle reigning domestic norms on sexual identity that makes a translation gender specific. Translating gender often exposes the specific priorities and limits of differing cultural codes.

A case in point would be the translation of Mahasweta Devi's Bengali short story 'Draupadi' by Spivak into English, and Leela Sarkar into Malayalam. Spivak's translation is accompanied by a 'Translator's Foreword' where she explains her motives for and her approaches to the act of translation, along with detailed notes. One can see here an attempt to attribute to the function of translation certain emancipatory possibilities capable of transforming the literary subaltern into the historical gendered subject. Leela Sarkar uses many of the translational strategies of Spivak, like retaining the English words in the original. Yet, the Malayalam translation lacks the feminist punch of the English one. The 'menacing appeal of the objectified subject to its politico-sexual enemy—the provisionally silenced master of the subject-object dialectic—to encounter—"counter"—her' (Spivak 1981, 391) is diffused in the Malayalam translation. For example, Spivak's English translation says, 'She looks around and chooses the front of Senanayak's white bush shirt to spit a bloody gob at and says, "There isn't a man here that I should be ashamed. I will not let you put my cloth on me"' (402). In the Malayalam version Draupadi says, 'Are these any men here, why should I be ashamed? All here are those who refuse to permit me to wear clothes, what to do? What will

even you do? Then, come on counter me, here counter me ...'
(Devi 1997, 52; my trans.)

Spivak's Draupadi says, 'I will not let you put my cloth on
me' (402). This powerful assertion, together with other syntax
changes, makes her translation extremely potent, one pulsating
with radical politics. Spivak's Draupadi pushes Senanayak with
her two 'mangled breasts' while Sarkar's Draupadi 'continued to
push Senanayak with her two breasts'. Just one adjective 'mangled'
by Spivak, serves to bring out the axiomatics of colonialism and
masculism that is so central to the story. Thus, while Spivak
attempts to inform the act of translation with a critique of sexism
and colonialism, Sarkar 'modestly' seeks to efface her presence
in the space of translation in the larger cause of 'fidelity' to
the original. A woman, as signifier and signification, can thus
oftentimes be 'lost' in translation. The brilliance of Spivak's
translation is that it re-reads and re-writes Devi in order to assert
her agency in both determining and gendering meanings, devising
strategies to make the feminine subject more and more visible
in language. Not provoking the reader, or remaining immune
to the intentions of the original, serves to dull the political
potential of translational acts, and results in translations that
remain handmaidens to the reigning norms and codes of the
target language and culture. Mahasweta Devi's *Stanadayini* was
translated by Spivak as the 'Breast Giver' and another translator
as 'The Wet Nurse'. Spivak argues that the second title 'neutralizes
the author's irony in constructing an uncanny word; enough
like "The Wet Nurse" to make that sense, and enough unlike to
shock' (1993, 182). She argues that the attempt of 'treating the
breast as organ of labour-power-as commodity and the breast as
metonymic part-object standing in for other-as-object the way
in which the story plays with Marx and Freud on the occasion
of the woman's body—is lost even before you enter the story'
(182). Mahasweta Devi's use of proverbs 'that are startling even
in the Bengali', and their omissions by the translator of 'The
Wet Nurse' in what appears a refusal 'to try to translate these
hard bits of earthy wisdom', contrasting them 'with class-specific

access to modernity', leads to 'the loss of the rhetorical silences of the original' (182).

Translating gender, undertaken as a politically conscious act, could help subvert the prevailing notions around 'feminization of translation'.

Macaulay's now notorious views on native Indian translators as 'a class of persons, Indian in blood and colour, but English in taste, in opinions, in morals and in intellect' (Macaulay 1835), who had to be protected from the influences of their hereditary prejudices can be applied in reverse here. Translators who are masters of other linguistic repertoires, but who remain Malayalis in taste, opinion, morals and intellect, in short ones who cater to their own dominant cultural ideologies and who vindicate their native patriarchies could derail the feminist project of translation. Thus, translations that could open a window to new languages and discourses become a cork to seal and brew indigenous cultures. The shift from translation as resistance to resisting translations marks the trajectory of the function attributed to translation from postcolonial strategy to a tool enhancing social narcissism and cultural cannibalism.

On Translating Queer Using Translation as Metaphor

The word 'queer' has its origin in Western anglophone worlds and does not find a lexical equivalent in Malayalam. This does not mean that 'queerness' as 'a concept or cultural referent, does not exist in non-Western languages or cultures' (Spurlin 2014b, 299). Malayalam has a 'normalised' queer register with 'polite' equivalents of queer terms which are common in other cultures. Radical attempts at queering the language are kept at a minimal level in Malayalam translations, reflective of the cultural inhibitions inherent in inhabiting the differences so embedded in the concept of queerness. Terms like *transvanitha, transpurushan,* etc., used to denote transpersons are mere portmanteaus, or more the hybrid form of a Malayalam word with a typical English prefix. The lack of Malayalam lexical registers for queer identities redirects to a reluctance to mobilise a queer discourse in the mainstream. The sentence 'she/he/they is a transperson' would translate *avar oru transvyakthiyaanu* in Malayalam—but among the three words 'trans', *'vyakthi'* (person) and *'aanu'* (is), the word 'trans' still remains intact like a misplaced entity when there is an abundance of root words in the Malayalam lexicon. The dearth of a register capable of linguistic compounding and bringing meaning to a normal sentence so as to flexibly denote and represent queer cultures and their discourses indicates an otherisation that seeps into the lexical, social and semantic levels of language. On the flipside, it is ironical that the language has 'proper' ethnic registers and vocabulary when it comes to cuss words and derogatory remarks, with no necessity to borrow from other languages. Language is 'ideologically layered' and the 'act of translation leads to new cultural systems realized through a semiotic process of codification, of decoding and recoding, of deterritorialization and reterritorialization, of production and mise en scène with new functions' (Spurlin 2014a, 203). The theoretical orientation of translation studies can be broadened by bringing in queer theoretical perspectives, challenging and engaging with the notion of the source or the original.

It is in this context that the issue of how queerness is translated in the cultural terrains of Kerala becomes pertinent. I use translation here, more in a metaphorical sense, in the manner that Cultural Studies theorists like Homi K. Bhabha and Stuart Hall do. Bhabha posits translation as the performative nature of cultural communication, calling it a language not *in situ* but *in actu,* which continually enunciates 'the different times and spaces between cultural authority and its performative practices' (1994, 228). Hall uses it as a metaphor for representation, whereby acts of cultural communication recognise 'the persistence of difference and power between different speakers within the same cultural circuit' (1997, 111).

The queer body poses many representational dilemmas to the translator, which also unsettles the binarist logic around gender and sexuality. As Spurlin (2017) notes, the dismantling of the 'gendered binary further calls to mind the performativity of translation to the extent that translation does not merely facilitate communication across languages . . . , but is a site of struggle in the negotiation and production of meaning, always already capable of new possibilities of counter-translation' (176). For example, the queer male body in Malayalam cinema, however naively represented, deconstructs the existence of an *a priori*, essentialist masculine subjectivity and thus can be seen as potentially liberating for marginalised sexual groups like gays and women. As examples of non-hegemonic masculinity, they question and radically subvert the hegemonic hetero-normative masculine bodies that popular cinema churns out. Thus, the 'feminised' yet male, queer bodies on screen defeat the very logic of their creation as foils for a virile masculinity by exposing the collusions of rituals, institutions and apparatuses in formulating masculinity as a discourse of power and naturalising it. By positing the male queer body as a site of contention between the masculine and feminine, and eventually situating it as liminal and emasculated, there is in fact an undermining of the very nature of phallic masculinity linked to the male body. It has been argued that 'sexual politics and the politics of sexuality constantly connect and it is this connection that raises the question of individual identification' whereby 'homosexuality undermines masculinity yet empowers femininity so that whilst the openly gay male often loses some of the privileges of masculinity in terms of identity, discrimination and domestic power, the lesbian may gain some of the privileges of masculinity through increased independence, at least personally, from the primary though not the only oppressor, heterosexual masculinity' (Edwards 1994, 52–53). Edwards also points out that identification is critical 'as an indication of political intention as neither male or female homosexuality implies any political persuasion per se until it is opened up to societal discrimination', so much so that 'if one does not have an overt sexual identity in a society where heterosexuality is omnipresent, one essentially passes as heterosexual' with all the political implications that it implies for both males and females (52–53).

Moreover, the feminised queer male body creates a crisis in the 'male gaze' with which spectatorial pleasure is largely said to be aligned, for it looks at the male body in the classic feminine role of a passive object that leads to a sense of unease, in the process interrogating and unsettling the phallic male economy of both the cinematic apparatus and the dominant patriarchal culture in which it is situated.

I use queer as a politically strategic term to articulate a de-essentialised identity, deconstructing received heterosexist notions of gender and sexuality and seeking to express non-normative experiences of gender identity and sexual practices. The queer body is one that posits scope for a radical recasting of the social and cultural moulds of gender boundaries and therefore offers itself to political cogitation. Queer thus comes to represent various kinds of anti-heteronormative desires while also signifying that lesbian, gay, bisexual and transgender subjectivities all necessarily tend to transcend the limits of their categorisation. It is therefore theoretically a more enabling and potentially more un-limiting term that helps in conceptually refiguring and liberating sexualities. An analysis of queer images in Malayalam cinema would bring out the regional, contextual differences that configure sexual subjectivities that is often ignored while speaking of the larger Indian context which flatten out the specificities and subtleties of the asymmetrical social matrixes of power that structure these sexual subjectivities.

Masculinity is as much a performance as femininity is. A man 'performs his masculinity, but he is not working from some kind of originary or cultural script. Rather, his gender performance implicitly refers back to other people's previous actions which give his own actions authority and grounding' (Reeser 2010, 81). And yet the performance of masculinity guarantees its actor a dominance and power that is not warranted in femininity. Therefore, normative masculinity in any culture becomes the norm against which all gendered behaviour by men and women of that culture can be compared, contrasted, measured and legitimised or regulated. There are cultural variations in masculinities from one society to another even within India and therefore treating it as a stable category of analysis is an impossibility. Reeser elaborates that given masculinity's innumerable variations in time and in space, it is much more complicated than what it is believed to be, and consequently it can be studied 'not as a single definition, but as variety and complexity' (2). The spectrum of masculinities comes into particular relief 'when someone used to one definition goes somewhere else, whether on an actual trip or whether they travel by reading texts, surfing the web, watching films, or viewing paintings from another time period or cultural context', where such 'cross-cultural or cross-temporal differences' illustrate masculinity as particularly relative, and 'what is taken for granted is not at all a given, but a fabrication or a construct of a given historical and cultural context' (2).

Even within a particular socio-cultural or historic context masculinity changes its modalities and often critiques and destabilises itself before being contested or critiqued from outside. Therefore, anxieties regarding masculinity are ingrained in its very construction. The performance of masculinity thereby necessitates the de-valorisation of the possibilities of other, less-accepted, representations of the male. Therefore, in popular forms of representation like cinema one can see a constant surveillance of the boundaries that draw the contours of behaviour that can legitimately be privileged as male. This has led to a fear of queer bodies in popular cinema in India that reflects certain homophobic unease and cultural confusion regarding what is often seen by many as a form of masculine pathology which could pave the way for a crisis within masculinity, challenging the very nature of 'manhood'.

Popular Indian cinema's unwillingness to give space for serious discourse on the gay body reflects a causal gender problem, which echoes Susan Faludi's words: 'the fragility and intractability of our concept of manliness' (qtd. in MacDonough 6). I argue that many movies treat male homosexuality as a psychic disease of masculinity, of an inability to be man enough—the male body that femininity has conquered, overpowering and silencing the masculine. It is in such a context that 'translating' the queer body becomes a trope in cinematic representations, as one demythicising and exposing the chinks in the armour of hegemonic masculinity, revealing its tenacious, fragmented and precarious nature.

Even as the academic and intellectual world in India continues to be drawn into post structuralist debates around gender politics, popular cinema seems rather hesitant in dealing with queer desire in a serious manner. In the recent past, apart from Bollywood's occasional flippant flings like *Dostana, Kal Ho Na Ho, Girlfriend, Honeymoon Travels Pvt. Ltd., Dulhan Hum Le Jayenge, Ek Ladki Ko Dekha To Aisa Laga* and *Shubh Mangal Zyada Saavdhan,* there are not many films which can be defined as queer. Some serious attempts at queering Hindi cinema have also come up in movies like *My Brother Nikhil, I am, Bombay Boys* and *Aligarh.*

Translation/adaptation could be processes for critiquing the monolithic perceptions of hetrosexualised masculinity that are in currency in popular Malayalam literature/cinema. The power and dominant positionality attributed to hegemonic masculinity rests secure in its not being contested or critiqued. However, if one looks at recent popular culture there are more and more images of protagonists adopting gender ambivalent and gender fluid states that trouble gender and gender hegemony. Often the denaturalising of 'normative' heterosexual and masculine behavioural patterns, though effected through comedy or farce, nevertheless contributes significantly to challenging institutionalised representations of hetero-masculinity.

To begin on a poststructuralist vein, if identity is fluid then it would be impossible to argue for any kind of fixity of identification with words or images. Thus, it is possible to have more than one identificatory position with a literary or filmic representation. If subjectivity is a process in destabilisation then one is forced to concede to the precariously unstable position of the subject during the process of reading/viewing a text. Judith Mayne argues that film theory has been bound by the heterosexual symmetry that supposedly governs cinema so much so that it has ignored the possibility, for instance, that one of the distinct pleasures of the cinema may well be a "safe zone" in which homosexual as well as heterosexual desires can be fantasized and acted out. I am not speaking here of an innate capacity to "read against the grain", but rather of the way in which desire and pleasure in cinema may well function to problematize the categories of heterosexual versus homosexual. (1994, 176)

Popular cinema in India as a pleasure machine is one that caters to the teeming millions of Indian population. Yet it is also a sociolect, a discourse that is determined by different social groups in terms of age, class, caste or gender. Therefore, as a language, Indian cinema can even while constructing the socio-cultural-ideological popular, nevertheless be 'heteroglossic', offering non-normative possibilities that subvert or negotiate the heterosexual dominant.

It is in this context that I seek to read *Chandupottu* (2005), a popular film in Malayalam which offers possibilities of an anti-essentialist and subversive reading of gender politics in contrast to popular paradigms that create supposedly unintentional or 'innocent' significations around representations of the queer body and desire. I do not intend to look at films marking homo-social desire in Malayalam cinema, but rather seek to analyse a different kind of an attempt to destabilise, in however rudimentary a manner, the discursive link between the male body and phallic masculinity.

Chandupottu presents a queer-straight male hero whose 'straightness' remains a secret till the end of the movie. Dileep's character of Radhakrishnan alias Radha is one who completely topples hetero-normative imaginations of the ideal hero. Having a male body, in being biologically male but refusing to conform to attributes of maleness in his social and sexual roles, he is positioned beyond the male-female binaries of institutionalised heterosexuality. He is a character who constantly offers the possibility of 'gender fluidity', even as he engages in a play with the very same stereotypical indicators of gender while refusing to conform to this gender coding, and in the climax unsettles given notions of both straightness as well as gayness. Speaking for the multiple ways of being gendered and sexual for males, the movie at a very fundamental level helps in queering the notion of hetero-masculinity in Kerala. Radhakrishnan's male body cannot qualify for prevalent notions of masculinity as it has already been 'symbolically penetrated' at a very tender age by the virile villain who uses a phallic conch shell to pierce his ear drawing blood, an incident which escalates into a violence of untoward proportions, and which ends with the murder of Kumaran's father by Radha's father. In a patriarchal gender sign system this forcible violation connotes Radha's feminisation and sexual penetrability. Thus, Radha's body is a trope of the possibility of emasculation and feminisation of the male body.

Radha troubles the hegemony and therefore, is labelled, stigmatised and punished. Both within the diegetic space of the film and as far as audience perceptions are taken into analysis, Radha with his crossovers in mannerisms, gestures and behaviour is constructed as a latent homosexual. Radha is the film's hermeneutic code, forcing the viewer to deliberate upon the ambiguity of his sexual identity and keeping the question of his being homosexual or heterosexual in constant play while offering evidential support for both possibilities. Though the film takes a hetero-normative stance in the end, Radha complicates the reductionist approach to view all human sexualities as homo or hetero. Thus, Radha queers the heter-masculinity of mainstream Malayalam cinema in numerous ways, in the process disrupting dominant paradigms of masculinity.

Though Radha in the end proves to be straight while assuming queer identified characteristics, nevertheless, the film foregrounds a historical moment in Malayalam cinema as it struggles with powerfully coded hegemonic masculine bodies, and yet is able to produce a character such as Radha who became an instant hit in the box office. The rationale offered by the film for Radha's taking on queer characteristics and mannerisms is rather simplistic, for he is said to have had a grandmother who wanted a girl child as granddaughter and brought him up as one. Born a male but nurtured and dressed as a female child by a doting grandmother, Radha grows into a delicate mix of the transgender and the cross-dresser. I deliberately use the term cross-dresser over transvestite to denote Radha's desire for feminine clothes, cosmetics and accessories as not being fetishistic but instead propelled by a yearning for female accoutre and an admiration leading to an imitation of the women around him. He is always cynical about the boorish, uncouth men who inhabit his rural, coastal fisherfolk life. His father was imprisoned when he was a child. The film seems to attribute Radha's transgender desires to the absent dominant father.

Radha's cross dressing is an external expression of the internal cross-gender experience of his own self. That Radha uses cross dressing as a way to negotiate the binary gender culture around him evolves as a possible reading of the film. Yet this very desire of the other gender and his disavowal of his assigned gender destabilises these same gender binaries. It is also interesting to look at Radha as one who 'performs' gender in excess. That is, his performance of femininity exceeds that of most women and therefore posits the sheer performativity of gender.

Radha is first presented as a cross dresser in childhood and continues to exhibit feminine traits, gestures and manners as a young man too. In the exaggerated, theatrical and effeminate behaviour of the protagonist the movie affects camp. The hero is in semi-drag most of the time in comic and witty yet exaggerated female impersonation. His vermilion mark, beads and make up allude to his 'femaleness', and yet he is poking fun of both masculinity and femininity, making a joke of himself in the process.

The film uses camp to represent the queer hero; combining performance, artifice and exaggeration. He is a man but 'not a man', not a woman, but a 'woman'. As Sontag says, 'To perceive Camp in objects and persons is to understand Being-as-Playing-a-Role. It is the farthest extension, in sensibility, of the metaphor of life as theatre' (1966, 280). I also use camp as Benshoff and Griffin define it, as a 'subcultural reception strategy' for 'queering heterocentrist film culture', using 'visual and stylistic excess', with larger than life characters and situations, and 'overtly mannered performances of "natural femininity"', and "'overwrought" generic experimentations' (2004, 7).

The film makes clever use of camp, using it as a strategy by which queer sexuality can be represented in mainstream culture in a humorous and non-threatening manner. Due to its irony and humour, camp is much more acceptable to heterosexual viewers than other types of gay or non-normative sexualities. Thus, camp becomes a means for lessening the threat for male heterosexual viewers. In patriarchal, homophobic and misogynist societies like ours, humour is the only effective way of representing different (deviant?) sexualities. Camp imagery in *Chandupottu* is an effective ploy for making difference less offensive and innocuous. As Sontag points out, 'The whole point of camp is to dethrone the serious. Camp is playful, anti serious. More precisely, Camp involves a new, more complex relation to "the serious". One can be serious about the frivolous, frivolous about the serious' (1966, 288). Camp can thus be seen as a strategy for overcoming the possible rejection of a movie with such a theme as also a means to regulate audience hostility and censorship.

The film uses camp humour to play on the instabilities and incongruities of sexualities, thus exposing them as constructions. Though there have been a number of instances of queer and camp performances in Malayalam cinema, it is the first time that a whole movie can be called a queer camp movie. Critics have argued 'that it is difficult to base camp performance as masculinity: since camp is predicated as exposing and exploiting the theatricality of gender, it tends to be the genre for outrageous performances of femininity rather than outrageous performances of masculinity' (Rijswijk 2008, 321).

The queer discourse in the film uses camp as a useful style to express itself, though the ending establishes the essential ontology of the 'normal', of the 'un-queer' as inevitable and natural. The film uses camp to interrogate dominant representation, for social satire, and for critiquing the hegemonic. Nevertheless, this expression of camp has to capitulate to the same hegemonic representational logic and perform heteronormative desires and functions. As Morril argues,

> Camp results from the uncanny experience of looking into a non-reflective mirror and falling outside of the essentialized ontology of heterosexuality, a queer experience indeed. By this logic, Camp can be seen to be the aftermath of a shattering of representation, a queer discourse that results from un-queer proscriptions of same-sex desire.... But "the Camp condition" is only a momentary suspension, a provisional breach of un-queer logic. Since expression can only occur in representation, the subsequent articulation of the condition which produces camp sutures the subject back into the enunciative ties of dominant order. Through camp, the queer subject is reassigned his or her "place". (1994, 119)

The ending of the movie thus shifts Radha from the category of the non-reproductive to 'natural heterosexual' productivity and virility. However, the movie posits the possibility for the first time ever in popular Malayalam cinema that socialisation and upbringing can influence gender and sexuality, thus busting the myth of phallic masculinity associated with the male body. That the 'normalcy' of the belief that biological sex determines gender cannot be problematised in the conventional milieu of Kerala without resorting to camp is also a probability that the movie illustrates.

Throughout the movie homosexuality remains a possibility. The character of Radha constantly comments on and seemingly desires or flirts with hegemonic male bodies. For example, he speaks of the muscularity of men and begs Malu to marry someone with good muscles who can take care of her. Yet, there remains a flirtation with homosexuality, toying with it as a possibility, mainly for comic effect, while the stable assumption of heterosexuality is reinforced again and again.

The film also uses carnival as a way of reading non-normative genders, where laughter provides a release to the sense of repressed otherness linked to gender ambivalences about the material body. The text evinces a deep unease with its apparent blurring of the boundaries between male and female and yet offers space for transgressive potential because of its creation of carnivalesque possibilities for a positive reading of queer desire. It is interesting in this context to note that the film was advertised as a 'comedy'. In Hollywood, queer comedy is often associated with camp and this is what is affected by the director Lal Jose too. The family romance comedy is camp in its use of the exaggerated, theatrical and the unexpected in an ironic fashion that combines the ordinary and the bizarre. Yet, queer power loses out in the end as Radha has to discard his semi-drag comic role and don the costume of the more obviously masculine man. But the film can arguably be treated as a straight-queer comedy for its problematisation of the easy identifications of the male body with the phallic power associated with masculinity. Arguably, *Chandupottu* offers a new iconography for Malayalam cinema, using camp to yoke together the apparently disparate ideas of gender and sexuality in the manner of a metaphysical gender conceit.

The village folk's reaction to Radha—from the open shock and contempt of his jail returned father to the sadistic curiosity of the villain and his cronies, from innuendoes on his 'eunuch' state to the semi-rape and violation of his privacy—all represent common responses to queer as 'unnatural' and 'freakish'. Many characters display a voyeuristic desire to stare at his feminised body, simultaneously expressing desire and revulsion, horror, condescension or pity for what is considered to be 'perverted' or 'deviant sexuality'. During his Goan sojourn, Rosie and her brother Freddie repeatedly treat his condition as 'correctible' and changeable. Thus, though Radha embodies the tragic contradictions of the queer human subject and the film does capture a queer sensibility, the film remains too straight a narrative, in the end aligning itself with the popular Malayali box-office hit formulae. Nevertheless, it queers the straight and straights the queer; in the process, complicating both.

Using camp's strategies of playful subversion to parody the normalcy of possible heterosexual unions like that of Malu and the villain, the film privileges the abnormality of queer Radha to the normalcy of hegemonic masculinity of Kumaran. Thus, even while validating normative heterosexuality, the film nevertheless subverts the concept of dominant masculinity, and Radha's body becomes a politically viable space in which the concept of hegemonic masculinity is mocked and destabilised. And, as in the Bakhtinian carnivalesque, the queer body of camp also mocks at 'decent' boundaries and 'good' tastes, showing affinities for the garish, the vulgar and kitsch.

Chandupottu offers interesting insights on cultural translations of sexual alterity, yielding insightful readings on how popular cinema could devise new translational possibilities around queering hegemonic masculinities in Kerala. Though the resultant filmic text is deeply flawed and limited by camp, and thus partly abjected, it nevertheless does not expunge otherness, instead attempting to shift the queer from the domain of untranslatability into new registers of translation and representation. This section of the essay, thus, very tentatively probes the possibility of opening up to a 'queer turn' in translation studies, one that could offer a critique of sexuality and translation as categories which are interrogated through the dual process of translating sexuality and the sexualization of translation (Santaemilia 2018, 13).

REFERENCES

Beauvoir, Simone de. 1958. *Memoirs of a Dutiful Daughter,* translated by James Kirkup. Harper & Row.

———. 1988. *Simone de Beauvoir: Avarude Kathaparayunnu,* translated by Nitya Chaithanya Yathi. Mulberry Books.

Benshoff, Harry, and Sean Griffin, editors. 2004. *Queer Cinema: The Film Reader.* New York: Routledge.

Bhabha, Homi K. 1994. *The Location of Culture.* London and NY: Routledge.

Blum-Kulka, Shoshana. 2000. "Shifts, Cohesion and Coherence in Translation." In *The Translation Studies Reader,* edited by Lawrence Venuti, 298–313. New York: Routledge.

Chamberlain, Lori. 2000. "Gender and the Metaphorics of Translation." In *The Translation Studies Reader,* edited by Lawrence Venuti, 326–27. New York: Routledge.

Chandupottu. 2005. Directed by Lal Jose, performances by Dileep, Gopika and Bhavana.

Chaudhuri, Maitrayee. 2011. *Feminism in India*. New Delhi: Women Unlimited.

Devi, Mahasweta. 1997. *Mahasweta Deviyude Cherukathakal*, translated by Leela Sarkar. National Book Trust.

Devika, J. 2014. "Gender in Contemporary Kerala." *Economic and Political Weekly* 49 (17): 38–39. http://www.jstor.org/stable/24480117.

———. 2019. "Women's Labour, Patriarchy and Feminism in Twenty-first Century Kerala: Reflections on the Glocal Present." *Review of Development and Change* 24(1): 79–99. https://doi.org/10.1177/0972266119845940.

———. 2021. https://englisharchives.mathrubhumi.com/specials/world-translation-day-2021/feminist-writersmalayalam-literatureinternational-translation-day-2021-1.6046016.

Edwards, Tim. 1994. *Erotics & Politics: Gay male sexuality, masculinity and feminism*. London: Routledge.

Even-Zohar, Itamar. 2000. "The Position of Translated Literature within the Literary Polysystem." In *The Translation Studies Reader*, edited by Lawrence Venuti, 192–97. New York: Routledge,.

Gasset, José Ortegay. 2000. "The Misery and the Splendor of Translation.", translated by Elizabeth Gamble Miller. In *The Translation Studies Reader*, edited by Lawrence Venuti, 49–64. New York: Routledge.

Hall, Stuart. 1997. Introduction. *Representation: Cultural Representations and Signifying Practices*, edited by Stuart Hall. New Delhi: Sage.

Irigaray, Luce. 1985. *This Sex Which Is Not One*. New York: Cornell UP.

Jain, Jasbir. 2011. *Indigenous Roots of Feminism: Culture, Subjectivity, and Agency*. New Delhi: SAGE Publications.

Mayne, Judith. 1994. "Paradox of Spectatorship." In *Viewing Positions: Ways of Seeing Film*, edited by Linder Williams, 155–80. New Jersey: Rutgers UP.

Kodoth, Praveena, and Mridula Eapen. 2005. "Looking beyond Gender Parity: Gender Inequities of Some Dimensions of Well-Being in Kerala." *Economic and Political Weekly* 40(30): 3278–86. http://www.jstor.org/stable/4416933.

Macaulay, Thomas Babington. 1835. "Minute on Indian Education."

Mathew, George. 1995. "The Paradox of Kerala Women's Social Development and Social Leadership." *India International Centre Quarterly* 22(2/3): 203–14. http://www.jstor.org/stable/23003947.

McDonough, Carla J. 1997. *Staging Masculinity: Male Identity in Contemporary American Drama*. Jefferson: McFarland.

Morril, Cynthia. 1994. "Revamping the Gay Sensibility: Queer Camp and Dyke Noir." In *The Politics and Poetics of Camp*, edited by Moe Meyer, 110–29. London: Routledge.

Mukhopadhyay, Swapna. 2007. *The Enigma of the Kerala Woman: A Failed Promise of Literacy*. New Delhi: Social Science Press.

Nabakov, Vladimir. 1941. "The Art of Translation." *The New Republic*, 4 Aug 1941, newrepublic.com/article/62610/the-art-translation.

———. 2000. "Problems of Translation: 'Onegin' in English." In *The Translation Studies Reader*, edited by Lawrence Venuti, 71–83. New York: Routledge.

Osborne, Natalie. 2015. "Intersectionality and Kyriarchy: A Framework for Approaching Power and Social Justice in Planning and Climate Change Adaptation." *Planning Theory* 14(2): 130–51.

Pillai, Meena T. 2022. *Affective Feminisms in Digital India: Intimate Rebels*. New York: Routledge.

Raj, Rekha. 2013. Dalit Women as Political Agents: A Kerala Experience. *Economic and Political Weekly* 48(18): 56–63. http://www.jstor.org/stable/23527309.

Rakkuyilin Ragasadassil. 1986. Directed by Priyadarshan, performances by Mammootty, Suhasini, and Adoor Bhasi, Sooryodaya Creations.

Raveendran, P. P. 2023. *Under the Bhasha Gaze: Modernity and Indian Literature*. London: Oxford UP.

Reeser Todd W. 2010. *Masculinities in Theory: An Introduction*. Sussex: Wiley-Blackwell.

Rijswijk, Honni van. 2008. "Judy Grahn's Violent Feminist Camp." In *The Body & The Book: Writings on Poetry and Sexuality*, edited by Glennis Byron and Andrew J. Smeddon, 319–30. New York: Rodopi.

Santaemilia, José. 2018. "Sexuality and Translation as Intimate Partners? Toward a Queer Turn in Rewriting Identities and Desires." In *Queering Translation, Translating the Queer: Theory, Practice, Activism*, sdited by Brian James Baer and Klaus Kaindl, 11–25. New York: Routledge.

Saradamoni, K. 1994. "Women, Kerala and Some Development Issues." *Economic and Political Weekly* 29(9): 501–09. http://www.jstor.org/stable/4400866.

Sontag, Susan. 1966. "Notes on Camp." In *Against Interpretation*, 275–92. New York: Farrar, Straus & Giroux.

Spivak, Gayatri Chakravorty. 1993. *Outside in the Teaching Machine*. New York: Routledge.

———. 1987. *In Other Worlds: Essays in Cultural Politics*. London: Methuen.

———. 1981. "Draupadi." *Critical Inquiry* 8(2): 381–402.

Spurlin, William. J. 2014a. "The Gender and Queer Politics of Translation: New Approaches." *Comparative Literature Studies* 51(2): 201–14.

———. 2014b. "Queering Translation." In *A Companion to Translation Studies*, edited by Sandra Bermann and Catherine Porter, 298–309. Sussex: Wiley.

———. 2017. "Queering Translation: Rethinking Gender and Sexual Politics in the Spaces between Languages and Cultures." In *Queer in Translation*, edited by B. J. Epstein and Robert Gillett, 172–84. London: Routledge.

Venuti, Lawrence. 1998. *The Scandals of Translation: Towards an Ethics of Difference.* London: Routledge.

FIVE

Translating the Subaltern

Translations of self-writings underscore an act of mediation, begging deeper scrutiny into the patterns of connection and dissonance between their political ideations, seeming narrative resolutions, and the art and artifice of their structure and form, within which occurs the performative staging of the autobiographical subject. However, mediated autobiographies carry an inherent problematic that hinges on questions of the degree of control, consent and agency that it takes away or grants the enunciating subject.

Nalini Jameela, a sex worker from Kerala, told the story of her life to I. Gopinath and this was published in June 2005 by DC Books, Kottayam. However, she rejected the book and went in for another version of her life story with the help of a group of friends, and this was published again by the same publisher in December 2005. In 2007, an English translation of her autobiography was published by Westland. However, what is significant is that Jameela never 'wrote' her story; she only attempted an oral rendering of it. It is her scribes and translators who attempted the narrativisation of her life, translating and configuring new possibilities into it. Thus, even when a subject narrates her story in a mediated self-writing, the literary framework of that narration, the artifice of its form, often rests with her scribes. The attempts to create the fiction of a narrative artlessness, the apparent conference of agency to the sole voice of the 'author' without understanding the tone and tenor of the mediating consciousness, or questioning the ideological framework of the narration would be to conveniently circumvent issues of authorship and authority in marginal writings. Nalini Jameela, with her limited literacy, narrates the story of her life to a scribe. Does the transcribed/translated story still retain the perspective of the marginalised testimonialist? Who is/are the author/authors of *Njan Lymgikathozhilali* (I am a Sex Worker), *Oru Lymgikathozhilaliyude Athmakatha* (The Autobiography of a Sex Worker) and *The Autobiography of a Sex Worker*—the three versions of one woman's life story? Thus, writings on/ of marginality raise certain fundamental questions regarding translation, authority and representation. Such questions become more complicated when linked to works that are narrated orally and are then recorded, transcribed, edited and translated by academic mediators.

'I am a translation because I am a woman' (Lotbiniere-Harwood 1991, 95) is a statement that seems so relevant in the case of Nalini Jameela's three autobiographies. The first was 're-told', rather 'translated', by Gopinath and published as *Oru Lymgikathozhilaliyude Athmakatha*. This went into six editions in one hundred days and sold thirteen thousand copies. But Jameela rejected this first version and prepared a second titled *Njan Lymgikathozhilali: Nalini Jameelayude Athmakatha* (I am a Sex Worker: The Autobiography of Nalini Jameela) and was again published by DC Books, deepening the controversy about her life and work. A third version titled *The Autobiography of a Sex Worker* was published by Westland in 2007 and this was a translation into English with a foreword by J. Devika, though she does not state clearly which version she has translated. These three translations of one woman's life story help anchor the belief that identity politics is crucial to translation. After all, translation, as Sherry Simon points out is 'considered as a mode of engagement with literature, as a kind of literary activism' (1996, viii).

The translator's focus on the linguistic and cultural constituents of the foreign text invariably 'provokes the fear that authorial intention cannot possibly control their meaning and social functioning' (Venuti 1998, 31), which is true in the case of the many 'autobiographies' of Nalini Jameela. That there can only be an 'episodic originality' when the subjective experiences of the subaltern's testimonial are being converted to a literary discourse by the linguistic mediation of the 'liberal' translator remains a moot question in this translation. Examining the 'authorial intention' (31) redirects us to the agency question of the translated, within the translation, during the process of a mediated translation.

What each of these translations emphasises is how and where the translator is positioned in the context of cultural debates in Kerala and what kind of politics he or she brings into the text that helps or deters the conventions and codes of the literary and social culture that the book seeks to address. Moreover, the crucial question remains—can an autobiography remain an 'auto'biography after being sifted through so many layers of translations? In 'Conditions and Limits of Autobiography', Gusdorf puts forth a significant argument that 'autobiographical selves are constructed through the process of writing and therefore cannot reproduce exactly the selves who lived' (qtd. in Friedman 1998, 72), which raises questions on the very existence of the autobiographical project. This is based on two factors from Gusdorf's assertion—first, the autobiographical selves written by the speakers themselves are formed as a result of a 'construction'. Second, because it is a 'construction', they 'cannot be reproduced exactly' as they lived. This assertion compels a re-analysis of Jameela's life stories, prompting a probe into the problematic of mediated autobiographies. How does Jameela name herself in her different stories? How does she interrogate the role of language in 'fixing' her 'self', even as she attempts to name her experiences? If at all there is a self-naming, how is it contradicted by the representations of the 'author', by the paratextual apparatus that accompanies the strategies of the marketing of Jameela's life? In the very act of fixing her own identity as a marginal sex worker, how does she articulate her relationships to systems of knowledge, of representation and of capital in which her narratives are inextricably embedded, even as they attempt to move beyond them? While Jameela could be an 'effect' of others' stories, at least sporadically, she wrests the agency to be the author of her own story. Her entry point into the enacting of the subject of her autobiography is different in each version.

Nalini Jameela, as the source of action, as the site of a subjectivity, which is not in itself fixed but crystallises in the very act of telling her story, is a subject who is also defined by the narration. The three translators of her life create different subjects where each time the subjectivity of the translator exerts a particular kind of agency to combine with the subject and thus recast the subject as significantly different. Thus, in each version, the marginal subject is not only narrated but packaged and marketed differently. Moreover, another strategy used in the first two narrations is to conceal the role of the translator and make it appear marginal or render it invisible, thus creating the appearance of conferring agency upon the subject. The third version is a feminist version, which attempts to reveal the narrator and her relationship to the subject clearly.

What is intriguing in these exercises is the problematic of 'writing' itself as one which unfolds a larger Derridean critique underscoring the undecidability of linguistic and conceptual analyses. This undecidability inhabits the crucial markers of both the language and selves that are written into the different translations of her oral narratives. The first version makes self-writing and especially women's self-writing a mere reaction to conventional strictures of morality while the second version strives to open up multiple possibilities of women's self-writing as a revolutionary act. Nancy K. Miller compares a woman's text to an onion where 'To feel at ease with the onion, to enjoy the onionness would mean accepting a radical decentering and reorganisation of pleasure: finding pleasure not in the revelation of a centre, but in the process itself of the peeling away of layers' (1991, 36).

The first version of Jameela's autobiography is disturbed by the 'onion-ness' of the text. It constantly probes to find a core, an essence to the gendered identity of a sex worker resulting in certain unease. In all three versions of the autobiography, the voice of the enunciated subject is oppositional, radical and heretical. Yet the tone varies in tune to who the writing subject/scribe or translator is. In the first version, one can find the hijacking of Jameela's voice by an expansive and progressively inclusive liberal-humanist agenda which attempts to shape the narrative to fit the model. With a long drawn out account on the part of the scribe to establish his credentials as an activist that borders on hidden moralising assumptions around 'higher humanity', one can yet feel in this translation a covertly patronising moral idealism towards the condition of specific oppression of both class and gender and the ensuing bourgeois male condescension. That Jameela becomes only an occasion for many other axes to be ground becomes clearer as the text progresses.

Autobiography as a literary genre has an institutional and normative status representing established conventions to which both the writer and the readers subscribe. After all,

> Framing an autobiography means relinquishing the particularity of the life and merging with the genre. Shaping a life into an autobiography evokes earlier texts and readers who controlled their selection. A process of matching and shaping connects the subject's writing with the tradition in print. In this way the subject and his readers are parties to an autobiographical pact: they agree to a correspondence between the life and the Life. (Long 1999, 16)

I argue that in this version the evocation of the genre of autobiography makes it clear that the autobiographical pact is not between the subject and her reader but between the translator and his readers. The marginalised female sex worker is transmuted into the generic subject by the agency of the male narrator who bestows upon her the worth necessary for this transmutation and also affirms the continuity with the autobiographical tradition. Finally, the autobiographical subject who emerges is a cultural and ideological 'other', constructed discursively by the 'self-narrative' yet bearing the indelible authorising signature of a neo-liberal patriarchal discourse.

In the revised autobiography Jameela hopes that she can retain her own style even as she embellishes or modifies (the Malayalam term used is *parishkarikkuka*) her life story with the help of 'a group of friends'. The question is, what are these embellishments that she seeks to bring in to revise the story? This statement also hints that her 'style' was lost in translation in the first version of her autobiography. Reaching out to a larger sense of community and forging of an extended family complex of relations marks the second as different from the modernist, individualistic narrative of the first. Any opportunity to deride 'feminism', categorically taken to be 'Western' feminism, is never left unutilised in the first autobiography. To illustrate, there is a tirade against a feminist who refuses motherhood because, theoretically, it consolidates women's slavery (Jameela 2005a, 45). A feminist is defined in the first version as a woman who refuses to bear children and who is neither capable of deep love nor sex. The simplistic stereotypes of men and women, ossified prejudices, and the superimpositions of the aspirations and ideologies of the translator into Jameela's narrative, all make the first version a translated marginality using the self of the marginal as a camouflage for other things. In the numerous digressions and ruminations on the hypocrisies and double standards of morality practised in Kerala society, one can see attempts to 'mediate' Jameela. Thus, the first version of the autobiography can be called a 'synecdochic translation', where the translator twists the SL text to fit his needs. The synecdochic translator condescends to the SL writer, assuming that he or she did not quite know what he or she wanted to say or how to say it, taking upon themselves the task of preserving what is most representative (Robinson 2007, 191). The anti-authoritarian and radical streak in Jameela's voice is garnered to create the rhetoric of liberal male logic whose agendas and conclusions are pre-set. The first version stresses on gender equity and is reformist in agenda emphasising class while the second version is more subversive and radical. In the English translation, one can see how there is an attempt to look at the intersection of class and gender and the double marginalisation of the sex worker, both as a woman and as a poor labourer. The high individualism of the first version is mellowed down in the second by a consciousness that shared individual experience is crucial in the discovery of commonalities of existence. Thus, we can see how the political strategy of representing sex workers is different in each version. The second version of Jameela's autobiography, which brings the shared individual experience, unveils an uncommon dimension of representing a subaltern woman's self in her autobiography by recognising the reciprocity of her existence as any other social being in society. Building on this dimension that displays the social mutuality of the sex worker becomes seminal in the backdrop of the tabooed, stigmatised experiences of her subaltern self.

'The very sense of identification, interdependence, and community that Gusdorf dismisses from autobiographical selves are key elements in the development of a woman's identity, according to theorists like Rowbotham and Chodorow' (Friedman 1998, 75). The 'unconscious masculine bias' (75) of both the translation theorists who put forth individualistic paradigms in theorising autobiographical translations, as well as the patriarchal translators who emboss their neo-liberal patriarchal bias while translating marginalised female testimonials, is eschewed in the incorporation of the shared individual experience as in the second version of the autobiography.

When analysing the individual space and the interconnectedness of the translated self of Jameela from a social lens, it is also pivotal to review the gendered intricacies and material conditions in the formation of a subaltern woman's 'self' and her social consciousness. The material conditions of forming and the resultant gendered subaltern self, as both product and process of multiple translations/interventions of societal constructs, power matrices and moral imaginaries, result in an experience of one's own as never entirely unique, as 'she is always aware of how she is being defined as a woman, that is, as a member of a group whose identity has been defined by the dominant male culture' (75). The chiselling of gendered identities and consciousness is perpetually in the form of a shared individual experience. 'The vast mass of human beings have always been mainly invisible to themselves while a tiny minority have exhausted themselves in the isolation of observing their own reflections' (Rowbotham 1973, 27). Rowbotham's usage of the mirror metaphor, like Lacan's 'Imaginary' stage in the model of identity formation, denotes that a woman's identity formation is the development derived as the grand total from what she sees as a reflection in the mirror of cultural representation. But this mirror is the reflecting plane that actually displays 'the prevailing social order that stands as a great and resplendent hall of mirrors. It owns and occupies the world as it is and the world as it is seen and heard' (27). It is this gendered reflection sculpted as per the male-centric world order a woman often stares into. It 'does not reflect back a unique, individual identity of each living woman; it projects an image of WOMAN, a category that is supposed to define the living woman's identity' (Friedman 1998, 75). The gendered subaltern 'self', which is the source of 'agency' in the marginalised woman's autobiography, is itself shaped as a 'collective' construct inseparable from the social mantle. Thus, the translated self is always already a 'group identity', 'reminded at every turn in the great cultural hall of mirrors' (75) of their otherness. It is this socially sculpted 'collective identity' that then gets further translated through linguistic and literary mediations—leaving the autobiography doubly narrated. The agency of the translated 'other' and the degree to which it is sifted and transmuted after being twice moulded is a point of concern here.

However, it is significant that none of the translations are victim narratives, as novels and stories on sex workers often tend to be. Nowhere in any of the three versions does Jameela admit to low self-esteem, self-hatred or repentance.

In Devika's English translation, one sees the joy of the discovery of one woman by another—of inadvertent alliances. The first version of her autobiography could not be claimed by feminists previously both because feminism is derided in it and also because feminists led the most trenchant attack on Jameela's life and work. Devika writes in her foreword that: 'These feminist activists had little in common with me, though I too lay claim to that label' (Jameela 2007, xv). Thus, her translation is a conscious effort to bring Jameela's autobiography into the purview of women's experiences and women's writings. She tries to do this by highlighting common motifs and finding alternative patterns of signification. For example, Devika writes in her translator's

Foreword that Jameela's autobiography reveals the exclusions of the dominant home-central, self-controlled feminine ideal and challenges the prostitute stereotype. In her very title, she calls herself a *laingikathozhilali*, a sex worker, claiming the dignity of *thozhil*, a word that can mean both 'labour' and 'profession' in Malayalam. Jameela does not seek direct entry to elite womanhood. She rejects the description of herself as a 'prostitute' as defined by the forces of morality—but this is not so that she can claim a description that would situate her in the community of 'women'. That she chose a description defined by labour indicates the distance between elite-centred notions of 'womanhood' and the female labouring poor in Kerala (ix).

Devika's translation, to borrow a term from Showalter, is a 'gynocritical' translation—a translation which is undertaken with the conscious aim of studying the female experience and constructing a female framework for the analysis of women's writing. Devika uses a 'Translator's Foreword' to draw attention to her own identity as a woman translator and a feminist at that, taking pains to define her feminism. Thus, she emphasises the way in which she draws connections and non-connections with Jameela which helps her understand the project of the text better and also plan her translation strategies.

As a feminist historian and translator, Devika is active in focusing attention on the task of bringing out the gendered nature of the text and the subject. Through the foreword and an interview appended in the end, she clearly traces and critiques the re-formation of the 'translated subject' and places alongside it 'the translating subject' so as to specify the translating relationship. For example, Devika's translation omits Nalini Jameela's apology to her readers in the Preface to the second version, significantly titled 'My written Tests' as 'I Try Out Writing'. Omitting the apologetic tone of Jameela's preface might have been a conscious decision to confer more power on her narrative and valourise the agency. Here, the pendulous agency of the translated, ramified by the twice-encoding of the narrative, gets placed on firmer ground.

The change in the Preface title in the translation also highlights a feminist desire to seize more power for the gendered subject. Thus, as pointed out by Simon, feminist theory highlights a renewed sense of agency in translation, which nevertheless cannot be understood 'as that of a free and unfettered writing subject', but rather as something in relation 'to the various sites through which the translating subject defines itself' (1996, 25). The definitions of these sites remain tenuous with the most important aspect of the 'enunciating position' of the translator being the project, where feminist translators willingly acknowledge their interventionism through a recognition that 'gives content to the "differences" between original and translation, defines the parameters of the translation process and explain the mode of circulation of the translated text in the new environment' (25).

Her lengthy 'Translator's Foreword' and the interview with Jameela at the end of the book might make Devika look like an 'intrusive translator'. But it could also be a conscious effort at foregrounding the translator's intrusive presence by making use of a strategy called 'supplementing', which, according to Simon (35), might be called 'hijacking' by others. This highly 'visible and explicit form of interventionism' (35), along with the translator's foreword and her interview with the author, seeks to prompt the reader to read between and outside the lines of the text, thus enhancing their understanding of the subversive practices and potential of the text. It is made clear that the translator's interest in the translation is not a mere coincidence but the result of a conscious understanding of a cultural and political task. Thus, the gesture of making the translation 'visible' is a conscious political one, aimed at both exposing the ruse and patterns of nationalist/patriarchal ideologies operating in the text, as also contesting them. This also helps us investigate how the gendered social roles of the translator and the translated are significant in understanding the patterns of their narration and translation.

When Devika states that Jameela is a friend and for reasons of friendship she undertook the translation project, then she is also signalling the role of translation in forming networks of solidarity around women's progressive causes. Thus, the translation becomes a striking example in Malayalam literature of the collaborative efforts of women to create, translate and critique radical women's writing in Kerala. This deconstructs and challenges the male-centric theoretical ideation of standardising 'individualism' as a paradigmatic chassis to carry forward the autobiographical narrative.

Absolute individualism to be utilised as a material of one's life writing 'is an illusion' and 'a privilege of power' (Friedman 1998, 75) for a marginalised female identity developed and living in a bourgeois-patriarchal-casteist social order. The collaborative efforts in Devika's version are a perturbation from defining 'agency' as an isolated individualism devoid of the 'senses of commonalities' as in Gopinath's version. This collective method by women in women's writing is a generic bolstering to the whole of women's writing in literature and a foregrounding of those that are excluded from the canons of autobiography and 'those writers who have been denied by history the illusion of individualism' (75).

If the first version of the autobiography attempted to create 'feminism' as an 'other', Devika's translation attempts to broaden the scope of 'feminism' by asking the question of who its women are. This kind of interrogation becomes a strategy to bring in excluded or less invoked women like Nalini Jameela into the gamut of a re-signified feminist politics. Thus, the project of translation also becomes a radical critique of feminist theory and practice, allowing us to navigate better the diverse ways in which, today, both theoretical studies and popular cultures nominally invoke a certain degree of gender equality and yet work to reconsolidate gender norms. She also analyses the process of feminist interpretation of women. Devika uses the translation project and Nalini Jameela as a fundamental way of rewriting feminism in contemporary Kerala.

Even in a self-written autobiography, it is argued that the 'autobiographical self is a fictional construct within the text which can neither have its origins anterior to the text nor indeed coalesce with its creator' (Anderson 1986, 56). If this is the case with self-written autobiographies what would happen in an autobiography where the 'Source Text' consists of twelve cassettes of taped interviews, some of which are apparently 'lost'? What is lost in the translation from this 'Source Text' to *Oru Lymgikathozhilaliyude Atmakatha* is the central act of self-naming. Interestingly, the self-claimed autobiography is named *Njan Lymgikathozhilali* where the obvious emphasis is on '*Njan*' or 'I', thus asserting her selfhood. As Anderson says, 'In a sense women's autobiography is both a reaching towards the possibility of saying "I" and towards a form in which to say it' (65). Thus, all three texts can be seen as points in Nalini Jameela's journey towards herself where she seems to be struggling with the problem of saying 'I'. In the second version, she writes,

> Many asked me if it was right to make such revisions. I don't know if there are rules about these things that apply to everyone around the world. Even if there are, and I happen to be the first person to change those rules let it be so! After all when I started sex work, I didn't do so by custom! ... I want to do everything to make my autobiography match my standards and style. (Jameela 2005b, 7)

However, that this is almost ideally impossible in translation is what the three texts illustrate. One can see how, along with that of Nalini Jameela who remains the 'translated', there are the voices of different translators who, without overtly drawing ideological lines, have yet brought contending voices into the text. The autobiography, or rather autobiographer, thus remains a contested site where translator and translated from varied positions try to outline the fundamental characters of women's oppression, the social and historical causes of that oppression, the autonomy of women's organisation, the analysis of patriarchy, etc. The first autobiography, even while appearing to empower the female sex worker, seeks to dominate the movement and as is literally evident in the text, overpowers the voice, style and language of the 'autobiographer'. The three stories explicate how the same story can change when viewed from different perspectives and ideological positions. As Brian Finney says, 'Each new attempt at autobiography will tell a different story since the story has changed in the course of telling and as a result of it' (1985, 13). Thus, the very project of telling the story to a scribe or the translator's engagement with it changes the story and a new Jameela is created as a result of this very act. 'We assume that life produces the autobiography as an act produces its consequences, but can we not suggest with equal justice that the autobiographical project may itself produce and determine the life' (De Man 1984, 63).

All three versions of Jameela's autobiography, read together, proclaim the autobiographical self as only an 'effect' each text creates and not an anterior, referential self. Thus, what is busted is the myth of the autobiographical self of Jameela, as a unified subject, as the source of meaning in her narrative. Jameela is foregrounded in these narratives as a functional construct whose life has only a pre-narrative quality. It is Gopinath, her set of friends and Devika who make narratives of her life by translating it and thus configuring new possibilities and meanings into it. Barbara Godard refers to the metonymic or contingent nature of translation by which it does not seek to carry meaning across but instead remakes meaning (1995, 73).

The three versions of the autobiography—by Gopinath, Jameela's set of friends and Devika—are all involved in what Godard calls a 'transferential process of translation' where the reading subject becomes the writing subject and the text carries the presence of the translator with it. Thus, the reader is not reading Jameela's life alone but either that of Jameela and Gopinath, Jameela and her writer friends, or Jameela and Devika.

This is not to say that one version of Jameela's autobiography is better than, or more correct, or that the others are unethical or appropriative in a negative manner. What is to be emphasised is that writing practices such as translations and especially translations of marginal lives and narratives are by and large mediations which operate entirely hrough ideology.

A widening of the definition of the translating subject becomes significant in a context where 'meaning is no longer a hidden truth to be "discovered", but a set of discursive conditions to be re-created' (Simon 1996, 13). Thus, 'Who translates whom?' and 'From where?' are as important as the 'What' and 'How' of translation.

The writing/translating of marginalised selves is a process involving plural subjectivities where authorship is only contingent—a wrestling over power between the enunciating subject and the writing subject with gradual intimidation of the former by the latter since the former's knowledge of the conventions of the genre is regulated and 'subsidised' by the latter. So I argue that in Jameela's translated marginality as 'auto'biography, the autobiographical pact between author and reader is invariably broken as the autobiographical subject is not the 'author' and can neither claim knowledge of the terms and conditions of the pact nor often verify the fulfilment of the contract.

I would prefer to privilege subaltern autobiography as a movement rejecting representational discourses of the hegemonic to a possibility towards self-embodiment using a self-reflexive language. But translated marginalities are co-opted narratives illustrating the impossibility of the autobiographical project. If 'telling' is just one step in mediating the gap between 'self' and 'life', then writing is an arduous trek that requires careful planning and charting. If autobiographies can be seen as a Hegelian effort to know the 'self' through consciousness and to illustrate the knowledge, then 'writing' is an essential part of 'knowing the self'. Translated marginal selves like Nalini Jameela's can fulfil the knowledge of 'selfhood' only partially because they do not 'write'. Instead, they are forced to inscribe themselves into another's language, soliciting the knowledge of their selves by others.

> If the autobiographical moment prepares for a meeting of writing and 'selfhood', a coming together of method and subject matter, this destiny—like the retrospective glance that presumably initiates autobiographies—is always deferred. Autobiography reveals gaps, and not only gaps in time and space or between the individual and social, but also a widening divergence between the manner and matter of its discourse. That is, autobiography reveals the impossibilities of its own dream: what begins on the presumption of self knowledge

ends in the creation of a fiction that covers over the premises of its construction. (Bentskock 1998, 146)

In the translated subaltern autobiography, the enunciating subject is not the writing subject. The primary act of bringing the subject into language rests with the writing subject who 'presumes' to know the 'other' and in the process also attempts to differentiate this self/other from others. Here, language becomes not merely a method of communication but the very symbolic structure within which the writing subject is constructed and into which he/ she tries to fit in the enunciating subject. Thus, the self of the 'enunciating subject' has already become an 'other' in the very act of writing the 'auto'biography—an 'other' translated from a state of marginality into the language of 'authority' of the writing self. The marginalised subject's entry into the dominant language is an act necessarily mediated by the writing subject. By eliminating incongruent elements in the enunciating subject's discourse, by making it ordered and coherent, the writing subject manufactures a text that appears seamless and whole. Thus, though Jameela exerts her 'agency' in rejecting the first version which had sold around thirteen thousand copies and went in for a second version of her autobiography, as an autobiographical subject one has to question her agency to know, express and regulate her 'self' without falling prey either to the politics of the publishing industry or the dynamics of the consumption of marginality in its economic and political context.

The subjective experiences of a marginalised woman like Jameela, when orally communicated in impromptu parlance, are cast under the framework of an immediate register containing rawness and imperfections, which can be attributed to being the 'originality' of the author's rhetoric, that is enormously different from the grammar and narrative style the market of the publishing industry demands. This 'natural parlance' is rigorously domesticated to expunge perceived 'inauthenticity, distortion and contamination' (Venuti 1998, 31). The linguistic, political and cultural mediation in the attempts to translate Jameela and her subjective experiences into the more 'intelligible' idioms of mainstream discourse compels a tri-vectorial probing set on control, consent and agency—whether it is confiscated or left intact with the enunciating subject. This probe obviously dapples the level of clout Jameela's self holds over the autobiographical self or the question of how congruent both of them are after being mediated and subsequently draws the conclusion that the autobiographical self is only an 'effect' of each translation. But a broader and largely 'unrecognised' ambit of explicating the portrayal of the self and agency in marginalised women's life writing is inaugurated through the versions of Devika as well as Jameela's friends as they are 'collective' ventures of a camaraderie of women, rather than a one-to-one enterprise of the subaltern narrator and the translator.

Finally, we also need to read Jameela's autobiographies keeping in mind the image in vogue today in Kerala' academic and critical discourses of the 'marginal other', the vindication of which has become both a fashion and a necessity harnessed to the public exhibition of political correctness. Nalini Jameela has become a 'rewarding' research in the academic circles today because of the feeling the texts generate that we have a better understanding of the condition of the sex worker in Kerala while actually, we remain enmeshed in the narrative coils of the 'stories'. Thus, if Jameela aspired to avert her 'marginality' through the act of telling her story, the writing that 'stages' her speaking seeks to keep her marginality secure. At this juncture, one has to go back to the question of 'Can the Subaltern Speak'. As John Beverley points out, what Spivak was trying to illustrate in her essay was that

> ... behind the good faith of the liberal academic or the committed ethnographer or solidarity activist in allowing or enabling the subaltern to speak lies the trace of the colonial construction of the other—an other who is conveniently available to speak to us (with whom we can speak or feel comfortable speaking with). This neutralises the force of the reality of difference and antagonism our relatively privileged position in the global system might give rise to. (2005, 431)

Elzbieta Sklodowska's arguments regarding the 'testimonio' can be applicable in the case of Jameela's life story too, as a staging of the subaltern by someone who is not a subaltern and not as 'a genuine and spontaneous reaction of a "multi form-popular subject" in conditions of post coloniality', but rather as a 'discourse of elites committed to the case of democratization' (1990–91, 113).

The very fact that an academic study such as this essay on Nalini Jameela's life, written from positions of privilege, is itself ironic, for conceding its provocation and radical otherness in the academy, it is yet to be pointed out that the oppression endured by a real sex worker cannot be represented by these commodified literary texts or in the university, for 'literature and the university are among the practices that create and sustain subalterernities' (Beverley 2005, 432). However, the existence of marginalised women's autobiography specifically as a genre is justified as an essential project in women's life writing because, as Joanne M. Braxton indicates, oftentimes such autobiographies become the marginalised women's 'letters of liberation, addressed first to herself, then to the community that surrounds and supports her, and, finally, to the hostile outside world' (2009, 131).

The epistemological authority that the autobiographical narrative secures in Jameela's case is not solely because of subaltern agency as it embodies the experience of the marginalised sex worker, but also due to hegemonic agency, because this particular experience has been packaged in a certain manner and presented in a literary form to a lettered audience and promoted as a legitimate voice representative of the oppression faced by sex workers in Kerala. Thus, writing itself is an act of deferring agency from the autobiographical subject and is complicit in attempting new modes of control over the subaltern's desire for agency.

The narrative of subject formation that mainstream academic discourses and publishing industries confer on subaltern women needs more irreverent critique that would seek to defy and transcend the hard borders in genre categorisation, even while exploring new dimensions and possibilities that afford more justice to their life narration, notwithstanding limited mainstream linguistic capabilities. At the same time, these innovative attempts at life writing are capable of bringing marginalised identities and their experiences to visibility with the caveat that even while they might capitulate to the capitalist imperatives of the publishing industry, they nevertheless attempt to nurture solidarities and alliances through collaborative efforts. In each version, the voice of Nalini Jameela is partly a construct of the text and seeks to appropriate the reader as much as we tend to believe in its 'authenticity'. It is a voice 'carrying the trace of the other', however interpolated it be by the market and hegemonic intellectuals at multiple levels.

REFERENCES

Anderson, Linda. 1986. "At the Threshold of the Self: Women and Autobiography." In *Women's Writing: A Challenge to Theory,* edited by Moira Monteith, 54–71. England: Harvester.

Bentskock, Shari. 1998. "Authorizing the Autobiographical." In *Women, Autobiography, Theory: A Reader,* edited by Sidonie Smith and Julia Watson, 145–60. Wisconsin: U of Wisconsin P.

Beverley, John. 2005. "Our Rigoberta? I, Rigoberta Menchu, Cultural Authority and the Problem of Subaltern Agency." In *Postcolonialisms: An Anthology of Cultural Theory and Criticism,* edited by Gaurav Gajanan Desai and Supriya Nair, 427–47. New Brunswick: Rutgers UP.

Beauvoir, Simone de. 2011. *The Second Sex.* New York: Vintage Books.

Braxton, Joanne M. 2009. "Autobiography and African women's literature." In *The Cambridge Companion to African Women's Literature,* edited by Angelyn Mitchell and Danielle K. Taylor, 128–49. Cambridge: Cambridge UP.

De Man, Paul. 1984. *The Rhetoric of Romanticism.* New York: Columbia UP.

Finney, Brian. 1985. *The Inner I: British Literary Autobiography of the Twentieth Century.* London: Faber and Faber.

Friedman, Susan Stanford. 1998. "Women's Autobiographical Selves: Theory and Practice." In *Women, Autobiography, Theory: A Reader,* edited by Sidonie Smith and Julia Watson, 72–81. Madison: U of Wisconsin P.

Godard, Barbara. 1995. "A Translator's Journal." In *Culture in Transit: Translation and the Changing Identities of Quebec Literature,* edited by Sherry Simon, 69–82. Montreal: Véhicule Press.

Jameela, Nalini. 2005a. *Oru Lymgikathozhilaliyude Athmakatha* [Autobiography of a sex worker]. As retold by I. Gopinath, Kottayam: DC Books.

———. 2005b. *Njan Lymgikathozhilali: Nalini Jameelayude Athmakatha* [I, a sex worker: The autobiography of Nalini Jameela]. Kottayam: DC Books.

———. 2007. *The Autobiography of a Sex Worker.* Translated by J. Devika. Chennai: Westland.

Long, Judy. 1999. *Telling Women's Lives: Subject/Narrator/Reader/Text.* New York: New York UP.

Lotbiniere-Harwood, Susanne de. 1991. *The Body Bilingual: Translation as a Rewriting in the Feminine.* Toronto: Women's Press.

Miller, Nancy K. 1991. *Getting Personal: Feminist Occasions and Other Autobiographical Acts.* New York: Routledge.

Robinson, Douglas. 2007. "The Tropics of Translation." In *Transatlantic Literary Studies: A Reader,* edited by Susan Manning and Andrew Taylor, 189–93. Edinburgh: Edinburgh UP.

Rowbotham, Sheila. 1973. *Woman's Consciousness, Man's World.* Harmondsworth: Penguin Books.

Simon, Sherry. 1996. *Gender in Translation: Cultural Identity and the Politics of Transmission.* London: Routledge.

Sklodowska, Elzbieta. 1990–91. "*Hacia una tipologia del testimonio hispanoamericano*" (Towards a typology of the Hispanic American testimony). *Siglo XX/Twentieth Century* 8(1–2): 103–20.

Venuti, Lawrence. 1998. *The Scandals of Translation: Towards an Ethics of Difference.* London: Routledge.

SIX

Autobiography as Translation

As a writer who shook the literary and social conventions of Kerala by writing the self as a breathing and desiring female subject in ways that the region had never witnessed before, Kamala Das radically altered the canonical structures of writing and feeling in the region. Through words that echo the intensity of felt emotions, she wove a daring world that challenged socially prescribed distinctions of the public and private. By critically analysing Kamala Das' autobiographies in Malayalam and English, which continues to haunt, unsettle and laugh at everything conventional about Malayalam's literary and cultural repertoire, this chapter attempts to study translation as a linguistic and embodied act that foregrounds the transactions and dissonances between the language of thought, the language of cultural reference, and language of writing. To this end, the chapter looks at self-writing as a conscious and curated process of self-translation that plays between the semantic codes and cultural nuances of the languages that she employs.

While Kamala Das has never been a writer to shy away from expressing her intimate thoughts, desires and conflicts, as evident through her autobiographies *Ente Katha* (1972) and *My Story* (1977), the many differences in the style, nature and texture of her self-narratives also provide considerable insight into her 'untranslatable' subjective presence both as self and process, their constant negotiations with society and imagined social readers. Autobiography as a genre attempts to reify the 'narratable self', or 'that which she already was', affirming the 'constitutive worldly and relational identity from which the story itself resulted' or the 'relations of her appearance to others in the world' (Cavarero 2000, 36). Given this, it is interesting to observe the ways in which these autobiographies become culturally-coded sites of self-articulation, which cannot be dissociated from the subject's perception of her socio-cultural agency. In such a context, it becomes pertinent to tease out the ways in which the narrating subject can be transcreated through the 'vital slippages', as Udaya Kumar calls it (2016, 18), between the narrative worlds of *My Story* and *Ente Katha*. Here, narrative worlds do not imply only the linguistically articulated world of the autobiography but also the feelings and thoughts that exist before it is ascribed the material form of words.

Madhavikutty's (Kamala Das' pen name in Malayalam) *Ente Katha* is believed to be an autobiography of a woman who opted to write rather than die. Thus, writing becomes an act of self-inscription in a language and culture that tried to silence her sexuality. *Ente Katha* created a furore in Kerala society in the seventies by valourising the female body. For the first time a woman used the Malayalam language blatantly, throwing to the winds a culture's preoccupations and values, and in the process critiquing all its dominant discourses. Her potentially subversive act of invoking the semiotic in Malayalam language and literature paved the way for writing the female body in a way radically different from male writings in terms of linguistic structure and content. But when Madhavikutty translated her story as Kamala Das's *My Story* in English, she must have encountered serious problems transcreating the female body written into the source language. The strategies by which the category 'Malayali woman', her multiple subject positions in *Ente Katha* and the cultural contingency of her experiences of oppression, get translated into the linguistic, historical and cultural specificities of a language such as English, form the scope of this paper. It is an attempt to analyse the process of translation by which the discursively constructed Madhavikutty of *Ente Katha* translates herself into the Kamala Das of *My Story*. Here, the chapter also acknowledges that languages do not remain isolated, self-contained entities but are ever-evolving cultural artifacts that emerge only in contact with the politico-economic structures around them. In the case of an ambidextrous bilingual writer like Kamala Das, who wielded English and Malayalam with equal grace and aplomb, the writer persona gets constituted through the sensibilities and aesthetics inherent in language structures, thus shedding light on the multiple ways in which 'languages erupt into each other, [in] unforeseen ways sudden languages happen at once' (Chandran 2018, 89). Hence, it becomes possible to go beyond questions of whether *My Story* is narrativising a Malayali identity, because to reduce Das and her cultural sensibility to a single point of reference, which is Kerala and Malayalam, would be tantamount to discounting her heteroglossic narrative subjectivity, formed through competing linguistic thought structures that always already seep into each other.

An autobiography is considered a genre of literature where the umbilical cord between the story and reality, the writer and the text, the signifier and the signified is yet intact. Kamala Das is one of the few writers in India who could snip this cord with élan, explicating in the process that all writings are constructed and all realities staged in language. *My Story* is not a literal translation of *Ente Katha*, which was originally serialised in the Malayalam magazine *Malayalanadu* in 1972. And yet the title *Ente Katha* translates as *My Story*. Kamala Das later famously denied *Ente Katha* to be a true story, stating that parts of it were fictitious. So whose is the voice that narrates *Ente Katha/My Story*? By positing this self as a fictional construct, by problematising it, Kamala Das actually poses a problem of identity, a problem linked to language, of writing one's self in two languages, in the process attempting to evolve a third—a language for writing the woman into existence. By celebrating the fictionality of her autobiography Das reiterates modern theories on the genre which stress the 'tautological nature of autobiography', pointing out that the 'autobiographical self is a fictional construct within the text which can neither have its origins anterior to the text nor indeed coalesce with its creator' (Anderson 1986, 59).

James Olney speaks of how it is impossible for an autobiographer to write the image double of her life, instead having to create herself afresh at every moment within the text (1980, 241). This might be the reason why Das chose not to go for a literal translation of *Ente Katha* into English but a creative retelling, aiming for textual equivalence. As she herself states in an interview, 'I have certain firm views about translation, I don't go in for a word-to-word translation. I always try to retain the spirit of the original in translation' (Raveendran 1998, 177). However, she adds that she finds it

> difficult to translate people who do not give me the freedom to reconstruct the work because without adding a little or subtracting a few lines I wouldn't be able to manage. I wouldn't be able to make it a finished work because I find in most regional literature certain inadequacies that come with the writer being a little bit too pompous to be a success. Because there are posturings which do not appeal to me. I would like a writer to be as honest as he or she can be. (177)

It is possible to speculate from textual evidence that *My Story* or parts of it were written first, which then formed the base for the translated/adapted/retold *Ente Katha*. The editor of *Malayalanadu*, V. B. C. Nair, reminisces in an interview about Kakkanadan's translation of the first chapter of *Ente Katha* from English ("Interview" 2004, 15). Madhavikutty herself says, 'I dream in English, I am afraid' (1989, 15). If this be the case, the very act of writing *Ente Katha* becomes an act of translating the self from the source language of English, to the target language of Malayalam, a reclaiming and recentering of identities in a new linguistic and cultural territory. Many studies have claimed that autobiographical memories are archived in the language in which it is experienced and that bilinguals often 'translate between their languages in order to access memories' (Puente 2015, 588). This brings to the fore the layered possibilities of translation, as a textual and imaginative practice, in Kamala Das' self-narrative and its self-translation. Here, translation becomes not only an active process involving a culturally-embedded linguistic system of reference but also a more impalpable, yet active, cognitive and psychological process of recollection. Given this, Madhavikutty becomes a being in translation, whose self-narratives reveal the interplay between her ideational repertoires, linguistic registers and cultural coordinates. Chapter 2 of *Ente Katha* begins thus:

> Yesterday evening in our visitor's room my husband told the Marathi poet Purushotham Rege, 'Kamala has started writing her autobiography'. He asked me to bring the first chapter and read it aloud to Rege. I did not comply to his request. I felt it would be like taking out a one-month-old embryo from the womb and exhibiting it. I never show my poems or stories to anyone before their publication. (Madhavikutty 1989, 18)

The first chapter of *Ente Katha* reads, 'When my friends came to know that I have started writing pieces of my autobiography, some of them said that no one less than forty years of age should attempt to write an autobiography' (1989, 13, my trans.). It is significant that no such references to the writing of an autobiography come up in *My Story*. That Kamala Das had started writing her autobiography and her friends knew about it contradicts the popular belief that it was a story written by a woman from her deathbed. Though this could be partly true, yet the textual evidences suggest that Kamala Das had started writing her story much before she reached the hospital bed and formed a contract with the editor of *Malayalanadu* to serialise *Ente Katha*. So it raises the question of which is the original text and problematises the notion of fidelity to the 'original'. In *My Story*, Das narrates her early education at home at the age of six:

> We had two tutors: Mabel, a pretty Anglo-Indian, and Nambiar, the Malayalam tutor. The cook was partial to the lady, served her tea on a tray... to Nambiar who came much later in the evening he gave only a glass-tumbler of tea and a few sardonic remarks. Nambiar in our house, moved about with a heavy inferiority complex and would hide behind the side-board when my father passed through the dining room where we had our Malayalam lessons. We learned our vernacular only to be able to correspond with our grandmother who was very fond of us. (1977, 9)

But in *Ente Katha* she is only four when the two tutors come to teach the children. The Anglo-Indian Mabel becomes the

Mangalorean Mrs. Sequeira. The Nambiar of *My Story* who 'received only tea and sardonic remarks' is fortunate enough to receive 'Parippu Vada' with his tea in *Ente Katha*. And yet it is Nambiar's inferiority complex in *My Story* that is attributed to the Malayalam language in *Ente Katha*. Madhavikutty writes, 'In those days we felt that Malayalam Language had Nambiar's colour and his inferiority complex' (1977, 16).

As Foucault argues 'all manifest discourse is secretly based on a "already said"; . . . this "already-said" is not merely a phrase that has already been spoken, or a text that has already been written, but a "never-said", an incorporeal discourse, a voice as silent as a breath that is merely the hollow of its own mark' (1972, 25). It can be argued that *My Story* is the as yet incorporeal discourse, the silent breath that permeates *Ente Katha*. The consciousness of an 'I' that performs/lives its gender in *Ente Katha* has an altogether different angle of entrance—that of an English language and education. The inferiority complex, which marks the learning of the vernacular is first attributed to the tutor in the English version and then to the language itself in the Malayalam version in what I argue to be a gradual systematisation of concepts, knowledge and experience in language.

Ente Katha displays more difficulties of narrating the self because Malayalam provides a cultural frame of reference within which the story is situated. In English the frame of reference is removed spatially and culturally and hence the emotional problems associated with remembering and narrating are fewer. For a woman the weight of patriarchal ideology is more intense and excruciating in her own native language than in English. Hence, telling the story is easier in English where value systems, cultural concepts and social norms that model experience are different. As language changes the ideological contexts too change, the process of processing memory changes, and techniques of cognitive mapping change. That *Ente Katha* is significantly less in volume than *My Story* reveals the ideological problem of narrating a woman's story in Malayalam where the acts of remembering and reiterating have painful emotional overtones. Thus, the methodology of remembering the past is weighed down by a political and cultural load in *Ente Katha,* while in *My Story* the process is easier.

The English version of the autobiography has afforded Kamala Das a neutrality whereas the Malayalam version carries the weight of markers of native codes like religion, ethnicity and gender. *My Story* is a good example of cultural code mixing where English is used 'to neutralise identities one is reluctant to express by the use of native languages or dialects' (Kachru 2000, 322).

My Story skillfully uses the English language to provide referential meaning while escaping Malayalam's cultural overtones and connotations, thus helping in the process of an identity shift—obscuring Madhavikutty, culturally conditioned by Kerala society and discursively constructed as 'a Malayali woman', in order to foreground the culturally neutral, more universal identity of Kamala Das. Thus, Kamala Das's transcreation of her story skillfully uses the English tongue to manipulate and control the normative and regulatory codes of Malayalam. The values and norms of English have been used to nullify traditional hierarchies of caste, class and gender. Thus, in *My Story* the cultural power base of *Ente Katha* is mitigated to a certain extent. English's 'power of alchemy linguistically to transmute an individual and a speech community' is what becomes evident in *My Story* where English transmutes the 'self' by providing more modernised registers to write the woman in (Kachru 2000, 326). Here, it is possible to see that Kamala Das adopts different narrative perspectives as she switches between languages. Through the apparent narrative divergences in the two self-narratives, one can discern the ways in which subjective identities remain constituted and embedded within language. The strategic omissions and additions that distinguish Das' self-narratives also hint at the larger cultural politics involved in discursively constructing and performing one's identity. As a result, linguistic mediation becomes a political act that encodes culturally-coded meanings to written words and lived worlds. Since autobiographies are mediated accounts produced through the triune of the 'author-narrator-protagonist' (Puente 2015, 587), these self-inscribed accounts reveal the subject's inner deliberations with the internalised thought structures as much as it gives insight into the socio-cultural negotiations that curate the conscious externalisation of subjectivities.

In conjunction with the argument that language and social models greatly influence the narrativisation of the self, this chapter seeks to illustrate how linguistic and semantic processes, linked to social models affect the construction of gender identity in such a way that the same identity might be projected differently while narrating the same life story in two different languages. By using the possessive pronoun My/*Ente*, Kamala Das/Madhavikutty fuses the author, narrator and character into one self. By denoting it as Story/*Katha* the writer consciously or unconsciously veers more towards a similar genre of the life-story than autobiography *per se*. Though both genres are the product of a process of narrativisation, fictionalisation and textualisation,

> [t]he life story develops specific traits; the orality of the genre produces a system of formal and structural recurrences and the interactional system as well as the stress on the social self, produce references to socio-symbolic discourse and the social imaginary through which a culture by means of language, maps and deciphers the world, a dimension also present in autobiography, but heavily marked in the life-stories. (Chanfrault-Duchet 2000, 63)

In the life story, unlike an autobiography, the author/narrator presumes an interaction with an audience, an audience that shares her models of experience and codes of culture. Though Kamala Das arranges all the important rites of passage charting the course of the evolution of the self and narrates all the events according to a chronological and causal scheme in *My Story*, *Ente Katha* displays a certain reluctance to the usual patterns of constructing the life story. It is more complex in its narration. The linear, confessional mode of narrative in *My Story* links it to a modernist form of writing while *Ente Katha* displays postmodern preoccupations in its part non-linear narrative relying on what appears to be a more disjointed memory. The preface to *Ente Katha* titled 'A Sparrow's Sorrow' is absent in *My Story*, and it is in this introduction to her life that Madhavikutty attempts to subtly negotiate the social contract in the act of writing one's story in the Kerala society of the early seventies. She writes in *Ente Katha,*

> Though I loved my husband deeply, he was unable to love me. At the moment of sexual intercourse with him I wished he would gather me in his arms after the act. Had he caressed my face or touched my belly I would not have felt to that degree the intense rejection I felt after each sexual union. When a woman relinquishes the first man in her life in order to walk up to the bed of another, it is not a contemptuous or immoral act, it is an act of pathos. She is one who is humiliated, wounded. She needs to quench herself. (1989, 8)

In subverting the conventions of a woman's autobiography Kamala Das shows how a woman constructed in accordance with the rigid codes of expectations of femininity can yet deconstruct herself in order to reveal the constructedness of herself. The one-page preface to *My Story* is stretched to nearly six pages in *Ente Katha,* a rather strenuous exercise considering the fact that the Malayalam version as a whole is much shorter than the English one. Madhavikutty in the preface to *Ente Katha* takes great pains to place her narrative identity inside the world of textual conventions yet outside it. More of a testimony than a confession, Madhavikutty here seems to address a culture whose expectations of conformity to an ideal of the feminine she cannot cater to. In contrast, the preface to *My Story* ends thus: 'This book has cost me many things I hold dear, but I do not for a moment regret having written it. I have written several books in my lifetime but none of them provided the pleasure the writing of *My Story* has given me. I have nothing more to say' (1977, n.p.). It is significant that this preface is found only in the Sterling edition published from New Delhi in 1976. The DC Books edition published from Kerala in 2004 omits this preface. The preface to *Ente Katha* begins with,

> A few years ago, one day in the afternoon, a sparrow flew into my room through the small window. Its breast hit the turning blades of the fan and the bird was thrown down. Hitting the windowpane, it clung to the glass for a few seconds. The blood from its breast stained the glass. Today let my blood ooze down to these pages, let me write in that blood. Let me write without the burden of a future, as only

one can write, making each word a compromise. I would love to call this poetry.... I always wished I had the strength to write this. But poetry never ripens for us, we have to acquire the maturity for it. (Madhavikutty 1989, 7)

By capturing the subtle emotional overtones of the narrator through the imagery of the bleeding sparrow, *Ente Katha* charts the affective imagination and emotional states of the narrator. Here, the familiar felt emotions are translated into the written social language in such a way that the gendered subject's identity is reified by deploying language as a flexible and sensorial medium. As a result, language here serves as a tangible externalised metaphor that actively registers Das' embodied emotions. The description of the bleeding sparrow in *Ente Katha* seeks to poignantly articulate the inarticulable affective worlds inhabited by the narrator through the synaesthetic evocation of emotions that seamlessly bleed into each other. The fluttering bird that later becomes a bleeding lifeless mass represents the narrator herself and the intensity of the imagery signifies the radical 'contingency' and 'sociality' of emotions (Ahmed 2002, 22). Here Madhavikutty is seen to renegotiate Kamala Das's relationship to the act of writing. The last sentence seems to emphasise that society needs to change in order to accept her writing. She turns the tables on societal norms and yet the pressures of conformity catch up with her as is evident in her many denials later on to the veracity of *Ente Katha*.

The self that is outwardly projected in *My Story/Ente Katha* is a self that tries to fit in, to conform, at least on the surface. This self is seen to situate and organise society and culture. Yet there is a progress towards a self that attains boldness in negotiating its relationship with the external world. What is achieved in the end is a new sense of identity, a woman who discovers her sexuality and who learns to revel in her multiple selves. But even here there is a difference in the two texts. *My Story* is more unapologetic and direct in its narration while *Ente Katha* is informed by a sense of *inter subjectivity*—a consciousness of the self as framed and limited by its interactions with the symbolic order. A wariness towards the audit culture is omnipresent in *Ente Katha*. Probably Madhavikutty is more conscious in her negotiations with the culture of the Malayalam language and its literary repertoire, knowing fully well that there are greater issues at stake in the autobiography's encounter with the social order here than in English. A mere look at the chapter headings will illustrate this point. The Sterling edition of *My Story* has fifty chapters some of which are titled—'I was infatuated with his charm', 'Women of good Nair families never mentioned sex', 'Was every married adult a clown in bed, a circus performer?', 'Her voice was strange, it was easy for me to fall in love with her', 'His hands bruised my body and left blue and red marks on the skin', 'Sex and the co-operative movement', 'I too tried adultery for a while', 'I was never a nymphomaniac', etc. Again, strikingly, all these headers are changed in the 2004 DC edition of *My Story*. For example, 'I was infatuated with his charm' is changed into the innocuous title 'The village school', while 'Women of good Nair families never mentioned sex' becomes 'The Feudal System'. None of the original titles find place in the Malayalam version which has chaste headers like 'The meaning of the word love', 'The season called beauty', 'Morality and rebirth', etc. Here we have a writer/ translator beset by different levels of cultural intervention while writing/translating in two different languages. Even the year and place of publication assume important dimensions. A female identity constituted by an intense awareness of sexuality is seen to be narrated, however subversively, with an acute awareness of the policing medium of the culture which a language represents. Thus, the expectation of conformity to a feminine cultural ideal is more on Madhavikutty than on Kamala Das, and hence disguises and ambiguities at the structural and narrational level of the text are more in *Ente Katha* than *My Story*. This leads to a situation where what is written has not been translated and what is translated has not been written. Madhavikutty's cultural identity often acts as a block in *Ente Katha*, forcing her to take more circuitous routes of narration. For example, the first meeting with her would-be husband, his sexual advances, their engagement, the subsequent visit to Calcutta, his crude attempts at sexual games, are all described in a simple, chronological straight forward manner in *My Story*. But in *Ente Katha* these incidents are compressed into two pages with philosophic ruminations and forward jumps in time. In all parts of the narrative where gender roles are crucial, *Ente Katha* displays a marked transferential tension at play, which is not so evident in *My Story*. For example, in the description of the rape where the old maid servant plays accomplice to the rapist, the whole incident is left ambiguous in *Ente Katha*, leaving the reader doubting the veracity of the incident. In *My Story* however, the narration leaves no doubt about the reality of the incident. 'The autobiographical tongue in any bilingual context is unlikely to tell the kind of homogenous and singular truth which critics of autobiography, quite contradictorily, seem both to disdain and desire' (McElroy 2000, 253). The process of historicising the subject and illustrating her dependence on the social order is more evident in *Ente Katha*, which offers innovative possibilities as far as the question of the specificity of women's writing leading to a feminist narratology is concerned.

Born in rural Kerala, brought up and schooled in Calcutta, married to a bank officer in Mumbai, spending a life divided among the cosmopolitan cities of Calcutta, Mumbai and Delhi, Kamala Das alias Madhavikutty projects a translated self, living in translated words. An intellectual self fashioned in the English tradition, yet bearing the weight of Malayalam's linguistic and cultural history, her autobiography is both a writing to and translating from the language of patriarchy. Probably it is this translatedness of being that helped Kamala Das challenge the authoritive codes of languages and culture. Translation here could be a metaphor for any activity in language that destablises cultural identities and received notions of selfhood, in the process questioning the notion of finality in translation. She thus uses translation as a tool to deflect the power of language, not only to reflect but also to construct reality. If Madhavikutty is Kamala Das in translation, what she does in *Ente Katha* is to earn the right to 'transgress from the trace of the other' (Spivak 1993, 179).

Kamala Das's self-translation of the story of her life reveals a writer who is forced to mould herself and her story according to two contradictory sets of cultural and linguistic norms. Culture here becomes a category more of enunciation than representation. Bhabha's description of translation as imitation comes in handy here, as

> Translation is also a way imitating, but in a mischievous displacing sense—imitating on original in such a way that priority of the original is not reinforced but the very fact that it can be simulated, copied, transferred, transformed, made into a simulacrum and so on: the 'original' is never finished or complete in itself. The originary is always open to translation so that it can never be said to have a totalised prior moment of being or meaning an essence. (Bhabha 1990, 210)

For Kamala Das, translation becomes a foundational activity where the unfinished original, both as self and text, is reworked and renegotiated in another culture and language. So fidelity is never a major concern with people like her who write from 'liminal' and 'hybrid' spaces. The neurosis of nostalgia that one finds in her autobiography is yet not the complete truth. For she is never really at home in Nalappat, often having to escape to Mumbai and then back to her ancestral home again. For an identity, carrying this trauma of dislocation, divided between the other tongue of English and the mother tongue of Malayalam, translation is an activity that best describes her being. Various studies have shown that the correspondence between the language in which memories are encoded and recollected can often help in retrieving 'more numerous, more detailed, and more emotional' memories (Bartolotti and Mariam 2013, 15). Since language constitutes and mediates the essence of the subject's identity and experience, Kamala Das' negotiations with her sense of self and belonging shows not only the culturally-bound linguistic metaphors with which she articulates herself but also the porosity of linguistic registers as it sifts and translates experiences and emotions.

Critics like Mary Jean Corbett argue that the autobiography is a way of attaining both literary legitimacy and a desired subjectivity

(Corbett 1992, 11). But the problem is whether this desired subjectivity is different for a writer while writing in two different languages. The literary tradition of the autobiographical genre in Malayalam has been dominated solely by men, especially men like V. T. Bhattathirippad and E. M. S. Namboothirippad who have played great roles in the public sphere in Kerala. For such great literary and social figures the autobiography was an unproblematic genre by which they could acquire a desired subjectivity as seekers/ producers of knowledge necessary for social amelioration. *Ente Katha* challenges the gendered separation of the public sphere from the private by exposing the so called domesticity of the woman as a social construct. And yet, again and again Madhavikutty apologises or attempts to justify herself. For example, she writes in *Ente Katha*,

> There are various reasons why I do not subscribe to the laws of morality prescribed by the society. The foundation of this morality is the mortal body. I believe that a supreme or salutary morality ought to be created in the immortal soul or if not, at least in the human mind... By telling lies, acting, cheating and hating many, I too could have covered myself in the blanket of society's pseudo morality and procured for myself a place of warmth and security underneath it... In a way writing such an autobiography truthfully, without hiding anything, is a striptease.... (1989, 87–88, my trans.)

These apologies and attempts to spiritualise the body are not to be found in *My Story* and betray an unconscious fear of social ostracisation associated with writing the female body. This register of anxieties, this culturally conditioned paranoia is more pronounced in *Ente Katha,* where Madhavikutty employs several such strategies of philosophising and justifying the trauma of female sexual transgression even as she attempts to transgress the patriarchal norms of representing the female. Despite this, what stands out in both versions of Das's story is the female body as real, an essence which is unsymbolisable, an unrepresented, unrepresentable space that challenges the patriarchal text from the margins. What comes through is a quest to retrieve this body lost in translation in the symbolic language. Within the discourse of autobiographical writing, Kamala Das uses the body as a space of difference, a space from where she could think femininity beyond the control of the phallic subject.

It is the marginalised semiotic aspect of Malayalam language that runs through *Ente Katha*. The poetry in *My Story* that is integrated into the text of *Ente Katha* makes it at times a non-rational discourse of the self which threatens the order of the symbolic language. Unlike in the male autobiographical tradition in Malayalam, Madhavikutty uses the irrational discourse of the semiotic to deconstruct women's marginalisation from the socio-symbolic contract. Yet it is important to note that such forms of subjectivity which attempt to subvert dominant discourses are at all times dubbed neurotic and immoral and punished by society. V. B. C. Nair says in an interview that Madhavikutty behaved like a 'street woman' when she stormed into his office alleging that he had twisted her writing to suit his purpose ("Interview" 2004, 15). The choice of epithets is highly significant and suggests the cultural saliences the word 'woman' takes, offering an insight into society's negative attitude to woman and her body. The implication is that the female body should be cloistered at home; in the street it acquires the connotation of free availability. This imputation about an eminent writer in Malayalam is indeed shocking. No wonder the writer felt compelled at some point in her life to say that she had written the autobiography at the behest of her husband for the money he wanted, and that she was truly a *pathivratha*, obedient in her life to her husband (Suraiya 2002). The very usage of the term 'street woman' by a man of some social standing is indicative of the male bias in the Malayalam language and its underlying cultural assumptions marked by the stamp of patriarchy. In such a culture the woman's body can only be seen as a tool to oppress her. Such a culture endorses masculinity as dominance and femininity as acquiescence to male dominance, and sex as another act of conquest over the feudal holding of the female body. So the writer whose story reveals that it is the 'discursive production of the nature of woman's bodies' that is 'central to the reconstitution of social norms of femininity, the patriarchal subjection of women and their exclusion from most aspects of public life' is punished by the patriarchal power structures (Weedon 1987, 108).

What Madhavikutty does in *Ente Katha* is a neat knocking down of the patriarchal ideological base of Kerala society. By exposing the limits of its domestic contract, the compromises inherent to its social fabric, the pitfalls of its system of education and above all the complete resistance to feminist gender critique, she problematises the relation between the female self and society. All the personal lampooning and hatred that forced Madhavikutty to disclaim the truth of her story points to the fate of all women in the public sphere in Kerala who attempt to construct discursively the experience of sexuality of Malayali women. Women's sexuality as a lexical gap in Malayalam literature and language echoes the dilemma of a culture still searching for ways to articulate the experience of womanhood. *My Story/Ente Katha* as the story of Malayali women, has to be *fictionalised* and made unauthentic to serve the purpose of all social and cultural agents paying allegiance to the symbolic powers. But together, through their open endedness and polysemy, they skillfully displace the masculine symbolic order, making us perceive the need to generate more discourses of the female self in order to reveal the other side of social history.

Mikhail Bakhtin points out 'Language is not a neutral medium that passes freely and easily into the private property of the speaker's intention, it is populated—over-populated—with the intentions of others. Expropriating it, forcing it to submit to one's own intentions and accents, is a difficult and complicated process' (2000, 278). Like Irigaray's impassioned plea for a woman-centred language, Madhavikutty's story has at its base the libidinal impulses of the female body narrated in a fluid language charged with feminine sexuality, embodying feminist resistances to patriarchal hegemonies of representation. Probably for the first time in Malayalam a woman attempts the *ecriture feminine*, rationalising the irrational, moralising the immoral and eroticising women's desire. *Ente Katha* in 1972 seems to be an anteredent to Irigaray's 'When Our Lips Speak Together'

(184–88) originally published in 1977. It almost reads like a forerunner to the essay, where Madhavikutty indeed begins a 'different' story in a language different from those of men, without letting 'convention' and 'habit' distract her. *Ente Katha* breaks the circle of conventional habit, the 'circularities' of male exchanges, knowledge and desire, by expressing multiplicities and speaking 'improperly'. Kamala Das cannot translate Madhavikutty for each is *several voices, several ways of speaking,* yet never separable from the other. Like Irigaray they assert that there is no possible *evil* in women's sexual pleasure, the only fault being stripping a woman of her *openness* and *marking her with signs of possession.* But women too should refuse to *submit* to male *reasoning,* refuse to feel *guilty,* for it is a male strategy to make women feel *guilty.* Eliciting Madhavikutty's confession that *Ente Katha* was written with the sole intention of making money, society finally succeeded in the strategy calculated to make her guilty for her story. Yet, in another interview to Shobha Warrior for the online portal Rediff, she reiterates that her autobiography was no fantasy. Kamala Das/Madhavikutty, in writing/translating her story, thus leaves *definitiveness* to the *undecided,* being what she becomes, *without clinging* to what she *might have been,* trusting only the *certainty* of the body.

As Judith Butler observes, 'individuals come to occupy the site of the subject and they enjoy intelligibility only to the extent that are, as it were, first established in language' (1997, 10). Given this, it is interesting to trace the ways in which the individual persona of the writer gets narratively interpellated and translated into two distinct, yet interdependent and overlapping, subjectivities, namely Kamala Das and Madhavikutty. To this end, this chapter has attempted to study the cultural politics that determine how the subject chooses to write themselves. By reading Das' *Ente Katha* and *My Story* as discursive sites that give insight into the narrative self as much as the manner in which they chart the cultural geography and ideological structures of the region, the study tried to understand the contours of the subject-in-translation, whose selves are to be discerned not only through that which is verbally articulated but also through unspoken impressions hidden amidst the rhetorical silences of the text.

References

Ahmed, Sara. 2002. "The Contingency of Pain." *Parallax* 8 (1): 17–34.

Anderson, Linda. 1986. "At the Threshold of the Self: Women and Autobiography." In *Women's Writing: A Challenge to Theory*, edited by Moira Moneith, 54–71. Brighton: Harvester P.

Bartolotti, James, and Viorica Marian. 2013. "Bilingual Memory: Structure, Access and Processing." In *Memory, Language and Bilingualism: Theoretical and Applied Approaches*, edited by Jeanette Altarriba and Ludmila Isurin, 7–47. Cambridge: Cambridge UP.

Bakhtin, Mikhail. 2000. "Unitary Language." In *The Routledge Language and Cultural Theory Reader*, edited by Lucy Burke, Tony Crawley and Alan Girvin, 269–79. London: Routledge.

Bhabha, Homi K. 1990. "The Third Space." In *Identity, Community, Culture, Difference*, edited by J. Rutherford, 207–21. London: Lawrence and Vishart.

Butler, Judith. 1997. *The Psychic Life of Power*. Stanford: Stanford UP.

Cavarero, Adriana. 2000. *Relating Narratives: Storytelling and Selfhood*. London: Routledge.

Chandran, K. Narayana. 2018. "To the Indian Manner Born: How English Tells its Stories." *Hermeneus* 20: 87–104.

Chanfrault-Duchet, Marie-Francoise. 2000. "Textualisation of the Self in the Life-Story." In *Feminism and Autobiography: Texts, Theories, Methods*, edited by Tess Cosslett, Celia Lury and Penny Summerfield, 31–75. London: Routledge.

Corbett, Mary Jean. 1992. *Representing Femininity*. Oxford: Oxford UP.

Das, Kamala. 1977. *My Story*. New Delhi: Sterling.

Foucault, Michel. 1972. *The Archaeology of Knowledge*. London: Tavistock.

"Interview with V. B. C. Nair". 2004. *Pachamalayalam*, 2 (3): 15.

Irigaray, Luce. 2000. "When Our Lips Speak Together." In *The Routledge Language and Cultural Theory Reader*, edited by Lucy Burke, Tony Crawley and Alan Girvin, 184–88. London: Routledge.

Kachru, Braj K. 2000. "The Alchemy of English." In *The Routledge Language and Cultural Theory Reader*, edited by Lucy Burke, Tony Crawley and Alan Girvin, 317–28. London: Routledge.

Kumar, Udaya P. 2016. *Writing the First Person: Literature, History, and Autobiography in Modern Kerala*. Hyderabad: Permanent Black.

Madhavikutty. 1989. *Ente Katha* [My story]. Kottayam: DC Books.

McElroy, Ruth. 2000. "Bringing it Home: Autobiography and Contradiction." In *Feminism and Autobiography: Texts, Theories, Methods,* edited by Tess Cosslett, Celia Lury and Penny Summerfield, 252–56. London: Routledge.

Olney, James. 1980. "Some Versions of Memory/Some Versions of Bios: The Ontology." *Autobiography: Essays Theoretical and Critical,* edited by James Olney, 236–67. Princeton: Princeton UP.

Puente, Ines Garcia de la. 2015. "Bilingual Nabakov: Memories and Memoirs in Self-translation." *The Slavic and East European Journal* 59 (4): 585–608.

Raveendran, P. P. 1998. "In Conversation: Kamala Das." *Malayalam Literary Survey* 20 (4): 15.

Spivak, Gayatri Chakravorty. 1993. *Outside in the Teaching Machine.* London: Routledge.

Suraiya, Kamala. 2002. "Mathavum Premavum." *Bhashaposhini,* Annual Issue.

Weedon, Chris. 1987. *Feminist Practice and Poststructuralist Theory.* Oxford: Blackwell.

Warrior, Shobha. 1996. Interview. *Rediff on the Net.* Online. Available: http://www.rediff.com/news/1996/3107adas.htm.

SEVEN

English and Postcolonial Translations

This chapter puts forth the proposition that there is an increasing propensity on the part of the corporate publishing world to woo the speech of the gendered subaltern, a process that has entailed multiple degrees of co-option. At a time when the 'popularity' of postcolonial theory within the academy has stamped the subaltern with a certain cultural value, making her a 'safe selling globalised commodity', one among the many 'culturally "othered" goods' (Huggan 2001, 6), it calls for academic alertness to the fact that many counter-hegemonic struggles themselves could be sucked in by the quagmire of neo-colonial agendas and transnational capital.

Subaltern narratives such as the Adivasi leader and social activist C. K. Janu's *Mother Forest* offer a radical critique of the deep chasm between the discursively constructed notion of the gendered subaltern and her own life as the subject material of a particular kind of history. That she probes, unsettles and punctures the discursively consensual homogeneity of oppressed Indian womanhood is indeed remarkable. Yet, when and what the subaltern speaks/attempts to speak is written/translated in English, it is imperative to look at how the language of hegemonic power, global currency and elitist identity articulates/silences her. Here, the pertinent question of whether one can be thought 'to be a postcolonial even before or without being translated into English?' (1998, 11) that Susan Bassnett and Harish Trivedi raise in the introduction to *Postcolonial Translation Theory* needs to be reframed in the contemporary market models of the translation industry to interrogate whether a gendered subaltern exists without being translated into English.

Lawrence Venuti speaks of three characteristics of minority literature: '... the deterritorialization of language, the connection of the individual to a political immediacy, and the collective assemblage of enunciation' (1998, 136). Many of the recent autobiographies by women in Kerala seem to fit into these schematics of minority. If one looks at the publishing history in recent years of 'gendered marginality' in Kerala for example, it makes one slightly uneasy. The increasing number of such books like C. K. Janu's *Mother Forest: The Unfinished Story of C. K. Janu* (2004), Ajitha's *Kerala's Naxalbari: Memoirs of a Young Revolutionary* (2008), Nalini Jameela's *The Autobiography of a Sex Worker* (2007), Sister Jesme's *Amen: An Autobiography of a Nun* (2009), among others, first published in Malayalam, their almost immediate translation into English and their record-breaking readership, point towards the possible institutionalisation of marginality as a fairly saleable intellectual commodity.

Underlying the genre of autobiography is the fundamental concept of authenticity which posits the idea that the writer is true to himself or herself as also that there is a movement towards self-discovery through experience. Here, the trajectory of self-discovery and its claim to veracity become ambiguous as the self that the writer 'discovers' from the fragments of past memories sequesters its character as the product of a conscious attempt of 'construction' which is tangled with the skeins of recollection and reminiscence. On the other hand, the dissection of authenticity as a trope, which assigns the values of accuracy and reliability to the 'self' precipitated in the autobiography, is imminent. In his attempt to dismantle the dichotomy of 'authentic texts' and 'non-authentic texts' in L2 pedagogy, Russell Simonsen insinuates that authenticity is a 'psychosocial creation' (2019, 246) which ascribes legitimacy to certain texts by banking upon subjective qualities such as accuracy and reliability moored in the language of the texts which is purported to be 'unsanitised' (252) and the socio-cultural purpose in the 'real world' at which they are directed (247–48) thus exposing the fallacy of 'texts being authentic by nature' (246). But authenticity has today also become part of a commodified representational mechanism through which 'selling' images of the 'other' are manufactured and manipulated by the intellectually dominant. Here, the texts from the margins with the languages and images of the 'other' in their 'unsanitised' avatar and their objective to serve 'the socio-cultural purpose' of inscribing their experiential lives into the mainstream imaginary fit into the seamless garb of unquestionable 'authenticity'. In this backdrop, it is essential to study 'the sociological dimensions of postcolonial studies: the material conditions of production and consumption of postcolonial writings, and the influence of publishing houses and academic institutions on the selection, distribution and evaluation of these works' (Huggan 2001, vii).

The representation of the gendered subaltern is a textual construct, which can neither be created nor often contested by her. The gendered subaltern who attempts to speak or inscribe herself into mainstream language and the social order does so by translating herself with the help of a translator from her own language into a hegemonic language and culture and thus essentially becoming a translation in the process. In the end, it is as though it is this act of translation which confers a privilege and status to her in the 'potential store of historical memory' (Asad 2010, 8).

Thus, the craft of translation becomes an act of social validation intricately connected to issues of power and authority yielded by the translator. This authority is further endorsed by the forces of institutionalised academics and a global publishing industry which offer the text of the subaltern certain currency. Thus, the power vested on the translator as an institutionalised power needs to be critiqued from various angles. One needs to look at the representation of the subaltern not as a simple act of representation but as a translation act contaminated by differential language power and mediated and constructed by institutional power.

What does the life story of an Adivasi woman, who mobilised her people and led them to a historic protest against the government, agitating for land for the landless tribal people, tell us readers? The book is called *Mother Forest: The Unfinished Story of C. K. Janu,* as told to and written by Bhaskaran and translated by N. Ravi Shanker. It primarily attempts to translate Janu's thoughts and her life from her language into English, in the process conferring coherence to a seeming incoherence, structure to what was loose and eclectic, thus attributing a semblance of 'symbolic' logic to a privileged ethnic semiotic. Janu apparently 'speaks' her culture to Bhaskaran and in her voice, he hears the 'silence of centuries' (Bhaskaran 2004, viii). So it is he who sifts these enunciations and constructs a text of it, 'helping' her break this silence. Thus, Bhaskaran encounters the language of the subaltern and uses his own language to map the 'Other', to fathom the 'Other's' speech, to organise its meaning, to create literary effect and to ask the right questions in order to extract the right responses from the 'Other'.

The English translator Ravi Shanker says his purpose was to retain the flavour of Janu's intonation and the sing-song nature of her speech in the translation. But that he is also engaged in reproducing the structure of a tribal language within the discourse of English and the point that these are in a sense 'unequal languages' is a matter of concern. That English is not flexible enough to accommodate the unaccustomed forms of speech or cultural acts of alien discourses, especially of caste and ethnicity is certainly true. Added to that is the fact that rather than subjugate itself to the transforming power of the 'other', Ravi Shanker's English remains curiously immune to the spirit of the 'other' so that the intention of the original is co-opted by the hegemony of English and its institutionally defined power structure even though the translator might remain open and emphatic. Here, language reveals itself as an asymmetric matrix of power, whereby translation becomes an act of violence that inflicts wounds of integration and acculturation. Talal Asad has pointed out that the languages of the Third World societies—including those 'of the societies that social anthropologists have traditionally studied'—are 'weaker in relation to Western languages (and today, especially to English)', and could more likely submit 'to forcible transformation in the translation projects than the other way around' (2010, 22).

He says that this is due to their greater ability to manipulate the weaker ones, as also the fact that 'Western languages produce and deploy *desired* knowledge more readily than Third World languages do. The knowledge that Third World languages deploy more easily is not sought by Western societies in quite the same way, or for the same reason' (2010, 22).

So what Bhaskaran and Ravi Shanker together do is an act of 'cultural translation' where the language of translation does not merely posit the notion of an English vs. a 'tribal language' but a hegemonic, culturally elitist academic 'play' versus a certain mode of life that, judged by the former's standards, would translate as 'primitive' and 'uncivilised'. 'The translation is addressed to a very specific audience, which is waiting to read about another mode of life and to manipulate the text it reads according to established rules, not to learn to live a new mode of life' (Asad 2010, 23). Thus, what Ravi Shanker translates is not the 'historically situated' speech of C. K. Janu—the Adivasi woman—but her culture to an English-speaking academic readership and, for this task, he has to first 'interpret' the 'meaning' of her speech and then re-inscribe and package it for the readers. However, it is interesting to note that the world view, almost a bird's eye view, of the ethnic life that Janu seems to present in the first chapter can hardly be the result of her conscious contemplation and speculation but a process nudged and prompted by the ethnographer and translator in order to construct a particular kind of discourse of the subaltern, that is then condensed, formatted, published and reviewed as a postcolonial text that 'centres' the margins. The attempt to translate it into English, however, is flawed. The apparently inconsistent and arbitrary switching of cases, beginning a sentence in the lower case—all seem ploys, sales tags for advertising some understanding of the gendered subaltern's language, her consciousness and her culture.

The discourse of English always already 'colonises' the gendered subaltern because it relies heavily on an Anglophone readership, a global market that is all too hungry for such images, shaped as it is by the horizon of expectation for writing by and about the postcolonial gendered subaltern. Here I invoke Mohja Kahf's arguments in a similar vein regarding writing about Arab Muslim women which she says is singularly dependent upon the environment of reception.

If Nalini Jameela's autobiography is titled *The Autobiography of a Sex Worker*, seemingly conferring agency upon her by emphasising her subjectivity and attempting to 'plant' her as the source of enunciation, the front cover of Janu's book stresses the authorship of Bhaskaran. The back cover of the book says 'Frank, guileless and deeply moving. Janu's unfinished autobiography is an eloquent testimony to her courage and her convictions'. Interestingly enough, the back cover of the Malayalam version proclaims it to be a biography of Janu. It says that the book recreates the life of Janu, the authentic daughter of the soil and is the most truthful and transparent biography that Malayalam has ever witnessed. This shift in genre from biography to autobiography in English seems a calculated strategy to foreground and claim a certain modernist preoccupation regarding the subjective. Authenticity is one of the most marketable elements of cultural difference in the publishing industry today. This move has also to be placed in the context of the newer and more subversive uses of autobiography which has staked an enviable claim, as no other literary genre has, of being the legitimate text of the subaltern, capable of speaking 'authentically' for both the individual and her marginal community. It is this claim to be the text of the oppressed that the English version seeks to appropriate, apparently projecting Janu onto the centre of her narrative and clearly positioning her as the 'enunciating' subject of the autobiography in order to highlight her subjectivity and agency.

The English text begins in lower case and the sentences are rather complicated. The translator says,

I wanted to retain the flavour of Janu's intonation and the sing-song nature of her speech in the translation. Initially I experimented with a form that roughly translated the first few sentences like this:

"where we all lived there was a time when work just meant *pullinge* out the paddy seedlings, *transplantinge* them in the fields *aand* such/

mostly work related to/paddy *faarminge*/plantation work become common much later/ work like *manuringe* coffee *manuringe* pepper *aand* such were simply not there/ most of the *toilinge* we did only in the rice fields/*carryinge dunge* to the fields *digginge* up the soil *withe* spades sowinge pullinge out the seedlings transplantinge them *weedinge wateringe reapinge carryinge* the sheaves of corn *aand* such" (italics mine)

Verbs are pronounced with greater emphasis than nouns in Janu's language, and I attempted to capture that in English. But many well-wishers, including the writer Paul Zacharia objected to distorting the language in this manner and advised me to keep it lucid. I reworked the draft and used the simplest language possible, keeping the flow of language close to the Malayalam that rolled off Janu's tongue. The upper cases in the first chapter, in a sea of lower cases, are used to indicate the stresses in Janu's spoken language. (xi–xii)

However, the discretionary use of lowercase, such as for 'I' and the articles of native life, while the uppercase is used for Coffee and Pepper and place names, Motor Pump, Chemicals, etc., almost becomes complicit at times with a syntactical and grammatical subordination of the subaltern. These stylistic and linguistic attempts must also be read together with 'received' notions amongst Anglophone readers of the gendered subaltern's subordination and silencing in language.

Thus, it is indeed the reception environment—of Left-liberal intellectuals, social activists, literary elite and the academics—who shape the language of representation, for it is after all they who have to decode it. Here, it is English that speaks the subaltern, not the subaltern who speaks English, turning itself into a framing narrative of subalternity. Thus, the text caters to the horizon of expectations of a hegemonic readership for whom the subaltern is a small 'i' and cannot be a bold, emphatic 'I'. These strategies of representation address a particular readership that is aware of the universalising tendencies of standard English and therefore requires both the enunciating subject and the language to strike poses that 'conform' to certain postcolonial positions which they have read about. The onerous task of constructing her in a specificity and difference is taken literally by an over-conscientious writer and translator who struggle to take into consideration the mediated nature of the enunciating subject as also the writing subject and the translating subject. Thus, this becomes a very good illustration of how theory constructs a discourse probably due to an intensely conscious awareness of the colonial baggage of English. Nevertheless, it is ironic that this subversive strategy itself can only be deciphered by a readership consisting of skilled and elite Anglophones.

A self-conscious nativisation of the English language to articulate the condition of subalternity can inadvertently turn back upon itself and exert a new control and authority over the subaltern which is exercised by a mediating postcolonial hegemonic intellectual. Thus, nativised English is used to domesticate the subaltern and placate the postcolonial reader. As Braj K. Kachru points out 'the real power of English language is in its "vehicular load", in the attitude toward the language, and in the deep and increasing belief in its power of alchemy linguistically to transmute an individual and a speech community' (2000, 326).

One could say that Ravi Shanker has made use of a kind of 'interlinear translation' where the stages of a translator's travel from the source text to a literal translation and finally into the published version is rendered more visible, drawing attention to the in-betweenness of the act of translation (Sturrock 1990, 996) as part of a responsible refusal to naturalise the gendered subaltern in standard English. While conceding to this method it is, however, necessary to point out that what becomes so objectionable is the patronisingly pidginised English employed by the translators that creates a museum effect which can hardly be said to garner respect for the gendered subaltern. Moreover, it points a finger at another kind of power—'the power to put on display, to dissect and analyze to the smallest detail', which is a symbol, 'indeed the actual realization—of the power to control and subjugate' (Shamma 2009, 47).

The English translation of Janu's life remains an interlinear, provisional version of her utterances out of which the postcolonial reader is prompted to construct a final free version. The rationale offered by the translator for this discretionary pidginisation of English is to retain the flavour of her original speech. Thus, what might have been an honourable intent, dissipates into the notion that only 'pidginised English' can correlate with the native tongue. This quasi-interlinear translation, I feel, also appears to construct a reading subject hegemonically valourised over the enunciating subject. There is the flaunting of a superior parole and a formal 'grip' over the source—grammatically, syntactically and semantically. Thus, to the gendered subaltern's disadvantage, her English autobiography remains 'a pedagogic contrivance' or even a 'model marked for display purposes only', and its 'flagrant inadequacy' and incompleteness 'points beyond itself' to a possibility of a better-formed utterance in the future (Sturrock 1990, 998).

It also highlights the role of the ethnographer and the translator whose acquired knowledge of the subaltern's life and culture can be borrowed by the reader to understand the pre-text of the subaltern. Thus, the problem of translating the subaltern is over-dramatised in this interlinear English, which struggles to reproduce Janu's speech which is rather 'telegraphic', into an 'unenglished' English. This defamiliarisation of English is a strategy calculated to make the subaltern not only sound native but also packaged to market it as the queer and the exotic that sells in a global cultural commodity circuit.

Thus, as Sturrock points out, the interlinear translation,

> is not permitted to reproduce a national language in a fluent form; rather, it approximates to those intermediary languages such as pidgin which have developed in like contexts in order practically to bridge the gap between existing languages. But as with pidgin, the inference is that one of these languages, our own, is both lexically richer and syntactically more advanced than the other, to confer with whose users in a middle tongue thus demands an intellectual sacrifice on our part. (1003)

Thus, Ravi Shanker's middle tongue is neither English nor Janu's tribal language but English masquerading as 'tribal'. (It is highly interesting to note here that neither the author nor the translator spells out which tribe Janu belongs to—using words like *Adivasi* and tribal alternately to denote her ethnic location).

Ravi Shanker does highlight the untranslatable characteristics of the syntax and lexicon of Janu's language and this would have sufficed without including the 'patronising Englishing' of the subaltern. In support of this translation one could argue that it does attempt to critique and transgress the discursive values and institutional limits of the English language culture paving the way for the manifestation of a cultural other. Translation scholars like Schleiermacher, Berman and Venuti have supported such translations. While one need not find fault with the ethics of such translations, what is disturbing is often the modes of its implementation as transparent/authentic representations of subaltern essence. The author and translator together believe that they have retained the syntactical and lexical peculiarity of Janu's language while this remains only an illusion and what comes through is a constrained translation, perfect in its collocations of English words but stilted in its construction of sentences.

While the attempt to evade linguistic homogenisation, however rudimentarily implemented, can be lauded, it is the play for the sake of play of signifiers, in the process flaunting their materiality that one finds a little problematic in the text. The gaps and fissures in syntax and diction instead of explicating the points of departure of the subaltern text from hegemonic culture values remain so at the linguistic level, giving rise to an easy and nostalgic idealisation of the gendered subaltern—making her a commodity of 'difference' (cultural difference?) without really problematising the target culture norms. Hence the translation remains at the preliminary level of a deliberate attempt at disrupting the fluency of the target language and fails to achieve what it might have set out to accomplish—that is, bringing in the differences in dialect, register, discourse and style of the 'other' in critically engaging with the target readership.

However ironic it might sound, postcolonial theory is becoming increasingly global in scope and ambition. 'Difference' has become an eminently saleable commodity under the tag of postcolonialism today. This could be the reason why a marginalised genre of writing like the autobiography has acquired a discursive value that makes it the very embodiment of literary modernism and seems to valourise it as an enactment of the self in opposition to the representational violence encoded by other forms of writing. Thus, autobiography has emerged as the most legitimate form of literary intervention within postcolonial studies.

However, when an 'autobiographical' subjectivity is attributed to the gendered subaltern, there is a need to critique the often absent presence of the subject within the narrative which is 'authored' by hegemonic intellectuals who, it is assumed, can better narrativise the alterity of the subaltern than the subaltern herself. The over-enthusiasm in the English version to hitch on to the fast-moving wagon of 'postcolonial autobiography' underscores a keen eye on marketability linked to a burgeoning area of intellectual activity. The words of Rey Chow become extremely relevant in this context:

> We need to remember as intellectuals that the battles we fight are battles of words. Those who argue the oppositional standpoint are not doing anything different from their enemies and are most certainly not directly changing the downtrodden lives of those who seek their survival in metropolitan and non-metropolitan spaces alike. What academic intellectuals must confront is thus not their 'victimization' by society at large (or their victimization-in-solidarity-with-the oppressed), but the power, wealth, and privilege that ironically accumulate from their 'oppositional' viewpoint, and the widening gap between the professed content of their words and the upward mobility they gain from such words. (1993, 17)

Chow argues that this was what Foucault meant when he said intellectuals need to struggle against becoming the object and instrument of power, raising the questions of why we should believe in 'those who continue to speak a language of alterity-as-lack while their salaries and honoraria keep rising', and how we could 'resist the turning-into-propriety of oppositional discourses, when the intention of such discourses has been that of displacing and disowning the proper?' (1993, 17).

How do we deal with a life story which is called biography in one language and an autobiography in another? The shift from biography to autobiography marks a global market demand for ethnic autobiographies which is one of the most commodified of literary genres today. The mainstream demand for subaltern autobiographies is precipitated, as suggested by Susan Hawthorne, by the voyeuristic tendencies of mainstream culture and the possibility of an indirect access to 'exotic' cultures whose differences are acknowledged and celebrated even as they are rendered amenable to a reading public (1989, 262).

Also, conceding the fact that 'one story cannot be "self present" to us, cannot be under the conscious control of the subject' (Anderson 2001, 126) we need to ask the question—whose is the voice that narrates the unfinished story of C. K. Janu? Is it Janu's? Is it that of Bhaskaran who claims to be, paradoxically enough, the 'author' of the autobiography and significantly enough owns the copyright of the gendered subaltern's book? Is it the voice of N. Ravi Shanker who confesses to fifteen drafts before the final version? Or as the feminist argument goes, as women have been trained through centuries to see themselves as objects and have been positioned as Other, autobiography is an impossible genre for women and especially subaltern women—'none of us as women, has as yet, precisely, an autobiography' (Felman 1993, 14). So even as we see hegemonic intellectuals like us and a hegemonic language like English appropriating the voice of the gendered subaltern, one can only seek to look beyond the autobiographical moments in the texts to 'moments of resistance or hesitation between discourses', 'between theory and autobiography' which might testify to the 'surprising irruptions' of the subaltern (14).

Mother Forest is neither a biography nor an autobiography, and it would be more appropriate to call it a testimony. 'What distinguishes testimony from autobiography, and what has generated much of its problematic character as a genre, is its mediated quality, the fact that an academic fieldworker must record, transcribe, and edit it' (Brooks 2005, 82). Brooks says that there are four categories: staging, acting, storytelling performance and dialogue that 'push testimonial language beyond ordinary circumstances and give it a quality of anthropological enactment' (184). The way Bhaskaran stages Janu's testimonio performance is highly interesting. The English translator recalls,

> I am back home after a wonderful trip to Wayanad to meet C. K. Janu, a vibrant young leader of the tribal people of Kerala.... We interviewed her extensively and she turns out to be one of the wisest people I have ever met. Her clarity of observation is amazing. And, her language for a woman uneducated in the traditional sense, is amazingly precise. (Bhaskaran 2004, ix)

And yet this 'amazing woman' needs an 'Author's Introduction to the English Edition', a 'Translator's Note', picture illustrations of 'tribal' life, a 'bio-data', the 'Text of the Agreement between the Government and the Agitation Committee of the Tribals', a letter from none other than Arundhati Roy 'supporting tribals' cause' and a 'Glossary' to make her more understandable.

The strategies used by the writer to 'flesh' out the interview scenario in order to intensify the performance are also interesting. 'We even spent a night in her small hut built on top of an encroached hill, where she lives with three women friends, 17 goats and a dog, and wild elephants keep calling' (x). It is this staging that helps us—Anglophone readers, bourgeoisie intellectuals and academics—to 'understand' the tribal activist Janu better. Thus, 'To read the testimonio is to decipher its special theatrical elements, its storytelling devices, the roles played by its participants, and the dialogical interaction between them' (Brooks 2005, 218). This re-visioning of the text as a testimony brings clarity to the distinct interplay of the 'textual grid' and 'conceptual grid' (Lefevere 2002, 75)—in this case biography/ autobiography/testimony and the 'authentic representation' of a subaltern woman respectively, as initiated by the writer and the translator by embedding certain markers of the gendered subaltern to elicit the desired response from the intended intellectual audience.

The question I seek to raise in this chapter is, can postcolonial academic impulses lay claim to ethical or moral legitimacy when they can be co-opted by hegemonic interests and transnational capital? Rejecting Western epistemological constructions of the other, we in India are devising newer and better strategies for 'our' subalterns to speak, but only through us. Is it that only we can confer epistemological authority over textualised subaltern experiences? The gendered subaltern in India can speak all she wants, but is it only our institutional authority as academics and our metropolitan English, with whatever degree of 'theoretical subversiveness' we assign to it, that can speak her loud enough for her to be heard in the global market? Here, Huggan's reiteration of Spivak's statement that 'when marginality, ... comes with the seal of academic approval, this may only help to commodify it, at the university and elsewhere in society' (Spivak 1991, 154 paraphrased in Huggan 2001, 23) becomes relevant. So the question remains—how far can our interests as UGC professors, intellectuals and social activists coincide with the identity politics and struggles for the socio-economic and cultural survival of subaltern subjects? Are advertent alliances possible between 'us' and the 'other', even while acknowledging that neither 'us' nor 'the other' can be homogenous categories but fluid entities caught in the flow of global capital, and in a constant flux of unequal power relations?

The idea of translation as significantly engaging with the production of a subaltern subject with agency, is a problematic, as is the concomitant mechanics of its representation. In his discussion of three works in Malayalam which includes Janu's book, P. P. Raveendran states that 'translation, as translation theorists are never tired of repeating, is a symbolic exchange that ironically leads to distortion and falsification of the original' (2007, 190). In the case of Janu, even the 'original' becomes a site of contestation, where C. K. Janu who appears as the spokesperson for the Adiya tribal community only speaks and does not write. The book itself is written by Bhaskaran, therefore proclaiming to have captured the caesurae in the recounting of her experience in her native tongue.

The book is in itself a translation of Janu's thoughts, thereby Janu, into Malayalam (a hegemonic language for the tribal communities), which later undergoes another round of translation to English, the language of the global market and the intellectually dominant. Hence, in the figure of the 'enunciating' gendered subaltern with 'agency' thus projected (or packaged?) in the English translation, the distortion is magnified, the falsification amplified and the exchange slanted. This heralds the need to dissect the 'process of dissimulation' (Birla 2010, 89) that facilitates the emergence of the 'subjectivity of a gendered subaltern with agency' under the veil of the English translation of a subaltern (auto)biography which carries currency in the global circuits of cultural commodities. Interestingly, this conundrum makes an appearance even in the course of writing this paper where citing the text in question becomes a sticky affair. The peculiar problem of attribution of authorship and agency is re-encountered in the reference list as while the text posits itself as 'the Unfinished Story of C. K. Janu', the phrase 'As told to and *written by Bhaskaran* [emphasis added]' in bold, white interface on the front cover nevertheless confounds us. Whilst the roles of the writer Bhaskaran and the translator Ravi Shanker have to be duly acknowledged in the entry, the position of Janu becomes dubious.

Almost twenty years have passed since the publication of *Mother Forest: The Unfinished Story of C. K. Janu* and the terrains of tribal representation have undergone drastic transformation. As Chandrabose observes in his paper 'Aesthetics and Politics of Poetry written in Tribal Languages of Kerala', the recent flurry of creative output in tribal languages undertaken by younger generations from the tribal communities in Kerala are attempts to mark their experiential lives in their own terms in difference to the standards set by 'civilised society' (modern society?) (2021, 26). They venture to shake off the overarching influence of the hegemonic language of Malayalam by devising strategies to appropriate the language, by instrumentalising its script to bring tribal languages into graphemic existence. More than often, they take up the task of translating these works from tribal languages into Malayalam, thus negotiating the terms of legitimacy and eliminating the mediators from the mainstream language who steered the course of translations earlier. However, the travails of representation, the cultural commodification and the co-option of the subaltern and the subaltern experience by the corporate publishing industry and the dominant intellectual audience that prevail, particularly in the context of its translation into the global language of English, need to be subjected to more rigorous scrutiny.

REFERENCES

Asad, Talal. 2010. "The Concept of Cultural Translation in British Social Anthropology." In *Critical Readings in Translation Studies*, edited by Mona Baker, 7–27. London: Routledge.

Anderson, Linda. 2001. *Autobiography*. London: Routledge.

Bassnett, Susan and Harish Trivedi. 1998. "Introduction: of colonies, cannibals and vernaculars." In *Post-colonial Translation: Theory and Practice*, edited by Susan Bassnett and Harish Trivedi, 1–18. Taylor & Francis e-library. doi.org/10.4324/9780203068878. Accessed 15 Mar 2023.

Bhaskaran. 2004. *Mother Forest: The Unfinished Story of C. K. Janu*, translated by Ravi Shanker. New Delhi: Women Unlimited and Kali for Women.

Birla, Ritu. 2010. "Postcolonial Studies: Now that's History." In *Can the Subaltern Speak: Reflections on the History of an Idea*, edited by Rosalind C. Morris, 87–99. New York: Columbia UP.

Brooks, Linda Marie. 2005. "Testimonio's Poetics of Performance." In *Comparative Literature Studies* 41(2): 181–222.

Chandrabose, R. 2021. "Aesthetics and Politics of Poetry written in Tribal Languages of Kerala." In *Indian Journal of Multilingual Research and Development* 2(4): 25–38.

Chow, Rey. 1993. *Writing Diaspora: Tactics of Intervention in Contemporary Cultural Studies*. Bloomington: Indiana UP.

Felman, Shoshana. 1993. *What Does a Woman Want? Reading and Sexual Difference*. Baltimore & London: The John Hopkins UP.

Hawthorne, Susan. 1989. "The Politics of the Exotic: The Paradox of Cultural Voyeurism." *NWSA Journal* 1(1): 617–29.

Huggan, Graham. 2001. *The Postcolonial Exotic: Marketing the Margins*. London: Routledge.

Kachru, Braj K. 2000. "The Alchemy of English." In *The Routledge Language and Cultural Theory Reader*, edited by Lucy Burke, Tony Crawley and Alan Girvin, 317–29. London: Routledge.

Kahf, Mohja. 2010. "Packaging 'Huda': Sha'rawi's Memoirs in the United States Reception Environment." In *Critical Readings in Translation Studies*, edited by Mona Baker, 30–45. London: Routledge.

Lefevere, André. 2002. "Composing the other." In *Post-colonial Translation: Theory and Practice*, edited by Susan Bassnett and Harish Trivedi, 75–94. Taylor & Francis e-Library. doi.org/10.4324/9780203068878. Accessed 17 Mar 2023.

Raveendran, P. P. 2007. "Translation as Hoax: Art, Othering and Life Writing." *Indian Literature* 51(1): 187–201. https://www.jstor.org/stable/23347895.

Shamma, Tarek. 2009. *Translation and the Manipulation of the Difference: Arabic Literature in Nineteenth-Century England.* Manchester: St. Jerome Publishing.

Simonsen, Russell. 2019. "An Analysis of the Problematic Discourse Surrounding 'Authentic Texts'." *Hispania* 102(2): 245–58. https://www.jstor.org/stable/26867581.

Spivak, Gayatri. 1991. "Theory in the Margin: Coetzee's Foe Reading Defoe's Crusoe/Roxana." In *Consequences of Theory*, edited by Jonathan Arac and Barbara Johnson, 154–80. Baltimore: John Hopkins UP.

Sturrock, John. 1990. "Writing Between the Lines; The Language of Translation." *New Literary History* 21(4): 933–1013.

Venuti, Lawrence. 1998. "Introduction." In *The Translator: Studies in Intercultural Communication*, special issue, Translation and Minority 4(2): 135–44.

EIGHT

Translating the Popular

This chapter seeks to interrogate the translations of representations in popular imaginaries, particularly translating gender into the popular, critically situating feminist and post-structuralist critiques of the popular in rigorous conversations with the representational problematics of gender. Patrick Cattrysse's interventions in mapping the similarities between translation and adaptation clearly demarcate 'cultural phenomena' as one of the pivotal axes that interconnect the two. Both are essentially interactive-representative processes that produce cultural products which involve primarily 'the interaction of users with texts in a socio-temporally defined context and argues that both are teleological processes, in that they are influenced by source and target (con)text conditioners' (Perdikaki 2018, 169). In such a contractual economy, a culture's representations of itself, 'womanliness', 'femininity', 'female-ness', and 'womanhood' are all often the most heavily invested areas of desire and control where the disjuncture between what is real and what is imagined is indeed acute and vast. Such representations interpellate women into normative codes of subjectivity that seek to naturalise their subordination in real life too.

Without looking into the ethico-political difficulties underlying the problem of representation, this paper tries to study how both the novel and the film subscribing to the hegemony of representational realism, work coercively in structuring women's representations, though the degree of such coerciveness is perceived to be much more pronounced in cinema than in the novel. What is often lost in such translations of gender representations from novel to film are the 'traces' of the other—muted voices and elided spaces caught up in the violence of the gaze. The very nature of the cinematic apparatus makes it an area of cultural practice where the stakes for women are especially high. The constitution of woman as a sign and spectacle, the degree of inscriptions/erasure of the signifiers underlying the sign woman, and the successful eliding over of the lived experiences of her life by hegemonic specular and libidinal codes—all work differently in cinema and are much more ideologically laden and equipped to sabotage the subjectivities of women as historical subjects.

Over the last few decades, following what is described by Mary Snell-Hornby as the 'cultural turn in Translation', the diverse forms of research engendered in the discipline have come to openly critique the reductive linguistic location of the practice. Today, translation and its multimodal manifestations occupy the subversive realms of transgressive political activity, especially with feminist and queer curation of the genre. Against the inter-semiotic translation's polemic traditions made visible in recent times, it will be generative to look at early masculine (exclusionary) practices vis-à-vis women and their socio-semiotic function within these 'texts'. To this end, there will be an attempt here to look at some of the issues which surface when the sign 'woman' is translated from the semiotic system of literature to that of narrative cinema, using two texts to illustrate the point. The first one is Thakazhi Sivasankara Pillai's novel *Chemmeen* which received the Kendra Sahitya Akademi Award in 1958 and was translated into more than twelve Indian languages and over thirteen foreign languages. The second is Ramu Kariat's film of the same name, which won the President's Gold Medal for the best film in 1966 and which was largely a faithful adaptation of the novel. The question that I seek to address in this paper is how differently do these two texts, or in the parlance of Translation Studies, the source text of *Chemmeen* the novel and the target text of *Chemmeen* the film, represent women?

Located in the unique schema of the socio-cultural milieu of Kerala, the inter-semiotic translation of *Chemmeen* represents conceptual metaphors of femininities and masculinities coded into the collective memory of the region by which it is able to translate 'complex meanings in an embodied gestalt' that the target (con)text conditioners—readers/viewers—'understands in a reflexive manner' (Fahlenbrach 2016, 13). Marx specified two senses of representation; *Vertretung*, or 'speaking for', and *Darstellung* or 'making present' (Marx 1962). Often representation becomes a complicated issue because of 'slippage between these related but discontinuous senses of the term and the consequences of their complicitous closure around positivistic notions of presenting the real' (Ganguly 2015, 62).

That Thakazhi's *Chemmeen* is often called 'misogynist' is interesting considering the fact that he was a progressive reformist writer who sought to portray the marginalised and the uprooted. The social reform movements in Kerala had a great role in shaping the oeuvre of writers like Thakazhi. Yet these emancipatory impulses are not echoed in the novel as far as the woman question is concerned. *Chemmeen* mystifies women through its sexist stereotyping, attempting to create an ahistorical feminine essence that links her to the primordial elements of nature and thus seeks to keep her sexuality in check.

The anxieties that one feels over the novel is heightened by the fact that it came at a time in Kerala's history when real women had just started feeling the bind of being women with the entailing necessity to nurture, prove and wear one's femininity, as well as the need to function ably as individuals in a social order where the challenges for women were greater. Into such a social milieu comes a novel by an acclaimed writer which as a cultural artefact is the carrier of a social mythology that is dangerous to women—that the life of innumerable fishermen who go out into the sea are dependent on the chastity of their women; the Savithri myth negatively retold in the backdrop of coastal Kerala.

Roland Barthes calls myth a stolen language that transforms meaning into form. Through the skillful use of myths, the sign woman appearing in representations becomes already laden with meaning, postulating a certain kind of knowledge, historicity and function. Thus, the reality of women's oppression and the conflicting issues confronting women are all impoverished and tamed by the connotative denotedness of myths. The chastity myth as used by Thakazhi in the novel, is a corruption or derailment of proper language use, in the process aiding and abetting the seduction of the female subject by ideology. Thus, like Freud's formulation of the 'riddle' of femininity, what Thakazhi in effect tries to do in *Chemmeen* is to seek an answer to the question of what femininity is for men. This question is the central axis, the impelling desire on which the narrative revolves—the story of how Karuthamma is constituted a woman by the dominant discourse of culture. The desire inscribed in the narrative is thus the desire of Chembankunju, of Pallani and Pareekutty. Karuthamma might be the object of that desire but never its subject. The works under discussion share a distinctly masculine gaze catering to the peculiar patriarchal '(con)text conditioners' in Kerala. As Laura Mulvey asserts, 'the spectator identifies with the main male protagonist, he projects his look onto that of his like, his screen surrogate, so that the power of the male protagonist as he controls events coincides with the active power of the erotic look, both giving a satisfying sense of omnipotence' (Mulvey 1999, 716). The male locations inhabited in the source text *Chemmeen* and its relatively faithful adaptation are rooted in the narrative authority that subordinates women and their social interactions to the mythic realms that continue to service patriarchy and its fantasies. The privileging of this gaze further legitimises the connection forged between the deeply masculinist traditions articulated in the text and the (con)text conditioners—the viewer/reader.

In the novel, Karuthamma is not allowed entry into the language, being repeatedly silenced by the father. Thus, it is a social discourse that speaks for her to which she herself has no access. She is constantly reminded of her body—that her breasts, her buttocks, have come of age. Therefore, the novel slowly and skillfully charts and maps her body to bear a particular kind of meaning which, though gained only through external relationships yet constantly reminds her of her 'inner essence'. When translated to the film the very first shot of Karuthamma marks the meaning she bears—her body is constructed as the object of the gaze—a multiple site of male pleasure, where Karuthamma equals her body.

Thus, the cinematic apparatus, always already compromised in the ideology of vision and the sexual difference, has constructed, cannot but construct, Karuthamma as an image, spectacle, and object of sexuality.

Clothing within the representative economy of visual registers participates in a complex system of meaning-making through the assemblage and manipulation of sartorial materiality subject to socio-cultural, often aesthetic, sensorial, and affective responses. Stella Bruzzi's *Undressing Cinema: Clothing and Identity in Movies* (1997) mediates how clothing and fashion are deployed in cinema to supplement its narrative vision as 'spectacular interventions that interfere with the scenes in which they appear and impose themselves onto the character they adorn' (xv). The film *Chemmeen*'s iconography is very different from the novel in that Karuthamma is sartorially draped almost exclusively to serve the scopophilic fetishes and anxieties of Malayali men's desires. As Mulvey writes, 'the determining male gaze projects its phantasy onto the female form which is styled accordingly. . . . Woman displayed as a sexual object is the leit-motif of erotic spectacle' (1999, 715). The white *mundu* and the blouse that Karuthamma is adorned with draw attention to her and her body, simultaneously objectifying her and fantasising about her. The dress and its inhabitations by Sheela, suggestive of a voluptuous corporeal body, a male fantasy, closely plays with the traditions of 'visual fiction' (Hollander 1980, xv).

Kariat's portrait of Karuthamma—as a fair woman, yet placed in the lower rungs of class and caste with evident focus on her breast and waist—displays this figure as one evidently created to be available to the male gaze. The ocular location of Karuthamma's dressed body epitomises the phenomenon of 'to-be-looked-at-ness' (715) as defined by Mulvey, whereby the female figure 'coded for strong visual and erotic impact' (715) or attired to elicit desire from male eyes, punctuates the screen. Karuthamma in the film embodies an erotically configured female passivity and availability much more in tune with the scopic gaze than in the novel. She is curated as a visual spectacle of conspicuous male consumption.

In both the novel and the film, Karuthamma is associated with acquiescent speech, but in the film, the co-relation of acquiescent speech to an acquiescent body is what makes possible the erotic violation on screen. The taut body of Sheela's Karuthamma marks the transformation of the central female subject of a coastal community drama into an objectified erotic figure created on demand to the visual and erotic desires of Malayali audiences—the (con)text conditioners.

The trope of the female body is at the centre of the problematics of translation/adaptation from novel to film in *Chemmeen*. What is highlighted in the film is an attempt to portray the female body as a corrupting influence—as the cause of all social problems in the text. Thus, the film resonates with a certain fear of women's bodies and also women's desires. What Pallani does at sea is to capture a great shark, which is, in fact, a metaphor for the monstrous feminine. Therefore, what the movie articulates has more to do with the tensions concerning masculinity and the taming of the monstrous feminine than the portrayal of the social reality of Purakkad or the woes and joy of the fisherfolk of Thrikkunnapuzha.

Kariyat's Pareekutty—the Muslim trader—evinces an anxiety about 'manliness'. In stark opposition to the powerful, virile manliness of Pallani or Chembankunju, Pareekutty is an effeminate, decadent figure. Thus, in the film, an almost primitive, savage manliness constitutes the male body as a source of power, which seeks to capture and channel the elemental force of women's sexuality. Both the novel and the film speak of women's chastity as the sacred force that holds the sea secure so that it would seem as though the 'damming' of feminine bodily power is crucial in damming up the elemental forces of nature. Significantly enough it is, however, the marginalised Muslim subalternity of Pareekutty which becomes ensnared by the charms of the female body, and he is left singing on the beaches of Purakkad, torn between repression and expression.

The climax of the film is classic in its urge to express a primitive male rage which also signifies the conflict between nature and culture. The shark is symbolic of the feminine energy that men want to repress or kill. But the futility of killing these bodies or getting rid of them becomes evident as the sea throws up all buried bodies in a telling image where the shark and Pallani are symbolically entangled in death as the bodies of Karuthamma and Pareekutty lie entwined on the shore.

Thakazhi's Karuthamma is 'imagined' by the reader as a member of the Araya community. But the filmic image of Karuthamma translated onscreen transcends the story and character. She is a wish incarnate as far as scopophilic pleasure is concerned. One of the first sentences she utters in both the novel and the film is a coy comment on the intensity of her lover's 'gaze'—a gaze that is focused unquestionably on her fair and ample bosom. The big dark mole on the breast in the movie serves to accentuate active scopophilia. In page after page in the novel Thakazhi struggles to portray Karuthamma's pleasurable unease at the gaze of 'Kochumuthalali' which she realises is focused on sexual parts of her body. But Ramu Kariat translates this Karuthamma in a single shot where he has the star Sheela wearing a lungi and blouse, so styled as to highlight the contours of her body. Karuthamma on-screen—coded for strong visual impact and erotic fascination—becomes, in fact, a leitmotif of erotic spectacle throughout, both inside and outside the story. Yet as spectacle, as sight, Sheela's Karuthamma seems to have no meaning by herself. It is only in the differential emotions and concerns she evokes in others that a meaning is created for the sign woman. For Pareekutty, she carries the value of love, for Chakki of motherly anxieties and tenderness and for Chembankunju, the economic potential of striking a good bargain, and permeating all this is the star value of Sheela the actress and her sex impact and appeal on the celluloid. The translated Karuthamma, the fair female form displayed on screen connoting male fantasy and catering to his pleasures, is the object of the combined gaze of both Pareekutty and the male spectators. However, as the narrative progresses, the film forces the male spectators to identify with Pallani rather than with the emasculated Pareekutty, for it is Pallani who marries and thus possesses Karuthamma. However, as Mulvey points out, the female figure in such situations poses a deeper problem in psychoanalytic terms. Karuthamma connotes the threat of castration where the 'woman as icon, displayed for the gaze and enjoyment of men, the active controllers of the look, always threatens to evoke the anxiety it originally signalled' (1999, 718). Thakazhi uses the myth of the Araya woman whose chastity brings her man back safe from the sea and holds the seething sea secure in its place. The cinema taps into this narrative structure to resolve the castration anxiety of the male protagonists. The adept use of the myth of chastity makes Karuthamma guilty. Thus, we have Pallani in scene after scene 'investigating' Karuthamma, attempting to 'demystify her mystery' through sadistic assertions of control and subjugation.

However, the film also goes beyond Thakazhi's use of the myth of chastity. It combines this myth with the myth of the *Yakshi*, the beautiful temptress of numerous folk tales and myths of Kerala, whose beauty lures men but castrates and kills them. It is this fear of the castrating female that is inherent in the Yakshi myth that the film uses. *Chemmeen*, the novel and more so *Chemmeen* the film deals with male castration anxieties. Karuthamma in the film, shown wandering on the beach in the night or standing on the beach in darkness bidding adieu to Pallani's lone rendezvous into the sea, is a figure that suggests dangers closely associated with female sexuality. Barbara Creed points out that in many myths around the world, the threatening aspect of the female genitals is symbolised by the '*vagina dentata*' or toothed vagina which, when offering pleasure, could also devour the male penis, thus becoming executioners of men (1993, 105).

The film is an attempt to domesticate the toothed vagina. Numerous images in the film create a horror of the terrible vagina— Pallani's confrontation with the Scylla-like devouring whirlpool in the sea, his attempt to grapple with and break the vaginal teeth of the great shark—all point to the male fear of female sexuality as a trap, a yawning hole that threatens to devour men.

That *vagina dentata* is crucial to the iconography of the film is established beyond doubt by the last shot—that of a huge dead shark with a close up of its bared teeth, dead and stranded on the beach. That this shark has been instrumental in killing Pallani, as Karuthamma was in killing both Pallani and Pareekutty is what the close up shot of gaping jaws and teeth juxtaposed to the dead bodies of Pareekutty and Karuthamma conveys. The image of the *vagina dentata* is equally applicable to the sea—Kadalamma as the terrifying mother who threatens symbolically to engulf the fisherfolk, posing the threat of psychic annihilation. Karuthamma like Kadalamma is linked to the primordial elements of nature—to the primal fear of obliteration and loss of identity by being swallowed up by the monstrous feminine.

Ramu Kariat also does not fail to pursue the second avenue open to the male protagonists as elaborated by Mulvey, that of fetishistic scopophilia. That both the novel and the film are fetishistic is beyond doubt. Nevertheless, the success of the film, its huge popular appeal is probably owing to the fact that it is able to tap much more into this fetishistic gratification using the image of '*chemmeen*' or the catch from the sea as a fetish for the woman, the 'catch' from the land. Sigmund Freud describes fetishism as arising when another replaces the normal sexual object, which bears some relation to it, but is entirely unsuited to serve the sexual aim (1962, 153). This substitution might be some bodily part, or an object linked to their sexuality, which in this case is the fish. In the film, the song sung by the women folk where they compare Karuthamma's eyes to fish underscores this idea.

The film creates a narrative enigma which is not as prominent or pronounced in the novel. The question of whether Karuthamma loves Pallani or Pareekutty, whether she does not forget or forgets Pareekutty creates a strategy of exchange and equivalence in the film. Often the fish or the 'catch', creating an 'insistent impression of display in the *mise-en-scene*, marks out a process of fetishistic substitution' (Cowie 1997, 276). It is Karuthamma who becomes fetishised in this process of substitution. Throughout the film Karuthamma and the fish, the catch is in a 'circulation of substitution and exchange' where one can decipher 'the palpable over investment in or excessive value on the visual within the image' (268). Marcus Bartley's camera captures the fishing boats coming in again and again to create multiple connotations of objects circulated and exchanged.

Thakazhi's Karuthamma is an already translated being, translated from real life into the 'symbolic' order of Malayalam novels, where meaning and significations are already fixed, and all thought and action of the female subject are patterned within a given discursive field. The further translation of this Karuthamma onto the celluloid thus becomes a process of double manipulation where an already subjugated 'other' is submitted to the dominant power of 'images of Malayali women' created and nurtured by Malayali audiences as an authentic representation of women.

Chemmeen won the first Sahitya Akademi Award for Malayalam novel and the first National Award for Malayalam cinema—all at the cost of what the Karuthammas of Kerala paid for re-presenting them and projecting their images as empty signs in the gendered, commodified systems of exchange that canonical literature and popular cinema often become.

Feminist interventions into translation practices, and contingent cultural transfer and contamination have critically re-examined the location of the translator from its misogynist sexist locales. Luis von Flotow remarks that 'Gender awareness in translation practice poses questions about the links between social stereotypes and linguistic forms, about the politics of language and cultural difference, about the ethics of translation' (1997, 14). Inter-semiotic translations like *Chemmeen* are a curious study that can locate how cultural signifiers and vernacular locations of gendered anxieties get reinscribed and circulated to produce and reproduce regional symptoms of hetero-patriarchal, scopophilic desires, and desirings.

REFERENCES

Bruzzi, Stella. 1997. *Undressing Cinema: Clothing and Identity in the Movies.* New York: Routledge.

Cowie, Elizabeth. 1997. *Representing the Woman: Cinema and Psychoanalysis.* London. Macmillian

Creed, Barbara. 1993. *The Monstrous Feminine: Film, Feminism, Psychoanalysis.* London: Routledge.

Fahlenbrach, Kathrin. 2016. "Introduction: Embodied Metaphors in Moving Images." In *Embodied Metaphors in Film, Television, and Video Games: Cognitive Approaches,* edited by Kathrin Fahlenbrach, 13–25. New York: Routledge.

Flotow, Luise von. 1997. *Translation and Gender: Translating in the 'Era of Feminism'.* Ottawa: U of Ottawa P.

Freud, Sigmund. 1962. *Three Essays on the Theory of Sexuality.* Translated by James Strachey. New York: Avon Books.

Ganguly, Keya. 2015. "Accounting for others: Feminism & Representation." In *Women Making Meaning: New Feminist Directories in Communication,* edited by Lana F. Rakow, 60–79. New York: Routledge.

Hollander, Ann. 1993. *Seeing Through Clothes.* London: U of California P.

Marx, Karl. 1962."The Eighteenth—Brumaire of Louis Bonaparte." *The Marx Engels Reader,* edited by Robert C. Tucker, 594–617. New York: Norton.

Mulvey, Laura. 1999. "Visual Pleasure and Narrative Cinema." In *Film Theory and Criticism: Introductory Readings,* edited by Leo Braudy and Marshall Cohen, 711–22. United Kingdom: Oxford UP.

Perdikaki, Katerina. 2018. "Film adaptation as the Interface between Creative Translation and Cultural Transformation: The case of Baz Luhrmann's *The Great Gatsby.*" *The Journal of Specialised Translation* (29): 169–87.

NINE

Translation as Adaptation

From the framework of a non-discipline like cultural studies, translation need no longer be seen as an act that unfolds solely at the lexical level, but as a process that is inherently political, and one that imbues a text with multiple cultural and social significations that go against the grain of disciplinarity. Consciously or otherwise translators 'translate texts and utterances that participate in creating, negotiating and contesting social reality' (Baker 2006, 105). This chapter seeks to look at adaptations as acts of translation that accentuate or remould the socio-cultural and political narratives encoded in the source text as demanded by new texts and contexts.

Any attempt to step beyond the traditional understandings regarding adaptation would necessarily need to trace the tenuous boundaries and convergences between the processes of adaptation and translation. Such an act broadens our perception regarding the processes by critically locating the politico-cultural transformation undergone by a text in adaptation. It has been pointed out that the study of adaptation 'encourages the theorist to look beyond purely linguistic issues and helps shed light on the role of the translator as mediator, as a creative participant in a process of verbal communication. Relevance, rather than accuracy, becomes the key word, and this entails a careful analysis of three major concepts in translation theory: meaning, purpose and intention' (Bastin 2019, 8), all three of which are located squarely in the terrain of the cultural and ideological. A cultural turn in translation would, therefore, seek to 'acknowledge adaptation as a type of creative process which seeks to restore the balance of communication that is often disrupted by traditional forms of translation. Only by treating it as a legitimate strategy can we begin to understand the motivation for using it and to appreciate the relationship between it and other forms of conventional translation' (8). This move could thus help reclaim the political, social, institutional and economic matrices that necessitate a translation in the first place, helping retrieve the cultural ramifications that are often missed in conventional discourses around the concepts of translation.

Adaptation reconfigures the semiotics of a text, necessitating a close scrutiny of intertextual and inter-semiotic connections. For example, in looking at adaptations from literature to cinema, one would need to reconceive literary and filmic texts as 'affective economies that communicate with each other, and with audiences, through the transmission of affective intensities, and the adaptive process as a dissemination of those intensities from one medium to another, where they take root and induce change from within' (Hodgkins 2013, 2). In this regard, Hodgkins conceptualises the process of adaptation as a 'generative drifting of affective forces between works, between mediums', which enable the critics to steer away from the traditional notion of fidelity (2).

The displacement of a written text to celluloid not only involves the transition between two media, but also involves 'a larger, millennial movement across philosophical traditions and cultural spaces' (Shohat 2004, 23). There are images, symbols and ideas which are enmeshed in a written text that cannot be visualised in a conservative social and cultural milieu. At the same time, the visual medium offers immense possibilities that carry certain narratives beyond the limited scope of the textual medium. This chapter intends to study the modalities by which such acts of adaptation bear imprints of culture and power hierarchies existent in both the source and target cultures.

The texts selected for the study are *Pallivaalum Kalchilambum* (1954), a short story by M. T. Vasudevan Nair, and *Agnisakshi* (1976), a novel by Lalithambika Antharjanam, and their cinematic adaptations, *Nirmalyam* (1973) and *Agnisakshi* (1999) respectively. In any endeavour to look into the literature/ film interface in regional Indian cinema, *Nirmalyam* (1973), a strikingly fresh debut film based on the short story *Pallivaallum Kalchilambum* (Sacred sword and anklet), makes a fascinating topic for study; for more than a half century after its release, it still remains a socially and psychologically valid document in the history of Malayalam cinema. It is also interesting that for the first time a noted writer donned the cap of a director to attempt an adaptation of his own short story into film. *Nirmalyam* is a powerful illustration of the inter-semiotic nature of film and the scope and potency of such a trait. The translation from *Pallivaallum Kalchilambum* to *Nirmalyam* involves a colossal appropriation of histories and milieus, of peoples, languages and cultures. In fact, this adaptation is a subversion of many literary conventions and canons as established by class hierarchies.

Pallivaallum Kalchilambum is a 'cinematic' story in the dexterity with which it alternates description and dialogue, in its skillful narrative control and felicitous handling of time and psyche. Though the adaptation of his own story might not have been a difficult task for a versatile artist like M. T. Vasudevan Nair, he has created a fine piece of filmic art that is yet clearly linked to its literary source. M. T. offers a story to the readers of *Pallivaallum Kalchilambum* and prompts them to create a world from it. But in *Nirmalyam* he presents the spectator with a world and leaves it to their imagination to weave a story from this world. Thus, while *Pallivaallum Kalchilambum* attempts to create an effect first on the level of signification and then perception, *Nirmalyam* moves from perception to signification.

The technical awareness of literary form and style that runs through *Pallivaallum Kalchilambum* bears upon M. T's cinematic style too, as also his use of the language of film. In the short story one can feel the strength of a writer who has a keen sense of the throbbing pulse of the written word. In *Nirmalyam* one meets a director who has grappled with and almost mastered the power of technologised visual image to communicate beyond any written language. Though in M. T.'s later scripts one comes across a celebration of the word as dialogue, *Nirmalyam* is an example par excellence of artistic restraint of the verbal language. There are no extraneous scenes or conversations and the director's economy is as striking as his craftsmanship. The restraint of the spoken word concentrates the spectator's attention more closely on the visual aspect of the medium and enhances its effect. The flashback scenes function to valourise a past, where the supposed agents of its glory like the *velichapadu* and the Kathakali artist indulge in nostalgic reminiscences around a lost tradition and a lost age, embedded within a striking visual narrative that buttresses its ideological anxieties. The technologically generated cinematic experimentations around visual juxtapositions, flashbacks, diegetic sounds and musical score engender and communicate the affective intensities of a generational loss to the spectator. Going beyond the restraints of the written word, a visual economy invested in validating a feudal logic, conditions and compromises the quotidian realms of the cinematic present, one that is coded to construct new meanings out of the cultural signs embedded in the narrative. In fact, a person familiar with M. T.'s oeuvre can perceive in the film the exhilaration of a writer who has discovered a new language, which expands the horizon of his writerly expectations.

Between the short story and the film is a time span of nearly two decades. This period (the sixties and the early seventies) were marked by seething changes in the socio-economic history of Kerala. The changes in the interplay of institutions, expressions and repressions, all taking place in the complex and varying fields of power, can be seen by reading both texts. The short story ends with the oracle trying to sell the sacred sword and the anklet of the divine goddess. But in the cinema it is the vagrant son who attempts the sacrilegious act. M. T. adds to the cinema the existential dilemma and ennui of the youth of the post-sixties era in Kerala. The image of the angry young man who vents his anger on tradition, as also the infusing of a mood of radical rebellion in the youth who cultivate a studied irreverence for all social, familial, religious and cultural institutions is poignantly depicted in the film. The shadow of Kerala's Naxalite uprisings of the sixties and seventies looms large in the horizon, and without a single word or image, the adaptation captures the historical mood of Left radicalism in

Kerala, 'an ideologically inspiring endeavour which immediately attracted the youth who were politically baptised by revolutionary terrorism that had organic roots' (Chakrabarty 2015, 3).

Desperate for securing a job, the characters of *velichappadu*'s (oracle's) son and Unni Namboothiri are representative figures of the lost generation of the seventies. The images of joblessness and poverty in the film illustrate the lived reality of the lower middle class families of that time. The film shares the concerns and anxieties of the former feudal sections who lost their elite position in the social hierarchy due to political and economic reforms in independent India. There are subtle references about the land reforms introduced by the Communist government, from the vantage point of a privileged feudal class, which is skillfully communicated through the visuals of the decadent *tharavadu* (ancestral house). The short story in 1954 offered a sharp critique of the moral apathy of the social milieu. However, in between the short story and its adaptation, the social and political history of Kerala underwent radical restructuring due to multiple agrarian and land reforms following the Land Reform Bill of 1957 and the Agrarian Reforms Bill of 1958, that destabilised the hierarchical agencies of land-owning castes. Hence, in the movie adaptation, M. T. appropriates this transformed consciousness of an erstwhile feudal class and their anguish, fear and dejection. The narrative of the short story is further developed to accommodate the socio-political shifts of the age and thus, adaptation becomes a cultural process of appropriating and interpellating the target temporal context. Both the priest and the feudal *thampuran* (upper-caste landlord) in the story represent the spiritual ennui, withdrawal, and disinterestedness of Brahmin communities within what could be read as an ailing temple economy in the backdrop of the crisis of feudalism. Not dealt with in detail in the short story, this milieu is mapped in greater detail in the movie and hence becomes an intense account of the cultural dilemmas of the age.

The temple priest of the short story is yet a thriving man, who lives off the money from the temple earnings. But in the film the priest is as much a pauper as the oracle. He manages to eke out a better living by becoming a tea shop owner. This, again points to the ebb of the tide of faith and the more rational, sceptical outlook of the society of the seventies. The new priest is constantly studying in order to get a government job. Thus, priesthood has become just another form of earning a livelihood and has lost its spiritual piety and sanctity. The film repeatedly sabotages feudal discourses of power associated with networks of temples, rituals and customs. The uselessness of the *pallivaal* and *kalchilambu*, which are symbolic signifiers of the tradition and sanctity associated with ritualistic discourses, forms the central theme of the narrative. Their cult value has been replaced by a commodity value that needs to put it into an economy of exchange. The ideological resonance infused into the images of the *pallivaal* and *kalchilambu* in the adaptation, which had remained largely symbolic in the short story, transforms the cinematic apparatus by a massive investment in affect that creates an illusion in the audience of renouncing their ontological nature in order to embrace a subject position of ownership of the ritualistic artefacts, thus suturing the spectator seamlessly into the narration.

At one time it was believed that the *pallivaal* could scatter the seeds of the Goddess's wrath in the form of smallpox eruptions. In the erstwhile Madras Presidency, which included the Malabar region, the campaign against smallpox had begun as early as 1800, though people still feared and revered it as a divine displeasure. But by 1973, much of this fear had been allayed by the widespread use of modern medicine and vaccines. Smallpox was no longer an imminent threat in society. Even when the Varrier's wife, who belongs to the temple community, is infected, it is not regarded with as much consternation as in the short story, though it is shown to bring the wayward back into the fold of belief. The *velichappadu* thus had lost much of his power among his 'Mother's' children. But in spite of it he rallies his failing spirit in a last attempt at reorganising the scattered devotees.

In a brilliant piece of social satire, M. T. depicts the landlord of the temple as the landlord of a new order. Culture is his capital and he does a lucrative job of selling temple arts, which have shifted venues from the temple premises to the landlord's villa. The audiences are no longer devout masses but foreign tourists. The *velichappadu*'s father is symbolic of the past that is sick and paralyzed. Unable to react to the stimuli and needs of the present, he yet hangs on to the family and to life—an extra mouth to feed, a conscience bed-ridden but not buried. The selling of her own body by the *velichappadu*'s wife is again a powerful critique of the woman of the times. The wife in the short story is a pale shadow of a character. But in the cinema she becomes a potent image of subversion. The wife's sex work is tantamount to the *velichappadu*'s attempt to sell the holy ornaments in the final section of the short story. Here, M. T. depicts the female body as a metaphor for the pollution that contaminates the social fabric of Kerala. A largely masculine ideological and visual economy is operative here. The subplot of adultery, which was not a part of the short story, infuses a patriarchal logic into the adaptation, one that is tenable for the misogynist male libidinal economies of spectatorship in Kerala. Thus, the short story becomes a starting point for the script and the script takes off from a point where the short story ends.

As far as the 'spirit' of the short story is concerned, there is an attempt to maintain 'fidelity', whereby the basic narratorial aspects, the main characters and their interpersonal communications, the geographical, sociological and cultural information providing the story's context—are all the same. The parallel love story of the *velichappadu*'s daughter and the new priest adds a strain of melodrama. But as a cinematic whole, the perceptual, referential and symbolic codes of the adaptation are very much akin to those in the story. The very title *Nirmalyam* carries on the imagery of decadence, which seeps through the short story.

Controversial and yet pathbreaking in its own day, *Nirmalyam* continues to be relevant even today, because it poignantly recreates the spiritual and material realities of a crucial era in the history of Kerala. In the backdrop of a shift from an agrarian to a capitalist, consumerist society, the film attempts to portray the fragmented character of social and cultural 'realities' and 'identities'. M. T.'s narrative realism does not attempt to delineate social realities only in psychological or individual terms but seeks to probe the more fundamental social and economic structures. The narrative incorporates an agitational aesthetic where the gloom of an epoch, which is neither 'post'-feudal nor industrial, is highlighted. The film is modernist in its formal self-consciousness and thematic preoccupation with social and emotional dislocation and the portrayal of a break from tradition.

Both the film and the short story attempt a social examination that centres on a historical development. There is a broadly construed realism in representation and narration. M. T., the short story writer as a director, has understood the ideological nature of both apparates and this understanding equips him with a strong theoretical framework to examine the meaning of a film as created through an interaction between text and spectator. Thus, here is an adaptation that seeks to interpellate the spectator, not as an 'ahistorical' subject but as a subject of history, with political, cultural and economic investments in questions around religions, class, caste and gender issues in Kerala.

The interaction between the film text and the spectator can be greatly influenced by the fore-knowledge and anticipation of the stardom of the actor. The play of this intertextuality is significant in *Nirmalyam* owing to the almost conscious absence of the star image in it. P. J. Anthony, as the *velichappadu,* was not much of a celebrity, while Sukumaran, as the rebellious son, was a debutant. None of the other actors were 'stars'.

Within its dominant linear causality, the adaptation pulsates with a certain apocalyptic intensity. The circumstantial and psychological realism in the film coupled with its maintenance of continuity results in the creation of a coherent narrative structure. And yet it is not the revealing of the story but the story's revelations, enhanced by the medium, that makes it an interesting adaptation. The entire set of images in the film or the arrangement of signifiers on the screen constitute the narrative discourse of the film. It is from this narrative discourse that the spectator weaves a story.

Both the short story and the film follow the same basic narrative pattern but the film enjoys the singular narrative privilege conferred on it by the medium—it is iconic and mimetic, hence it shows before it tells. The *velichappadu's* postures, gestures, costume, gait and mannerisms, all automatically become visual reality on the screen, while the verbal description of the same would have probably cluttered and choked the short story. The filmic narration also goes beyond the short story's narrative discourse. M. T.'s emphasis in the film seems to be on a more dynamic interaction between the narrative discourse and the spectator. His task as filmmaker appears to be the creation of a new kind of an active spectator who would contribute to the construction of the narrative. The climax of the adaptation thus becomes a way of provoking the spectator, of addressing him/ her in a new way, so that he/she may be able to create a different kind of a film experience. The psychological effects are all there on the screen. It becomes the task of the spectator to search for the causes of these effects. *Nirmalyam* thus shows a concern for reaction rather than action. From the psychologically sensitive protagonist, one is forced to track back to the social forces and economic institutions which compel him to be what he is. As the very title connotes, *Nirmalyam* is an attempt to shed the 'remains' of a past that is ideologically compromised. And yet the future appears to be more fearsome than the past or the bleak present. M. T.'s protagonist struggles to navigate through a difficult moment in history and bears witness to an era of morbid transition. An existential angst, a sense of limbo, haunts even the title. The word *Nirmalyam* denotes the remains of an offering, especially of flowers offered/placed on an idol during pooja, which are then removed in the morning. Significantly the movie begins with the morning ritual of casting away the *nirmalyam* and cleaning the idol. The director thus attempts to portray cinematically a social situation where the last remains of the selfless devotion of the past is wiped away from an idol which will remain a stone—sans decoration, sans devotion and sans divinity.

That M. T. in 1973 chose to select *Pallivaallum Kalchilambum* as the source of adaptation for his first film speaks volumes about the political imperatives attributed to adaptations. It is in response to the need of an era, a social, cultural and historical necessity, that an adaptation becomes possible. Negotiating the mixture of castes and classes, customs and traditions, the adaptation goes beyond the original in deconstructing the post-agrarian society of the times. One has to look beyond the film text for social meanings of not only cinematic practices but also of the actual practice of production of the adaptational text. It is extremely interesting that in 1973, P. J. Anthony, a non-Hindu, entered the sanctum sanctorum of a temple for the actual shooting of a film. It represents a powerful attempt at the subversion of casteism, which also allows the star to be claimed by different audiences, thus shaping anew many reception contexts over time. This subversive act of unsettling the conservative ethos of a society is unequivocally linked with the adaptational logic of the movie. In the short story, there was only a narrative description of the oracle and his rejection of religious ideals. When the same character was adapted to the silver screen, the body of an actor outside the filmic subject's religion, assumes the agentic responsibility to carry out an unconventional act of transgression. Here, adaptation becomes a performative act, adding further to the process of destabilising the deeply inscribed strategies of power vested in hegemonic cultural codes associated with religion.

The production of a cinema involves the complex dialectics of technique and technology. A 'realist' cinema does not evoke 'reality' but only a semblance of it. The process of production is vital to the understanding of an adapted text, where its aesthetic of realism is, to a large extent, governed by the socio-economic conditions under which it is produced, as much as the ideological effect it seeks to produce in the spectator. As spectators/readers of the film text who inhabit a different set of conditions, our response to *Nirmalyam* would be very different today. M. T. himself has remarked that given the current social conditions no producer would be willing to produce a film like *Nirmalyam* and no distributing agency would be willing to fund such a project (Nair 1998, 14). Thus, *Nirmalyam* would be historically impossible today. Industrial structures, networked agents, market imperatives, and legal and policy regimes (Murray 2012, 6) are all forces which constrain and enable adaptation in a society. In the current neoliberal political economy, which has made its inroads into mass media like film, the market dictates the type of movies that a 'consumer' should watch. The rise of the culture industry and 'the installation of cinema as the only art form that could weave itself seamlessly into the production-consumption industrial model within a market economy has contributed to undermining its ideological and aesthetic values' (Pillai 2017, 52). All this, alongside the rise of a political society, has culminated in the massification of consumption and constituted a popular imaginary that internalised the logic of the market, which would make an adaptation like *Nirmalyam* impossible today.

Part of the success of *Nirmalyam* as an adaptation is owing to the Oedipal trajectory it traces. It is to be noted that after the *velichappadu*'s discovery of his wife's sexual betrayal, her face is seen framed in the curve of the *pallivaalu* (sacred sword), which often strikes one as a fetishistic symbol. Thus, it is implied that the *velichappadu*'s holy love is the cause of the unholy liaison. In the next shot the wife's words confirm this as she directly implicates the *velichappadu* and says that when he was wrapped up in the affairs of the goddess, he never ever thought of her and the children. He neglected their hunger. From this point there is a marked change in the *velichappadu*—he slips into an almost trance-like state.

The film's final spectacle has contributed greatly to its success. One is forced to watch spellbound the spectacle of a human body caught in the throes of an intense emotion and the final orgasmic release—the spitting on the idol and the masochistic orgy with the *pallivaal*, hitting it on the head and spilling blood on the screen. The *velichappadu* spits on the face of the Goddess. But it is his own blood which oozes into his mouth that he spits out. Thus, the act of spitting becomes a sacrificial offering of blood.

A rare combination of extreme devotion and defiance, it is the final resolution of an Oedipal desire. A sensational portrayal of the body spectacle—the intense love of the oracle for the Goddess reaches its emotional, physical and visual climax in the final scene. There is no speech and yet the rising crescendo of drums in the backdrop articulates the language of the orgy. The *velichappadu*'s body becomes the embodiment of agony and ecstasy, engendering a similar feeling in the spectator and thus leading to visual and narrative pleasure. Through an excess of sensation and emotion there is a manipulation of the spectatorial pleasure, which, however, serves a nobler cause than 'tear-jerking' melodramas or 'fear-jerking' horror movies.

Nirmalyam is an exceptional adaptation—for the excellence of its screenplay, the tautness of its construction and its thematic complexity. But what fascinates one even today is the boldness and integrity of its adaptational approach, and the coherence of its aesthetic experience. As an adaptation it cinematically epitomises a moment in Kerala's history and in the process becomes historical.

However, *Nirmalyam* offers a significantly different adaptational logic from a novel that was published nearly two decades after *Pallivaallum Kalchilambum*, Lalithambika Antharjanam's *Agnisakshi* (1976), which underwent a cinematic adaptation two decades later in 1999. *Agnisakshi* is an important literary text in Malayalam for the manner in which it writes the woman back into Kerala's reform project, not only in terms of women's roles and agency in the reform movement, but also in highlighting the high stakes it held for them, resonant with personal and political investment. It also enriches our understanding of Kerala's experience of modernity, not solely as a tryst with tradition that yielded linear narratives of history and development but as a more complicated, complex and contradictory process. *Agnisakshi*, as a text set against the backdrop of social reforms in Kerala and nationalist movements, acts as testimony to the fact that 'the evolution of a distinct feminist sensibility in the subcontinent and its negotiations with the larger thought structures of the region cannot be condensed to a linear progressive history' (Pillai 2022, 4), but it follows variegated trajectories that took inspiration from nationalist impulses as well as 'sub-national/regional and global patterns of gendered mobilizations and struggle' (4). There are strong undertones of Gandhian nationalism within the narrative of *Agnisakshi* where a woman as a sign is invested with the significations of the spiritual dimensions of the nation. Being symbolic of the nation, her desires have to be purged and transformed by and through a process of sacred objectification. The binaries of pollution and purity, associated with the female body in *Nirmalyam*, surfaces again in *Agnisakshi,* but through a distinct modality. The titles of both adaptations bear the significations of purity and honour that are deeply inscribed in the discourses of Indian philosophical thought.

In attempting to retrieve and reconstruct a lived and shared history of women's interventions in the public sphere in Kerala, *Agnisakshi* speaks volumes on the regimes of gender disciplining, and the manner in which orthodoxy shaped gender reform and traditions informed the notion of the modern subject. The literary text had already garnered a number of accolades including the Kendra Sahitya Akademi Award (1977), the State Sahitya Akademi Award (1977), the Odakkuzhal Award (1977) and the Vayalar Award (1977), before it was adapted into a movie by Shyamaprasad in 1999, himself a debutant director at that time. The film won eight state awards including the award for the best director, best film, best cinematographer, best actor and best supporting actress. It also received the National Award for the best feature film in Malayalam.

There are different temporal frames that *Agnisakshi*, the novel as also its filmic adaptation encompass. There is a span of more than two decades between the publication of the novel and the release of the movie. The narrative itself is scattered among the early decades of the twentieth century, a period fraught with the tensions of modernity in the wake of cataclysmic social changes in Kerala. It is also ridden by the anxieties around nation formation in the backdrop of the nationalist struggles, at a time when the state itself was technically in a nascent state of subnational imagination. It also looks on to the period of post-Independence ambivalences on the nature of the historical category called the nation, and its ensuing disillusionments. Thus, it roughly marks half a century of the most turbulent and eventful decades in the socio-cultural and political history of Kerala. But this was also a period that was fraught with important ramifications as far as gender history in the state was concerned. The systems of oppression like family and religion were punctured by the neoteric social consciousness engendered by the variegated conduits of modernity in Kerala. Concomitantly, 'the tensions between the dissolving matrilineal family and evolving, male-centred families shaped the new Kerala well into the twentieth century' (Jeffrey 1992, 17). The emancipatory political project that forms part and parcel of the novel *Agnisakshi* should be read within the scope of this critical juncture in the cultural history of Kerala. Nevertheless, the filmic adaptation, materially located in the ideological tensions, institutionalised cinematic frameworks and cultural practices of a post-liberalisation era, all of which come to bear upon its adaptational dynamic, foregrounds a representational schema that seeks to address the affective anxieties around globalisation.

When Antharjanam began writing in the early decades of the twentieth century, gender was a question that begged for resolution both within the nationalist paradigm and the reform projects in the region. Women's roles in society as also the division of spheres and ideals of femininity were all under discussion and negotiation. But by the time these trenchant issues reached the audiences of the film adaptation in the late nineties, compromises had been effected in what was almost a century of drastic social and political transformation. As far as gender and caste in Kerala were concerned, silences had set in and Antharjanam's analogous, complementary and often alternate female worlds became outmoded in what was a gender regressive turn of Kerala's experience of modernity.

Without being overtly caught up in how useful the fidelity approach in studying an adaptation might be, questions nevertheless have to focus on what happens when a text like *Agnisakshi*, with such radical emancipatory possibilities for women, is translated into the filmic medium where the language of popular cinema is often *not* amenable to feminist politics. A nuanced approach towards the portrayal of women in cinema raises pertinent questions of how these narratives are able to reflect their lived experiences. Ilana Dann Luna envisions 'film adaptation as a tool for gender subversion, a strategy that could be deployed to multiply meaning and critique the existing symbolic order of things, not as a singulative act, but as a reconditioning repetition' (Luna 2008, xvii). She goes on to argue that, 'dialogic processes, the interaction between a source text and its reiteration(s), between authors and at times across generations, could be capable of constructing alternate subjectivities that could act as contestations to previously established, reiterated, and regulated stereotypes of the gendered self' (xvii). In short, mass media has historically been the vehicle of disseminating gender stereotypes, aiding the construction of misogynistic and patriarchal cultural codes and norms. At the same time, there were attempts by the filmmakers to deconstruct or reverse these 'insidiously coded behaviours' by the acts which Luna calls 'repetitive rebellions' in movies.

The Malayalam film industry has witnessed a long tradition of adaptations. In the early years, especially in the fifties and sixties, many of writers from the progressive left in Malayalam including Thakazhi Sivasankara Pillai, Uroob, Ponkunnam Varkey and Kesava Dev, whose works were adapted into films or who wrote screenplays for some of the movies, exerted a strong influence in moulding a social-realist base for Malayalam cinema. As a result of the growth of Left politics and their cultural interventions in 1940s and 50s, 'it was purported that art's real mandate was to depict the life worlds of the masses—their sufferings, joys, and struggles' (Mokkil 2019, 61). There was a strong commitment from the part of novelists and filmmakers towards the political project of educating the masses. Hence, adaptations in early Malayalam cinema were ideologically informed and inherently political, rather than being a product to consume. This, however, was gradually dissipated for the more commercial and hegemonic strands that cinema embodies. Shyamaprasad has, over the years, perfected the art of adaptation which has become his forte. As an auteur, his thoughts on adaptation of a literary work into film might seem at odds with the aspirations of the literati:

> Most adaptations in Malayalam Cinema have focused on the story and plot of the literary piece from which it sought adaptation. Many adaptations including the most popular ones like *Chemmeen* have focused on retelling the story of the original. However, for me, making a story is not the primary concern of the director. A filmmaker is not a storyteller. He or she is one who revels in recreating the experiential world of the original. Therefore, cinema, as a more palpable and sensuous medium, seeks to weave together and entrance the senses. In this attempt to meld the word with images and perceptions, the story itself becomes secondary as far as a film maker is concerned. It is only a vehicle for transporting the viewer to another aesthetic plane. Thus, it is the language of cinema in which I narrate the tale that is more important to me, not the tale in itself. (Shyamaprasad 2013, interview by Meena T. Pillai)

These words echo the fact that a director has to be true to his medium more than anything else and it is not the story to be told but how it is told cinematically that becomes the hallmark of the auteur's style. This is where issues of fidelity come into play and pose the quintessential dilemma of any adaptation. Beyond the conventional understandings of the concept of fidelity, the affective turn in adaptation studies has opened up debates about the inter-semiotic dialogue between literary and filmic text. The theories of adaptation and theorists 'attuned to affect' carefully trace the affective structure of a text, to divine its immanent affective features, and then actively chart the 'transformational relays' forged by its intensive affective flows (Hodgkins 2013, 144). The affective lens helps to study the role of an auteur and the symbiotic and generative methods by which a text is metamorphosed in other mediums.

How far should a film be true to the source literary text? To the question of how faithful he had been to the letter and spirit of

Antharjanam's *Agnisakshi* and whether he considered faithfulness
to be a requisite at all, Shyamaprasad's words are significant:

> A film and a literary work are entirely different. So the task of
> the director is different from that of an author. A writer's task is
> conceptual in the sense that he/she is dealing with ideas and thoughts
> and has to devise ways of pushing that across. A director has to
> grapple with more concrete things than that. There is the need to
> create a real world of images on screen. For this s/he has to blend the
> visual and the acoustic in addition to monitoring other concerns like
> casting, dialogue delivery, location, setting and also understanding the
> technology of the medium. Therefore, a film maker's commitment
> cannot be uni-dimensional to the author. There is the commitment
> to one's self and art, there is also the commitment to the audience,
> but most importantly there is the commitment to the medium itself.
> While I read and enjoyed Antharjanam's *Agnisakshi*, I could create
> only my own *Agnisakshi* in the world of cinema. But then that is
> a new way of understanding the original. (Shyamaprasad 2013,
> interview by Meena T. Pillai)

The film is for the most part faithful to the novel and follows the
same structure and sequencing of events. The flashback mode is
used throughout, both in the novel and the film. There is also
a veritable borrowing of Antharjanam's dialogues. The indirect
first-person perspective of the novel, which is that of Thamkam,
is retained in the film's third-person narrative. While the novel
offers an explicit critique of patriarchy in Namboodiri *illam*s of
the period, the film limits in more than one way the exploration
of women's social inequality as also the overt challenges that
gender posed to social structures in the original text. The film
covertly seems to indulge in a neoconservative mainstreaming
of the emancipatory ideas in the novel, precisely using its locus
as a feminist text in Malayalam as also its romance, plot and
characterisation, to diffuse attention from the genuine feminist
concerns it seeks to echo. The trajectory that *Agnisakshi* the novel
traces in its filmic avatar in fact illustrates the patriarchalisation
of feminism, a project that has its roots in the earlier decades of
the twentieth century in the growth of the reform movement in
Kerala under the sign of the masculine

The implicit feminism of Antharjanma's *Agnisakshi* and its progressive, egalitarian foundations are eclipsed and toned down in the film adaptation where the emphasis is seen to shift subtly to masculine roles and the notion of 'dharma' in the masculine context. In that sense, the adaptational logic of *Agnisakshi* complicates the historical situatedness of women's emancipatory politics. The polite feminism of Antharjanam with its stress not on equality of the sexes but on the complementary roles of men and women in social life, is further tamed into conciliatory positions where the movie goers of the nineties, both men and women, can be appeased without overtly radical or subversive polemics coming into play to disrupt or disorient spectatorial pleasure. The film posits itself in a cinematic space where the critical concerns regarding gender, sexuality and woman's subjectivity are conveniently excluded. The movie limits itself to a comfortable narratorial course and is hesitant to accommodate the radical evolutionary trajectories of feminist politics in Kerala. Instead, the movie depoliticises the intricate engagements of the novel with the cause of women's political struggles, catering to an audience who are uncritical consumers of the filmic spectacle. In the 1990s, a more intensely political adaptation of *Agnisakshi* had the possibilities of raising critical questions that would complicate the dialogic possibilities of the complex relationships between nationalism and the gender reforms project in Kerala, historically putting the nation in dialogue with the region. In an age when the women's question seemed to have been conveniently resolved within the bounds of the modern developmental nation and to have almost disappeared from public discourse, the film seems reluctant to re-dig the grave. Therefore, it seeks to eschew the multiple axes of women's emancipation and motherhood, both in the private and public domains of life, which the novel constantly invokes, and chooses to limit itself to the tangled web of the relationship between Devaki Manampalli and Unni Namboodiri. Shyamaprasad himself has pointed out that,

> I have retained the basic structure of the story. However, there is a shift in focus from the social drama to the intensely individual and

personal traumas of the characters. I concentrated on the deep love between Unni Namboodiri and Thethi, a love that surpasses human understanding, and is yet so universal caught as it is in the bonds and bondages of life. Therefore, there is definitely my own touch in the style of narration and the treatment, as also in the selections and omissions I have made from the original. This is what makes a film a film, so uniquely different from the novel. At another level I have also used the story to experiment with the language of cinema, attempting to create new idioms and syntaxes for that language. So using the medium differently, putting my signature on it was also my concern, not the mere telling of the story of Unni and Thethi. (Shyamaprasad 2013, interview by Meena T. Pillai)

The language of cinema, as has been researched and analysed, is most often a male language, mirroring the dominant patriarchal conventions and ideologies of an age. Movies can be seen 'as vehicles of popular culture that carry and communicate consumption ideology the world over.... Feminists in particular have been cognisant of film's power as a vehicle for both encoding and enforcing society's views of "women's place"' (Sanyal 2022, 20). The semiotically encoded representation of women as a 'consumable product' informs the scopic and libidinal economies of spectatorship in India. 'Cinema can exploit women to conform to certain types while rejecting others, allowing them to be moulded and defined by hegemonic social structures, and in the process unconsciously assisting in the reproduction of these hegemonies' (Pillai 2010, 5). An auteur's position in reproducing a literary text might point to the fact that the underlying principles of selection might itself undermine the basic ideological premises of the literary text. The male director's words on the choice of an overtly radical feminist text is resonant with such differences:

I have always been fascinated by *Agnisakshi*, right from my childhood days. Going beyond the social drama and the period angle of a tale told in the backdrop of a Namboodiri *tharavad* in the first half of the twentieth century in Keralam and the abysmal changes in the world around it in the wake of the anti-feudal and nationalist struggles, there is nevertheless a story that is essentially timeless and universal. This is the story of transcending love, of one's duties and responsibilities in this world and of human dilemmas poised between these two. It is about choices or the lack of them, of numerous individual quests—social, religious, spiritual and emotional. It is also about one's personal failures to sublimate our desires, the existential angst of the human condition, and its predicaments. Therefore, the novel found an early resonance in my heart and I thought it encapsulated many of my experiences and the difficult choices in my life. It also projected for me many of the concerns and issues of the people of my parents' generation. I found myself captivated by this story and it haunted me for years. I mulled over it for a long, long time and thus was born my filmic response and tribute to Antharjanam's classic tale. (Shyamaprasad 2013, interview by Meena T. Pillai)

It is amply clear that the male director's choice need not necessarily be informed by the imperative to narrate either women's histories or women's subjectivities. Thus, the ideological traces of the male auteur in the film can come into conflict with those of the woman author of the literary text. Justified as 'timeless and universal', the auteur tries to free the narrative from its unique political and historical specificities. The disengagement of the film from its 'time' and 'space' evidently unties the narrative from its ideological function in a society. This is an instance where the male auteur's authority on the celluloid can also function to subtly jettison the female author's concerns in the written text and act as a testament to the gendered affective economies that surround a work of adaptation. Jack Boozer, in his introduction to the book, *Authorship in Film Adaptation* (2019), reiterated Robert Stam's view on directors as auteurs who 'orchestrate pre-existing voices, ideologies, and discourses, without losing an overall shaping role…a director's work can be both personal and mediated by extrapersonal elements such as genre, technology, studios, and the linguistic procedures of the medium' (Stam qtd. in Boozer 2019, 24). While adapting a literary work, artists could be affected by their own gender subjectivities and hence will undermine the nodes of subversion ingrained in a text. Thus, Antharjanam's image of the woman as reformer in direct opposition to the entrenched and received notion of man as reformer attains an irritant status in the movie through the very casting of Shobhana in the role, an actress whose popular films of the decade invoke an altogether different aesthetic and visual register. The director, in his attempt to combat the received popular imagery of an all too desirable feminine, does take pains to de-aestheticize her presence and strip her of the signs that are coded for male pleasure. Nevertheless, the star persona triumphs and the director and the actor together seem to fail in bringing Thethi's humanist spirit, radical reformist zeal and subversive energy to life. Rajit Kapoor, in contrast, as an actor who had successfully deflected visual excesses in his roles and inhabited alternative spaces of filmic representation seems tailor-made for the role of Unni Namboodiri. The film is unable to offer space for a female gaze which might never have been its object. To the question of whether there was a conscious ideological position that the film sought to represent or whether it tried to align itself with Antharjanam's political views, Shyamaprasad responds thus:

> I did not consciously attempt to bring in any ideological position. With regard to caste, I feel that the Namboodiri background is not the most important or essential aspect of the story, unlike what most critics who stress the community angle, do. In fact, I think the basic story would remain unchanged in a Muslim community too. So the all too familiar and human conflict between tradition and modernity, irrespective of Nair or Muslim or Namboodiri subject positions coming into play, is what fascinated me most. (Shyamaprasad 2013, interview by Meena T. Pillai)

A feminist critique of the film would point a finger at the fact that Shyamaprasad has highlighted the loneliness of the woman in the public sphere, thus validating women's confinement in the private spheres of life. However, he strongly and vehemently refutes this charge:

> It depends upon how you would want to interpret it. The female protagonist of the film is lonely by her own choice. One must not forget that Thethi is a very strong character. She does not want to be part of this whole drama of power, but is nevertheless a powerful person. One cannot merely look at her through the lens of gender

binaries. She is the one who is vested with action and it is her actions that impel the narrative of the film forward. I chose to omit the chapters of her life where Antharjanam portrayed her in numerous social roles. But the transformation from the Thethikutty, silenced inside the confines of her *mana* to the powerful and ennobling character of Sumithrananda Devi can be interpreted as an act of liberation and empowerment. (Shyamaprasad 2013, interview by Meena T. Pillai)

However, this omission is a serious one, given the fact that it charts precisely the journeys that Thethi makes, the trials and tribulations she faces and the transformation of the self they effected, through which Antharjanam offers a very strong and trenchant gendered critique of the reform movement in India. The role of women in the Indian national movement situates itself within a liminal space between progressive and conservative ethos. The confluence of these forces resulted in the formation of a 'moral/spiritual' feminine ideal among nationalist middle classes. On one hand, 'the new woman was to be educated', but 'unlike the Westernised or Western woman, her education should be specifically focussed on developing the "womanly" virtues of self-sacrifice and chastity and on her training as a wife and mother to nationalist men' (Parr 2021, 4). Amid all the patriarchal restraints manoeuvred by the social necessities, 'women's education provided opportunities for engaging with public life' (4). In fact, the discontents with nation and religion, the possibilities of motherhood outside the domestic pale, the strategic use of a welfare rhetoric by women to gain entry into the public spaces of the nationalist and reform projects and the legitimisation of such movements, come vibrantly alive in these omitted sections. The movie through its omissions seems to hold a brief endorsing the spiritualist, essentialist foundations of Hinduism. However, the novel's project seems to have been much more complex and nuanced than that. Without rejecting Hinduism, it sought to question its ancient misogynist base, choosing to work within the very same strictures and structures it tried to dismantle or subvert. Many of these early Hindu feminist leaders were able to overcome the hindrances of working within a Hindu society through a strategy of assimilation and accommodation where separate female institution-building programmes by women were to prove to be the vehicle for the movement for Hindu women's embracing of modernity, by both enabling women to mobilise in pursuit of their own welfare and contributing immensely to the transformation of women's public roles (Anagol 2008, 284).

Much has been said about the male reform project in Kerala in the context of modernity and the manner in which it reformulated both patriarchy and tradition. Antharjanam's *Agnisakshi* seeks to complicate and offer a more nuanced understanding of the 'enlightened paternalism' which was a hallmark of Kerala's reformist ideology. Thus, it was not her Namboodiri father's benevolence alone or Unni Namboodiri's interventions that took Thankam to college but also her personal ambition and struggle to carve a new self through education. Thankam is a new and gendered sign that radically unsettles the fiefdom of the male household with the Aphan as its feudal lord, administrator and chief-justice. The *nirahara sathyagraha* of fasting and non-cooperation that Thankam unleashes within the household in a sense replicates the Gandhian model of resistance. The nation's emancipation and women's emancipation both bring discontents in postcolonial India. Much, much later, Thankam invokes Devaki Manampally's speech that their legacy of woes, the inheritances of sorrows that she and the mothers and grandmothers of her generation inherited ought not to be passed on to the younger generation of women. This anxiety that the burden of the cross the women of their ilk carried might fall upon subsequent generations is echoed in Devaki's words, as also in the actions that mould her public and private life. All of this is depicted in the movie too. However, when the story seems to highlight the relationship between a man and his wife only, relegating everything else to the margins, this weight of anxiety and its ideological bearings seem to have been neutralised. Thus, a complex historical process is reduced to the myth of the steadfast spiritual masculine and a new cult of the individual feminine whereby the radical gendered spirit, invested in social issues in the original, seems to have been overshadowed by hagiographic narrations of the masculine ideal.

Agnisakshi, the movie, is not a woman-oriented adaptation while on the surface it might seem to be a largely truthful one. The problem here is also accentuated by the fact that Antharjanam's novel, when read in post-liberalisation Kerala, offers possibilities for reading it as both socially progressive and ideologically conservative. The meaning in the film text is produced not solely out of the signs that characters come to represent and the significations of their interactions but also the contexts and codes in which they are read. In fact, a post-feminist reading can unearth the part of an individualistic and headstrong woman's role in creating her own unhappiness and loneliness through a dysfunctional marriage, thus negating the personal sacrifices and historical functions that Devaki Manampalli undertakes to execute. However, the director's words that she is lonely 'by her own choice' illustrate the hollowing out of meaning from the historical implications of her life and choices. This creates a semantic void into which are filled new events of meaning as suited to the exigencies of a new age where the women whom Devaki Manampalli sought to 'liberate' have already been tamed by the myth of conjugal domesticity. Thus, a close analysis would reveal how Antharjanam's Devaki, who was an empowered sign resonating with the associative totality of the concept of women's quest for freedom from repression and its vibrant image, becomes a different signifier in the film through the cinematic image of the 'lonely' and un-domesticated woman. Emptied of its original radical aesthetic, it becomes easy for the film to construct itself as part of the dominant semiological chain of Malayalam cinema and its patriarchal semiotics where woman's bliss is always linked to the confines of the hearth and the home, and Devaki remains a figure to be sympathised with but never emulated. So the movie moves far away from a literary text which could treat domestic self-denial and feminist self-seeking as complementary, and which could offer spiritual solutions along with a rebellious zeal to transform the material and the temporal.

The movie at one level, remains rooted in the simple conventions of the sentimental and the melodramatic and seeks to revisit a feminine history under the aegis of a spiritual and paternal masculine. The director's comment in a newspaper review subsequent to the release of the movie is very telling. 'Agnisakshi is a spiritual film and the fundamental issue is spiritual identity', says Shyamaprasad. This turn to the emphasis on a 'national spiritual' in the era of globalisation, attests to the politics it seeks to instil. In contrast to *Nirmalyam*, the agentic role adopted by the director of *Agnisakshi*, seems to hollow out the radical potential of a historical text in order to suit the exigencies of the new economic and cultural logic of its reception.

According to Shyamaprasad, *Agnisakshi* is more than a period film and it tells the story of the transformation of a society caught between two worlds, the past and future. 'This film was basically made to highlight the plight of the common man and poses many questions about the nature of happiness. It is not about the Namboodiri women alone. It has a sense of timelessness about it', he says (*Agnisakshi*, a Spiritual Film). In another review Vinu Abraham points out that 'the eternal quest for inner peace, born out of disillusionment in life', is what *Agnisakshi* is all about and argues that 'the film accomplishes a better and detailed treatment of Unni by highlighting the thematic preoccupation of the novel—spiritual quest over materialistic pursuits' (Abraham 1998). The film which won eight Kerala state film awards, including the best film and best director, came under a lot of fire from Left ideologues and critics in Kerala who accused it of glorifying Indian spiritualism and vindicating Hindutva agendas by deliberately downplaying the radical portions of the novel and accentuating the spiritual (Radhakrishnan 1999). The movie's perspective evokes more empathy for Unni Namboodiri and the audience tends to be more sympathetic towards him than Thethi. To the question 'Do you think that you were fair to the female protagonist?', Shyamaprasad's response is revealing:

Well, as a male director and a man, my own subject positions and sympathies would be for Unni Namboodiri, more so because I could understand him and align my own choices and dilemmas with his. He embodied for me what I underwent in my life or what my father experienced in his own, a man caught between the past and the future, with a deep sense of commitment to his own destined roles in life. Unable to break free from his past or his lineage and tradition, he is nevertheless the most poignantly modern among all the other characters. He can understand the other and help free the other from the shackles of rituals and habits while offering himself in sacrifice for the other's freedom. (Shyamaprasad 2013, interview by Meena T. Pillai)

This answer is an interesting one, given the fact that the movie begins with a dedication, invoking the emotive vocabulary of motherhood, with the director dedicating the film to his mother Shantha Rajagopal (1929–98), thus drawing the informed reader into the same horizon of expectations that the literary original is believed to have attempted. J. Devika has critiqued this process of 'recuperation' of Antharjanam into the liberal humanist canon as the 'Muse of Motherhood' by ignoring the tensions that accompanied her complex rendering of motherhood (Devika 2008, 106). Through *Agnisakshi* Antharjanam 'articulates the dream of a public life informed by non-instrumental motherhood and motherhood informed by public life through tracing the life trajectories of Devaki Manampalli and Thankam Nair' (106). Significantly enough Antharjanam dedicates *Agnisakshi* to the sacred life of Devi Behan and all unknown women who made a service of their lives like her, as also her country, her community and the history of its emancipation. Antharjanam's Devaki, though childless, was mother to many untouchable children around the *illam*. There is a poignant description of her relationship with the maid Naniyamma's grandson Unnaman, whose scabs and sores she bathes with oil and soap, whom she feeds with *payasam* and *ada,* and for whom she buys books and a slate. These descriptions are compressed to one lacklustre scene in the movie where Devaki feeds the urchin Unnaman some leftover *ada* only to be chastised by her mother-in-law and finally laughed at by Unnaman and his companions. The movie also omits the section where years later the grown up Unnaman, now retired Subedar Padmanabhan Nair, comes to Thankam and begs her to give him Devaki's address because she was the one who made him human and he would like to fall at her feet and weep. 'Here, she is here. In my chest—in my mind. Young mistress's form is imprinted in my life's breath. Amme! I shall look at that and pay my obeisance to her' (Antharjanam 1976, 32). This omission robs the complexity of motherhood that the literary text envisages, its domestic politics and sentimental aesthetics linked to the political economy, and its reformist uses to install women in participatory roles in social and public life without it being an instrument of subordination in the private precisely through its consecration.

Also, the fact that the director himself accepts his presuppositions and lived reality as a masculine subject will definitely exert an influence over the process of adaptation. While speaking about women filmmakers' adaptations, Shelley Cobb reiterated Christine Geraghty's statement that 'Adaptations can be particularly productive texts for thinking about film authorship and the cultural politics of gender, but we must shift our view of adaptation away from the source as the standard' (Cobb 2014, 10) and instead one must 'explore the particular ways in which [film] adaptations make their own meanings' (10). The authorial identities are also instrumental in constructing the meaning out of the codes embedded in a text.

At another level however, the movie skillfully weaves Antharjanam's project of charting Devaki's journey as one from desire to woman's independence from desire, as also an emancipation from women's function as mirrors for masculine desires. Nevertheless, if Antharjanam's women were desiring subjects who refused to be straitjacketed into male parameters of desire or sexuality, the film, through its visual iconography and the tone and tenor of its treatment, seems to highlight this as a doomed project. It is in this partial or slanted inscription of women's desires, sans a stronger emphasis on its historical and material contexts that the discursive register of the film seems to privilege dominant discourses that delegitimise such representations. There seems to be a shift in emphasis from the position that female desire can be as fulfilled or as thwarted in the social domain as in the private and domestic to the position that women who 'sacrifice' their lives in the public sphere remain unfulfilled and joyless. This in fact re-emphasises a patriarchal conception of the feminine. Thethi's authority in the end seems solely premised on the repression of her womanly desires, and the pinched and harrowed face on screen, the visual structuring of that character, endorse such feminist authority to be meaningless and not to be aspired to by the women in the audience.

However, this kind of a feminist analysis should not miss the fact that normally a movie in Malayalam set in this period could afford endless visual pleasures through a controlling male gaze and an ample scope for scopophilia, which is not the case as far as this film is concerned. Neither the gaze of the camera nor the gaze of male characters within the film seeks to transform the woman into an object of desire or fetish. The film's visual strategies of representation definitely steer clear of the restrictive/cinematic constructions of women so characteristic of mainstream Malayalam cinema. The film gives us numerous brilliant instances of how a director can work around and often circumscribe the conditions of women's representability and pose subtle challenges to the patriarchal parameters of Malayalam cinema. The aestheticisation of the female body is not a concern in the film though the casting of Shobhana does invoke this history of aesthetics and its linkages to the erotic in Malayalam cinema.

The privileging of a Valluvanadan, elite Brahmanical dialect in many of the post-1990s films signifies an attempt to write the feudal, Brahmanical patriarchy (eased out by the socialist progressive concerns of earlier decades), back into the representational idiom of Malayalam cinema. However, Shyamaprasad chose to shoot the film in Ramapuram, a village where Antharjanam had actually lived. He points out that, 'I wanted my adaptation to be located in the same place. Thus, my choosing of Central Travancore was a conscious decision, though there was a lot of pressure to take it to a

Valluvanadan locale, which is a measure of popular taste in Kerala. I particularly wanted the unique ambience of Antharajanam's story to be retained in the film too' (2013, interview by Meena T. Pillai).

This is no mean task to achieve in a medium such as cinema, traditionally steeped in male desires. It is also interesting to note how the movie in complete conformity with the novel and in direct contradiction to mainstream spectatorial norms, is able to posit masculine domesticity as imbued with a superabundance of qualities, this being especially significant given the rise of hegemonic masculinity in Malayalam cinema by the nineties. It has been pointed out (Pillai 2013b) that Malayalam cinema in the 1990s has been characterised by a 'refeudalisation' of the public sphere and civil society. It has also been suggested that by the eighties and nineties the rhetoric of the popular in an overtly commercial cinema in Malayalam was successful in hitching female fantasies of empowerment and transformation to the pleasures of consumerism and the allure of commodity, signalling the final blow to the emancipatory possibilities that cinema could hold for the women of Kerala (Pillai 2013b).

The collusive tactics of capitalism, neo-conservatism and patriarchy together contribute to shaping this rather ironic social phenomenon. It is into this milieu that *Agnisakshi* makes an entry, characterised by a radical disjuncture from this aesthetics and ideology, precisely because it is an adaptation of a literary work credited with the aspirations for dismantling the patriarchal, feudal bases of a society. The film denies the male spectator, groomed in the dominant codes and conventions of popular cinema, any possibility of activation of scopophilic drives by denying him any chance to identify with the narrative hero.

However, as already argued the film also paradoxically enough taps into the homoaesthetic circles of interpretation in Kerala (Devika 2013) that leaves the specificities of Antharjanam's text moot or untouched, and helps its circulation and consecration within male circuits of desire which make pleasurable reading or viewing possible as a man. By subtly erasing the poetics of location

(Miller 1995), it feeds into the universalising tendencies of cinema that construct monolithic images of men and women. Female subjectivity becomes merely the ground of representation against which ample scope is given for developing the trope of the conjugal family premised on women's spiritual inner essences. Despite the fact that it does veer away from the dominant codes of cinematic representational traditions in Malayalam, it fails to capture the literary text's attempt to imagine a genealogy of women reformers or highlight positive images of female agency and power vis-à-vis the reform project in Kerala. Antharjanam had herself pointed out in the 'Author's Note' that if the book 'helps the women of a new generation to have a better understanding of women of an older generation, and persuades the older generation to perform a self analysis and other people to examine the tears and dreams of a bygone age, it will suffice'. Obviously the function of the adaptation has shifted grounds from this specifically gendered agenda to a more universal cosmic drama of individuals where the milieu, the medium and auteristic male sensibilities have tamed the progressive feminist aesthetics of the woman author's message in significant ways.

Thus, the movie adaptations of two seminal texts in Malayalam, *Nirmalyam* and *Agnisakshi*, offer two distinct cultural and spectatorial experiences, hinging on the requirements of their historical locations. *Nirmalyam* extends the revolutionary zeal of *Pallivaalum Kalchilambum* and appropriates the radical socio-cultural consciousness of a generation into the vocabulary of its cinema. On the contrary, *Agnisakshi* tames the possible gender politics envisaged in the age of its conception, creating ambivalent alignments with the revivalist imperatives within the political economy of globalisation. While the 'weak messianic power' (Benjamin 1969), of a past is redeemed or resurrected in the future by an adaptation such as that of *Nirmalyam*, it is hollowed out and a residual tradition that could have been insurrectional in the future of its adaptation like *Agnisakshi*, slips into a conformism that overwhelms and subsumes it.

REFERENCES

Abraham, Vinu. 1998. "A Trail by Fire." *The Week*, 18 Oct.

"*Agnisakshi*, a Spiritual Film." 1999. *Indian Express*, 15 Jan.

Anagol, Padma. 2008. "Rebellious wives and dysfunctional marriages: Indian women's discourses and participation in the debates over restitution of conjugal rights and the child marriage controversy in the 1880s and 1890s." In *Women and Social Reform in Modern India: A Reader*, edited by Sumit Sarkar and Tanika Sarkar, 282–312. Bloomington: Indiana UP.

Antharjanam, Lalithambika. 1976. *Agnisakshi: Fire, My Witness*. Translated by Vasanthi Sankaranarayanan. Oxford UP, 2015.

Baker, Mona. 2006. *Translation and Conflict: A Narrative Account*. New York: Routledge.

Bastin, Georges L. 2019. "Adaptation." In *Routledge Encyclopedia of Translation Studies*, edited by Mona Baker and Gabriela Saldanha, 5–8. New York: Routledge.

Benjamin, Walter. 1969. *Illuminations*. Translated by Harry Zohn. New York: Schocken Books.

Boozer, Jack. 2019. *Authorship in Film Adaptation*. Austin: U of Texas P.

Chakrabarty, Bidyut. 2015. *Left Radicalism in India*. New York: Routledge.

Cobb, Shelley. 2014. *Adaptation, Authorship, and Contemporary Women Filmmakers*. Hampshire: Palgrave Macmillan.

Devika, J. 2008. *Woman Writing = Man Reading?* India: Penguin Books Limited.

Hodgkins, John. 2013. *The Drift Affect, Adaptation, and New Perspectives on Fidelity*. New York: Bloomsbury.

Jeffrey, Robin. 1992. *Politics, Women and Well-Being: How Kerala became 'a Model'*. New York: Palgrave Macmillan.

Luna, Ilana Dann. 2008. *Adapting Gender*. Albany: State U of New York P.

Miller, Nancy K. 1995. *French Dressing: Women, Men and Ancient Regime Fiction*. New York: Routledge.

Mokkil, Navaneetha. 2019. *Unruly Figures: Queerness, Sex Work, and the Politics of Sexuality in Kerala*. Seattle: U of Washington P.

Murray, Simone. 2012. *The Adaptation Industry: The Cultural Economy of Contemporary Literary Adaptation*. New York: Routledge.

Nair, M. T. Vasudevan. 1998. "*Aa Chithram Athmarthamaya Udyamamayirunnu*" (That picture was a sincere attempt). Interview by E. M. Ashraf. *Kalakaumudi*, Dec. 27.

Parr, Rosalind. 2021. *Citizens of Everywhere: Indian Women, Nationalism and Cosmopolitanism, 1920–1952*. Cambridge: Cambridge U P.

Pillai, Meena T. 2010. "Becoming Women: Unwrapping Femininity in Malayalam Cinema." In *Women in Malayalam Cinema: Naturalising Gender Hierarchies,* edited by Meena T. Pillai, 1–27. Hyderabad: Orient Blackswan.

———. 2013a. "The Celluloid Women of Kerala." *Economic and Political Weekly,*48 (48): 140–41.

———. 2013b. "Matriliny to Masculinity: Performing Modernity and Gender in Malayalam Cinema." In *Routledge Handbook of Indian Cinema,* edited by K. Moti Gokulsing and Wimal Dissanayake, 102–14. New York: Routledge.

———. 2017. "The Many Misogynies of Malayalam Cinema." *Economic and Political Weekly* 52, (33): 52–58.

———. 2022. *Affective Feminisms in Digital India: Intimate Rebels.* New York: Routledge.

Radhakrishnan, M.G. 1999. "Film Under Fire." *India Today,* 12 Apr.

Sanyal, Devapriya. 2022. *Gendered Modernity and Indian Cinema: The Women in Satyajit Ray's Films.* New York: Routledge.

Shyamaprasad. 2013. Interview by Meena T. Pillai, 6 May 2013.

Shohat, Ella. 2004. "Sacred Word, Profane Image Theologies of Adaptation." In *A Companion to Literature and Film,* edited by Robert Stam and Alessandra Raengo, 23–46. Malden: Blackwell.